WHAT PEOPLE ARE SAYING ABOUT

BEAT THE RAIN

Gripping storytelling from the very start, this book draws you in and keeps you engaged, often on the edge of your seat, right till the bitter sweet end. *Beat the Rain* is a wonderfully written, fantastically pacey debut novel from an author with a truly compelling insight into the human condition and all its frustrating and often cruel twists and turns. The book is rich in characters, atmosphere and the element of surprise. It's serious and often sad but also laugh-out-loud funny all at the same time. A touching and sensitive portrayal of the interconnected mess of everyday life and love. One of those reads that leaves you wanting more.
Siobhan Kennedy, *Channel 4 News*

Emotional rollercoaster, psychological thriller – *Beat the Rain* ticks both these boxes for me. I was sucked in from the start. The sensitive characterisation, level of observation and Nigel's ability to not only touch on the plethora of issues that come from the train smash of life, death, family and relationships but also express so effectively the emotional highs and lows was compelling throughout. Absolutely compelling.
Caroline Follett

Intriguing, painfully honest and beautifully written.
Nina de la Mer, Author, *4.a.m, Layla*

Beat The Rain is an atmospheric and neatly paced first novel. Behind the scenes – shining through the two main characters' inner dialogues – is a refreshingly honest intelligence at work.
Poet Charlotte Gann, *The Long Woman, Noir (forthcoming)*

i

ROUNDFIRE
BOOKS

At Roundfire we publish great stories. We lean towards the
spiritual and thought-provoking. But whether it's literary or
popular, a gentle tale or a pulsating thriller, the connecting
theme in all Roundfire fiction titles is that once you pick them
up you won't want to put them down.

If you have enjoyed this book, why not tell other readers by posting a review on your preferred booksite. Recent bestsellers from Roundfire are:

The Bookseller's Sonnets
Andi Rosenthal
The Bookseller's Sonnets intertwines three love stories with a tale of religious identity and mystery spanning five hundred years and three countries.
Paperback: 978-1-84694-342-3 e-book: 978-184694-626-4

Birds of the Nile
An Egyptian Adventure
N.E. David
Ex-diplomat Michael Blake wanted a quiet birding trip up the Nile – he wasn't expecting a revolution.
Paperback: 978-1-78279-158-4 e-book: 978-1-78279-157-7

Blood Profit$
The Lithium Conspiracy
J. Victor Tomaszek, James N. Patrick, Sr
The blood of the many for the profits of the few... Blood Profit$ will take you into the cigar-smoke-filled room where American policy and laws are really made.
Paperback: 978-1-78279-483-7 e-book: 978-1-78279-277-2

The Burden
A Family Saga
N.E. David
Frank will do anything to keep his mother and father apart. But he's carrying baggage – and it might just weigh him down...
Paperback: 978-1-78279-936-8 e-book: 978-1-78279-937-5

Beat the Rain

Beat the Rain

Nigel Jay Cooper

Winchester, UK
Washington, USA

First published by Roundfire Books, 2016
Roundfire Books is an imprint of John Hunt Publishing Ltd., Laurel House, Station Approach,
Alresford, Hants, SO24 9JH, UK
office1@jhpbooks.net
www.johnhuntpublishing.com
www.roundfire-books.com

For distributor details and how to order please visit the 'Ordering' section on our website.

Text copyright: Nigel Jay Cooper 2015

ISBN: 978 1 78535 364 2
Library of Congress Control Number: 2015960667

A CIP catalogue record for this book is available from the British Library.

Design: Stuart Davies

Printed in the USA by Edwards Brothers Malloy

We operate a distinctive and ethical publishing philosophy in all
areas of our business, from our global network of authors to
production and worldwide distribution.

For Andrew, if he wants it

Acknowledgements

To my children, Florence and Louis, thank you for inspiring me every day. No words written or spoken could describe how much I love you. And you're right, if a baby was strong enough to carry the whole wide world, he/she might spin us around and around and tip us upside down and we could all be thrown into space and die. (Except, gravity. We'll talk about that when you're older).

Andrew, I'd never have finished this without your support. Thank you for putting up with me and believing in me when I didn't believe in myself. You inspire everyone you meet to strive to achieve his or her potential and I don't think you know how wonderful that is. Always be you.

To my parents, thank you for your continuing love and support and for being such wonderful grandparents.

To Caroline, you deserve an award for how many times you've read this novel during the editing process. Thank you for your feedback, your emotional support, guidance and unfaltering belief – you've been amazing.

To lovely Ali, thank you for your beautiful cover designs, they helped more than you know. Amanda, thank you so much for the author photographs and for your feedback on my first draft.

Thanks to Nina, Charlotte, Caroline and Siobhan for your endorsements, they meant such a lot. Thanks also to Charlie, Kate, Sam, Emily, Clare, Dr Dixon and Sara for reading and feeding back on my early drafts – it was really useful to see it through other people's eyes.

Thanks to everyone who downloaded my opening chapters and left reviews on the website – you have no idea how much it meant to me or how important they were in getting the attention of publishers.

Last but not least, thanks to John Hunt Publishing and Roundfire Books for publishing *Beat the Rain*.

Part One: The Unsaid

"I'm going to let it take me."

Chapter One

Louise does all of the things the bereaved are supposed to do; she's had enough practice. She gracefully accepts well-meant platitudes from people she can't stand; she smiles in the right places and pretends she's still able to care. Everything she's become is now an invention, a persona created to make other people feel better.

If she could, she'd never leave the flat again, she'd switch off her mobile, stop answering the door and lie in bed, endlessly staring at the ceiling. This morning she slept through the postman knocking as she dreamt of hot narrow lanes and enormous churches. She smiled and pointed out of the window, past the church, past the market stalls in the square, past the sea. She felt Tom's presence behind her, tried to turn around to see him, to kiss him. Then she felt her sheets clinging to her. Morning.

Tom would have heard the postman. He would have jumped out of bed like an excitable ten-year-old.

"A package, Lou," his gleaming eyes would have said.

"You're a grown man, Tom," she would have replied, barely glancing at him as he danced around the bedroom in nothing but his boxer shorts.

"What do you think it is?" he'd have asked.

"Same as every month, Tom," she'd have smiled. "Your books."

She stares at the yellow-white stained walls of their flat. Her flat now, she reminds herself, just hers again. Today is book day again. She has one every month but this one's early. She stubs a cigarette out on the faded mahogany dresser under the hallway mirror. This thing that she is, this woman, barely formed, stares back at her, like an alien, a shadow of someone who used to exist. Is loss something she's supposed to accept in her life, like other people accept doing a job they don't love or avoiding chips and chocolate cake? She checks her eyes in the hallway mirror to make sure they're not too puffy and braces herself before opening the front door, mentally preparing her 'outside' face, the one that can still smile.

Her days are alike, or different. It doesn't matter. None of them contain a version of her that isn't alone. She shuts her front door, looking away from Mr Carmichael, her ever-smiling, ever-gardening neighbour as he potters around in a pair of overalls. Louise has often wondered what he does for a living – he and his wife don't seem to work, they're always at home, gardening or singing in their front room around an enormous piano that seems much too big for the space. She feels lucky her flat is upstairs so at least she doesn't have to listen to them harmonising.

"Louise." He smiles at her with ceaseless hedge-trimmer hands. "How are you feeling today?" She ignores him and shuffles down the street, sinking into her jumper.

The post office is a thirty-minute walk or a five-minute bus ride away. She imagines the jolting, crowded red double-decker full of kids, old bag ladies and men with body odour and decides to walk. For the most part, her journey produces untroubled faces but occasionally, they become familiar. That's when everyone's smiles freeze.

"Louise, you look great," the familiar will say eventually, their frosty hands touching her jacket sleeve in faux concern. Louise will lick her dry lips in preparation.

"Do I?" she'll finally ask, sometimes genuinely. They'll nod as their fingers grip her arm more tightly.

"We were so sorry to hear about…" Then their voices will trail off. They all think she's dealing with it and she has become practiced in keeping her smile on long enough to reassure them they're right. She waits until they've scuttled away before allowing it to crack.

3

"Tell your fortune," someone says as she rounds the corner by the bank or pub or restaurant. A lucky-heather woman is standing in front of her, a rainbow headscarf and flowing dress billowing in the gentle breeze. With the morning sunlight glinting behind her, she looks somehow otherworldly and for a moment Louise is mesmerised.

"Some change for your fortune?" the woman says again and for the tiniest of moments, Louise thinks to herself, *Why not?*, then she shudders, remembering what her fate is like. She closes her eyes tightly for a second, as if this will help her break free from the spell she's sure the lucky heather woman has put her under.

"No," Louise says loudly, almost shouting and stepping away. Then, as her manners take over, she says quietly, "Thanks anyway," and continues her journey.

* * *

"What would you do if I died?" Tom asked her once, leaning over and smiling. His left hand invaded her top, resting on her breast.

"I wouldn't let you," she replied, thrusting her chest out and grinning.

"But if you couldn't stop it."

Fingers explored, she pulled him closer. "I'd fuck the postman."

Later, smoking cigarettes and shivering: "Promise you'll never leave me," she said. He kissed her, rolled over, slept.

* * *

"It's Louise, isn't it?"

Louise rounds another corner and is confronted by a woman who grabs her and hugs her tightly, as if she has found her long-lost sister. Louise wishes she'd caught the bus, at least people would have left her alone then.

"I haven't seen you for ages."

Louise stands motionless, arms by her side, not returning the embrace.

"It's me, Narinda," the woman says. "From school. You remember? Of course you remember. The old gang?"

"How are you?" Louise forces out eventually. Seeing her is almost as painful as losing Tom. Narinda is someone from an old life, one Louise wants no part of. Just seeing her has given her gooseflesh, reminding her of the person Tom helped her leave behind, someone she no longer recognises.

"Oh it's so good to see you again. How's...oh what was his name? Tom, wasn't it?"

"Dead," Louise says defiantly, cutting her off. Narinda rocks back slightly, clearly unsure what to do or say.

"Oh, I am sorry," she manages eventually.

"Bye, Narinda," Louise says quietly, pushing past her and continuing her journey.

As she enters the post office, the air conditioning dries her eyes. People are littered around, some waiting in the queue, some filling out forms with broken black biros with snapped silver chains hanging from the ends. Louise hugs her jacket to her chest and waits her turn and when she eventually gets to the counter, she looks away from the man and pushes the card under the glass along with a bill and driving licence as proof of address, hoping she's not going to have to have the same conversation as last month and the month before.

"Has Tom Gaddis signed to say you can pick this up for him?"

"He's dead."

A beat. Frozen features, unsure how to respond to her. "We can't release anything to you unless he's signed to say you can pick it up for him, you see."

"Can dead men sign forms?" Steely green eyes, staring

unflinchingly through the glass, daring the man to be a jobsworth. "You can see it's my address, you can see we live together…" A pause, reality sinking in for the twentieth time that day. "Lived together."

Luckily, today, the assistant simply looks at the note and says, "Cold, isn't it," and he grins a British yellow-tooth smile. "Sign here." He shunts a form towards Louise. Her fingers do the work and as he hands her the parcel; she clutches it to her chest and steps back out onto the morning high street.

Every month, she receives the company's 'choice' of book for Tom. It was in the small print when he signed for it – if he didn't choose one himself from their catalogue, they would send one of their own recommendations for him to read. She couldn't allow herself to cancel it, to cancel him. It's strange, though, because the books are early this month and the package seems different. She lets her arms fall back slightly to read the label. It's not the normal printed name and address at all. It's a handwritten one. Tom's writing: Lou.

* * *

"Why don't you like Lou?" Tom asked her once, slipping onto the arm of her chair.

"It's not my name."

Eyes smiled. "So?"

"I was christened Louise."

"Lou, Louise. Same name."

"Different name entirely. Different name, different pronunciation,"

"Pronunciation."

"What?"

* * *

She clutches the box tightly, swallowing and swallowing again, sure the spinning in her stomach will cause her to be sick. She drags herself upstairs and sits staring from the window, hugging the parcel so tightly it hurts her small breasts.

Time is suspended as she walks down their street. *Her street.* The parcel is warm in her arms, like it's emitting some sort of heat, some sort of *life*. As she walks into her front gate, Mr Carmichael is still pruning his hedges and deadheading flowers. He smiles and nods. Her fingers are freezing as she hunts for her keys to the flat, avoiding his gaze, pretending she doesn't feel like a madwoman screaming behind alabaster skin.

"They can teach you a lot, you know," he says.

"Sorry," she mumbles, trying to get her keys in the lock to avoid a lengthy discussion with him.

"Plants and flowers. Trees."

"Sorry, Mr Carmichael, I've really got to get in and..." Louise says without looking around, not even caring if she appears rude.

"When leaves die in autumn, the trees don't hold on to them," Mr Carmichael continues regardless. "They let them go, Louise. If they didn't, no new leaves would grow."

"Mr Carmichael, I..." she starts, glancing around at him and pursing her lips.

"And how sad that tree would look when spring arrived. Still bare."

Louise doesn't respond, she simply nods her head as if she's listened and walks into her flat. She mounts the stairs and stares down the end of the hall at her kitchen, swimming in washing up and ready meals. If Tom were alive he'd be angry.

"Ready meals?" He'd read an article in *New Scientist* once and had become obsessed with modified foods. "They'll kill you." He was probably right of course, but his abstinence didn't save him. She wonders what choices people actually have and which are illusions. His diet couldn't rewrite his death so what made him

7

think anyone else's could?

"The place is a pig sty," she hears him say in her head as she drops her handbag and jacket in the hallway. The package, which she has momentarily placed on the dressing table under the mirror, stares at her, uncomfortable out of her arms. The heating isn't on and she reaches out and touches the parcel gingerly; it feels warm. How can she get a parcel from him six months after his death? Somewhere, in the background, a telephone rings.

"Adam," she says quietly, leaning against the wall and cradling the telephone in her neck. She wipes her eyes as she glances through the open door into the sitting room. Similar to the state of the kitchen, the floor holds newspapers. Last week's dinner plate sits next to last night's, the night before that's. If she could care long enough she'd tidy up.

"Look." For the tiniest of moments, she thinks about telling him what is sitting on the hallway dresser but as quickly as the thought appears she releases it. This is hers, it's for her. It's her name scrawled on the parcel, not Adam's. *Lou.*

"Can I talk to you later, Adam?" she says finally. She can't look at anything other than the parcel. Since his brother's death, Adam usually manages to bring her back to the real world, but this morning he's an irritation, a barrier between her and the past. She nods her head as Adam says something, as if she's listened to him and has understood what he's said. She hasn't, she's already thinking about re-cradling the phone as her fingers fiddle with the corner of the brown-paper package, mysteriously back in her arms without her realising she's picked it up again.

"Yeah," she finds her lips saying, hanging up.

She opens the parcel with shaking and unfamiliar hands. The only thing that stops her tearing at it is his handwriting. That must be preserved. She walks into the sitting room and sits on the sofa, pulling the paper back, opening the top of the box. Lots of packing paper hiding...what? Her fingers grab and pull, throw the packing paper on the floor with the other rubbish. Inside the box lies a DVD and a bottle of red wine, bubble-wrapped.

* * *

Memories, one week before he dies:

"What did you buy that for?"

Tom flinches, darts his head towards the kitchen door as Louise stands there, back early from university, taking her jacket off.

"Jesus, you scared the shit out of me."

"Don't be ridiculous." She smiles, wandering into the kitchen and putting her jacket on the worktop. "What are you up to?" she continues playfully.

"I don't know," his thick red lips reply. He stands poised, holding a bottle of red wine half in, half out of a shopping bag.

"What did you buy that for?"

"What do you mean?"

"The wine."

"It's red."

"Yes. But what did you buy it for?"

"To drink. What else?"

"You like white. Are you cooking me dinner or something?" She puts her arms around the back of his waist, but he shirks her off.

"No." Irritation flickers in his voice, but is replaced immediately with a more conciliatory tone. He turns to her; grin lips, dark eyes. "It's not for now. It's for later."

* * *

Now is later. Her fingers pull the last of the bubble-wrap off, freeing the wine so it sits cool in her palm. She puts it down, snatching the DVD, which wears no label of its own. Her hands are like those of an alcoholic in withdrawal as she fumbles it into the machine and pushes the play button. On the floor in front of the TV, she can hear every whir of machinery. She clears herself a space on the floor and waits.

* * *

The first time Louise saw Tom was in the dirty pink-walled newsagents at the end of her road. He was standing at the counter, talking to someone in the aisle and then he glanced at her and she was hooked. She fell in love there and then. He looked so…safe, actually. If you'd asked her before, she'd have said it was his smile she liked, or the way his t-shirt was caught in his jacket, showing the tiniest bit of the skin around his midriff, or the way he was massaging his neck with his hand as the cashier took his money. But in reality, she simply knew in that instant that he could fix her – and she needed that after her dad's death.

After the newsagents, Louise didn't see Tom again for about two weeks. Then, as she was getting a coffee in a café at seven dials, she saw him. He was standing at the café counter, wearing his suit and tie, sweating.

"Coffee, please. And a slice of toast and marmite," he asked the woman behind the counter.

"White or brown?" she asked.

"Granary, please."

"Only got white or brown."

"Brown then, thanks."

Louise stood staring at him and it took her a few moments to realise he'd turned around and was looking right back at her.

"Work experience." He smiled, opening his arms out and glancing down at his suited body. "What do you think," he said, giving her a twirl and a wink.

"Oh, hi. Yeah. I saw you in the newsagents the other day," she said nervously.

"I remember." Tom smiled.

"Small place, Brighton," the woman behind the counter said jovially.

"Yeah, some bloke got his nose bitten off in the Zap Club the other day, did you hear?" Louise said. *Shit.*

"Um, no, I didn't," Tom replied, his gaze not leaving hers. "Listen, I've got to run, can't miss my train. But you want to go out? Cinema or something? Or pizza?"

"Yeah," she said, trying to remain cool and calm. "That'd be great. Do you want my number?"

* * *

"Lou?" Tom's voice. The television screen flickers. Her fingers tremble over the DVD controller. "Will you love again?"

"I don't have to. I've got you," she hears herself reply from the screen. He'd been recording her without her knowledge.

"But if you did have to. What then?" Dark screen before her. No pictures. Then:

Light. His smiling face. He sits in a clean sitting room, on the sofa that presses into her back. She looks over her shoulder, sure for a second he's sitting there, he's come back to her. But her version of the room is like a junkyard, he could never live there.

"That was as far as I got," she hears from the television. Her head darts back to it and her eyes swallow his moving image. His *living* image. Tom leans closer to the camera.

"I'm stupid, aren't I? But I can't tell you."

Chapter Two

Adam sits at his kitchen table staring at the telephone in front of him. Louise was anxious and dismissive. She could need time on her own, he supposes, but given the letter that arrived from Tom this morning, he suspects there's something else going on. He shivers in his t-shirt and stares at the telephone again before standing up and grabbing his keys and jumper. He's going to have to go to Brighton to talk to her, whether she wants to or not. They can't carry on like they are, skirting around the issue. If he's learnt anything from his brother's death it's that life is too short; you have to grab it while you can – nobody is guaranteed the long haul.

* * *

Losing a twin is something Adam can't explain to anyone. How can anyone not born half of a pair understand? Even Louise, suffering her own grief, can't get close to comprehending the complexity of Adam's emotions. Not that she's tried. But that's okay. In some strange place inside, the loneliness of his grief is comforting, like it is another aspect of being a twin that outsiders can never 'get'. It makes him feel closer to Tom. Their bond, their 'otherness' is still there, even if Tom isn't. But there is something else lurking deep inside Adam, another feeling, something uncomfortable, something guilt-laden that Adam has spent months working hard to supress – something he will never consciously recognise despite the profound effect it is having on him: Tom's death has offered him a release – it has given him the opportunity to just be Adam Gaddis. For the first time in his life, he isn't one of a pair, he isn't the less-charismatic twin, crouched in his brother's dazzling shadow. Emotionally, Adam under-stands this feeling but he can't allow it in, he can't allow the possibility of finding a positive in something so horrific.

The truth is that everyone preferred Tom to Adam. They didn't mean to and Adam doesn't blame anyone for it, but it was true. Tom knew it and Adam knew it. Some people probably didn't even know they felt that way – not consciously. But Tom had been the charming twin, the handsome twin, the accomplished twin. Somehow, Adam – who looked like Tom, spoke like Tom, dressed like Tom – had always been second best. In many ways, Adam hadn't even minded – the lack of attention and expectation meant he'd been able to relax a bit more than Tom, who always felt the need to perform.

"It's all right for you," Tom would say playfully. "Nobody *expects* anything from you. They all think I'm going to run the world or something."

When Tom died, Adam's parents went to pieces and he couldn't help feeling a sense of guilt, somehow, like his survival had created an imbalance in the world that only he could correct.

His parents had insisted on having Tom's body brought home to them. Adam realises now that he's never asked Louise how this made her feel. They'd all been so wrapped up in how *the family* was feeling, Louise had been excluded from everything, like her relationship with Tom wasn't worthy somehow because it had been cut short. What were a few years compared to a lifetime? But she loved him, she deserved to be treated better.

Would she have been happy with Tom's body being displayed in his parents' front room? She was in so much shock that Adam doesn't think she'd have had any reserves left to argue with her pseudo mother in law, anyway. The first few days after Tom's death were a fog of denial for all of them he supposes, days he can't replay in his mind with any accuracy. Even Adam hadn't known what his mother was planning.

"He's in the front room," she said. The words were hard for her, he could tell. They struggled dryly out of her throat, like it was cracked and bleeding, denied of moisture. "You should say goodbye properly, before the cremation."

"In the front room?" Adam steadied himself against the edge of the wooden kitchen work surface, his fingers becoming purple white with pressure. The freshly boiled kettle beside his mother was still steaming, making the white and green tiles beside it dewy.

When he finally mustered the courage to go and look at him, Adam loitered in the doorway for what seemed like hours. The floor of the room where they'd put him was covered with an old, Persian-style rug. It wasn't Persian, of course. It had never been near Persia, it was from the Sunday Wimbledon market. It was red and blue and gold, diamonds and paisley and the tassels had been cut off years ago as their mother couldn't bear having to brush them out every day. Adam stood in the doorway, staring at the rug and not daring to step fully into the room where his brother was 'resting'. Such euphemisms struck him as unnatural. He wasn't resting; he was dead. Adam has always felt people should be encouraged to deal with reality, not fiction. They should grieve for what's real, not imaginary. This repression, this obsession with pretending things were *other* than they were didn't work for Adam.

Against the back wall of the room sat a dark chestnut cabinet with glass doors to display the best china.

"Why can't we use those plates?" Tom had asked his mother once.

"Because they're for best," she'd replied.

"When will that be?" Tom had persevered as Adam sniggered in the background. As far as Adam could remember, the plates had never left the cabinet except when they needed dusting. That was Gaddis life. All show, never letting go.

Adam took a step. In the centre of the room, a dark, polished wood coffin held his brother, his mirror image, his true other half. The room was warm. He imagined the whole place should be cold and grey, devoid of life, but it wasn't. The fire was flickering, casting warm shadows on patterned wallpaper. The small figurines that usually sat cold on the hearth were bathed in an orange glow. As the flames moved, it seemed they might spring into action, stretching, dancing and pirouetting.

His parents had chosen silver handles for the coffin, something Tom would have approved of. He'd always hated gold, for some reason Adam could never fathom. Maybe it was because his first girlfriend, the first to break his heart at least, used to wear big gold hoop earrings. Adam doesn't know, he never asked. Now he'll never know.

Adam stood rooted to the spot, unable to step further into the room. He could see the satin interior of his brother's casket, light blue. He could smell something, not a horrible smell, but something he couldn't identify, something at odds with the room. Whatever it was, it didn't smell like Tom, it was neither the soap he used nor the overpowering special-occasion aftershave Louise had bought him for his last birthday. Adam peered forward and could make out Tom's white hands against his best black suit. They were lying clean and pale by his sides, not crossed over his chest. Holding his breath, Adam took another step and looked at his twin's face – a deathly reflection of his own features – inanimate and otherworldly.

Adam stared at Tom's face, pale and expressionless, nothing like his brother was in life. Adam couldn't look at him; he didn't want to see that. He didn't want to remember that. The thing in the casket – that husk, that hunk of meat – that wasn't Tom. Filled with something uncomfortably close to revulsion, Adam ran from the room and from his parents' house.

The funeral wasn't any better. His parents chose to respect Tom's wishes and cremate him, even if they'd gone with a church service, something Tom would have hated. Adam had stood there, detached from the proceedings, looking around the church, too large to be small, too small to be large. People squeezed into it as the rain poured down outside. It didn't fit.

Like a t-shirt washed on boil, it was cutting into him, stifling him and making it hard to breathe. In the months since his brother's death, he's tried to remember the service, tried to remember people's kind words – anything about that day that will blot out his brother's cold dead features. But he can't.

He can remember his mother, at first so composed that people remarked on it, on how well she was doing, on how strong she was. Then, as the coffin was carried in, it was like she had been attacked from within and gasps and tears clawed their way to the surface as she fought desperately to drag them back, to compose herself for her son, to show him that respect at least. But it didn't work and each time she failed to contain her sobs, they resurfaced again with renewed energy. Adam thinks that was the hardest thing to watch for many of the people in the church – their grief wasn't so much about the loss of Tom; it was about a mother who'd lost her son. That was a grief everyone could understand and empathise with.

He remembers the inappropriate cousins, the ones who got so drunk at the wake they forgot where they were, coming up to him and saying: "I've had such a good time, today, Adam. It was so nice to catch up with the family," as if he was going to grin and agree with them, slapping them on the back and buying them another pint.

But the rest of the funeral? He can't remember. He can't remember Louise, what she wore, what she said, almost like she was sidelined from the whole event. But he did sit with her afterwards.

"He made me smile, Adam," she said, leaning into his shoulder. "I didn't realise how important that was until I lost him, you know?"

To Adam, the whole thing is now like a scene from someone else's life, something that happened elsewhere that he's only got the vaguest notion of. But Tom's cold expressionless face in his coffin is perfect, he can remember that in detail. If he could change anything in his life at all, it would be that: seeing his brother's dead body. He'd give anything to have Tom's memory uncorrupted. Un-decayed. But there is no point in regrets, Adam now understands.

"You can't rewind, Ad," Tom used to say. "Learn and move on."

* * *

Adam walks along the main road, searching for a cab. There are many but most whiz past with lights extinguished. When one finally stops, the driver pulls the window down and looks out.

"Where to, mate?"

"South, to..."

"Sorry, mate."

He's pulled away before Adam can argue. Three taxis later and Adam is finally wrestling in from the cold. He's trying a new tactic and hasn't spoken to the driver to tell him he wants to go south of the river. He sits back into the leather interior, which smells of kebabs, turning his stomach slightly.

"Victoria, please." He winces and waits for a response. The taxi driver turns around.

"Sorry, mate, I'm not going south,"

"But that's where I want to go."

"I'm meeting the wife for lunch in Finchley. I'll never make it back in time."

"So why did you have your light on?" Adam says, trying his hardest to hide his irritation.

"Because I'm a taxi."

"That doesn't want to taxi?" Adam pulls on the door handle, more irritated by the second but the door doesn't open.

"Okay, mate. I'll take you, alright. Can probably make it back as long as we don't hit traffic."

Smug bastard.

"I don't want you to take me now." The door clicks open and Adam falls back onto the cold street.

Adam misses living in Brighton, wishes he hadn't quit his course the way he had, wishes he hadn't moved back to his parents' house in north London. He wishes a lot of things, but what's the point in that? He knows why he left, of course. Louise. In the end, he couldn't bear to be near her and Tom. Couldn't bear to see them together day in day out, so happy. He hadn't wanted them to split up, he hadn't wanted that at all – but at the same time, he couldn't have stayed and watched their love affair for another day longer. He's not sure he's ever admitted that to himself before now; he'd almost believed his own lies, the reasons he gave his parents about his course not being a 'good fit', about not feeling like he was achieving anything. In reality, it had hurt too much to be near them.

So he'd moved back to his parents' house. It hadn't been easy to do even then, but living there got worse after Tom died. Adam's relationship with his parents never recovered from his brother's death. His dad believes 'less said, soonest mended' and when he thinks about it, Adam probably takes after him more than he realises. But that meant they retreated into themselves and never mentioned Tom to each other – and that didn't feel right. Almost immediately, Adam felt awkward, like he couldn't mention his brother in his dad's presence in case it cracked the glass case of denial he'd built around himself. Who knew how far the glass shards would shatter and who they'd injure in the process? Better to remain quiet. Don't mention Tom. Less said, soonest mended. Except of course, they were all far from mended. They'd dressed their wounds to stop any outward signs of bleeding. Put up a front to make sure the world thought they were coping. Because that was the most important thing to do, wasn't it?

Adam isn't without sympathy for his mum, of course. She copes in the only way she knows how. He'd been with them when they found out Tom had died – when Louise had called to tell them. He's always loved her for that, for the fact she'd wanted to make the call herself, despite the fact she didn't get on with Janet. Adam and his dad had been sitting at the kitchen table eating sandwiches. The phone had rung and his mum had answered, smiling. Then her face had frozen. Then had come the silence, the calm, white silence. Adam can't remember how long this went on for, but as she tried to find the words to convey the information to her husband and surviving son, she couldn't get the words out. She hadn't needed to, they'd known. Adam often longs to go back to that moment, before Louise's phone call, before awareness, before they knew they'd lost Tom forever. His father had run over and grabbed his mum and held her to him. Adam had remained seated in unreality, a black-and-white figure in the middle of a blood-red vignette of family tragedy. Sometimes he feels like the colour never came back to his life, not fully.

But now Tom has sent him a letter from the grave. He's giving his blessing, his permission to move on. The only question is, will Louise feel the same?

Chapter Three

"I wish I could tell you," Tom is saying on the DVD, rather than actually speaking to Louise while he had the chance. "This is hard for me, Lou. I don't think you can share it."

Louise leans back, buttocks solid on the floor. On the DVD, he is sitting on the sofa that she can feel on her back.

"I don't feel like I'm dying." His lips seem to take up the entire screen as he speaks, like they might lean out and kiss her, giving her one last moment, one last touch. But they don't. Instead, he pauses and sits back, rubbing the back of his head.

"I guess you think that I took the bloke way out. Avoided the issues. Avoided you. Well maybe I did. Maybe I am. But you're so far away. It's like I live somewhere else." His eyes look away from the television at the floor.

"That's because you didn't tell me," Louise finds herself whispering. Her skin feels tight as her mouth shapes the words, painfully aware he can't hear her. The option he chose is all one way and she's not sure she can forgive him for that. He didn't allow her a voice and she's not that woman anymore. She won't ever be that woman again.

On the television screen, Tom sits silently stroking the stubble on his left cheek. Louise's eyes don't waver from the screen and as his lips start to move, she feels something. Not love, not loss but disgust.

"Why didn't you tell me?" bursts out of her and she jumps up and clutches each side of the TV screen before her. "Why didn't you let me help you?" She drops back and starts sobbing. "Why didn't you let me say goodbye?"

Silence. Or not. He's speaking. She's been speaking over him. Frantically, she grabs the DVD controller and presses the rewind button. His image contorts, moves backwards.

"...it's like I live somewhere else," he repeats. Pauses. "But I don't suppose you need to know that." He rubs his head again. "You want to know why I haven't told you. Don't you?"

Louise nods, watching his lips again, always his beautiful, full lips. She imagines they'll be the last thing she'll forget as his memory fades and the years pass.

* * *

"You can't rewind," Tom said to her once. She'd been moaning about something or other, wishing she hadn't gone into town because it'd been busy and she hadn't got the shoes to go with her dress that she wanted for the dinner party they were having that evening and Tom said: "Will you stop moaning. You can't rewind."

At dinner, their friends Steve and Sue wanted to play a word game. Each of them had to choose three words to sum up their partner, no more, no less.

"Passionate, intelligent and caring," Sue had said, beaming, proud that she'd distilled the essence of Steve into three words as requested.

"What about you, Tom? What three words would you use to describe Louise?"

"I wouldn't," he'd replied irritably. Normally, this would have been his territory, words. He and Adam both loved words. Language was their thing – Tom was a budding academic, his brother a budding writer. So normally, this would have been right up his street. But somehow, on this night, he was different. She should have seen the signs, should have known something was coming.

"Come on, Tom." Louise had smiled, slightly embarrassed.

"Come on what, Louise? You want me to diminish you by paring you down to three disembodied words? They'd be sufficient, would they? They'd sum you up? It's insulting."

"It's a game, Tom, for fuck sake…"

21

"Look, I didn't mean to upset anyone," Sue started.

"You didn't," Louise said, trying to smooth things over. "Tom, what's got into you?"

* * *

Now she knows. As the picture on his DVD fades back in, Tom is sitting at the kitchen table in his dressing gown. He's smoking and staring at a pair of glasses that sit on the table.

"We thought it was the glasses giving me the headaches." He picks them up and twirls them. "I went to the hospital. It's not the glasses," he says matter of factly, looking at the cigarette in his hands thoughtfully. "I haven't had one of these for years. Me and Adam gave up together." He pauses, corrects himself. "Adam and I." He puts the cigarette in the ashtray in front of him and looks directly at Louise. "I know I should tell you. But you're so happy. After everything, your mum, your dad. You're happy now, with me. Here and now. How can I ruin that?"

Louise's fingertips are cold and her nose is numb. She pulls at her hair and pushes it back away from her face, swallowing hard.

"So I'm reading *New Scientist*," Tom says. "It's a boy thing. Apparently." Louise produces the smallest of smiles and touches the television screen gently with her fingertips.

* * *

A month before he died:

"What are you reading that for?"

He was scratching his nipple, reading.

"What?"

"*New Scientist*."

"What about it?"

"Why are you reading it?"

"Because I want to."

"But it's boring."

His eyes grinned, followed by his lips. "How do you know?"

"It must be. It's a boy thing."

"What? Women can't read about science?" he said, getting up and grabbing her by the waist and tickling her. "For shame, Lou, for shame."

* * *

Back in her sitting room, eyes glued to the screen:

"I'm reading about things that I will never see. But you might, Lou." The television flickers. "I'm getting a headache," he says, shutting the magazine in front of him. "That's more terminal than it used to be." Louise reaches for the screen to touch his face again. "They want to operate."

A long pause.

"It would likely give me brain damage." He sits back. "I'd lose my language."

Louise can't see anything but his face, filling the screen with her fingers pressed against it. She's holding her breath, unable to tell how she's feeling or what she's thinking.

"Will you hate me if I don't tell you? If I let nature take its course?" He nods to himself, as if he's answered for her. Louise's fingers leave the television screen.

"I'm going to let it take me," he says simply, as if he's talking about something tiny like which yoghurt to buy or what TV programme to watch. He's talking as if his decision didn't have any consequence and that it doesn't matter that he didn't discuss it with her.

Louise scrambles back across the floor, to get away from the television, away from him. Leaning back against the sofa, she clutches her knees to her chest, frantic and sobbing.

* * *

Before Tom's funeral, Louise had stood on his parents' doorstep, not wanting to knock, not ready for the contact with Tom's mother Janet. It was November and she remembers vividly the geraniums either side of the front door were still thriving: red and pink blooms exploding from green stems and furred leaves. She had no idea if this was normal or not but it didn't seem normal. Nothing seemed normal.

"Thanks for coming," Janet, Tom's mother had said as she answered the door, as if there was a reality where she wouldn't have come. Louise and Janet had never had an easy relationship. Louise had bought her flat at 16 after her father died, courtesy of his insurance and the sale of their house. Tom had moved in with her when he started university and at 18, this was far too young for Janet's liking. Louise and Janet's relationship had been strained and uncomfortable at best – it certainly wasn't something either of them wanted to continue now there was no reason to.

Janet had been wearing a beige trouser suit, tailored to her tall, thin frame. Her hair, grey-blonde, had been sprayed rigidly into position, like a physical manifestation of her views.

"Hi," Louise had said eventually, lacking the will or the energy to challenge the assumption that she might not have come to her boyfriend's funeral. Janet had smiled, but it'd been unnatural and disconcerting. For a moment, they'd both stood still, gawky, like teenagers, unsure how to move or what their limbs were supposed to do. Neither had moved to hug the other; they'd never pretended affection and saw no reason to start now. Eventually, Janet had stepped back, ending the impasse by opening the door wider so Louise could get in without them coming into contact with her.

Later, after a service where she'd been almost entirely ignored, Louise had found a quiet corner with Adam, away from the insincerity of Tom's relations and other funeral goers.

"You didn't see him, Adam. On the kitchen floor, I mean, all twisted. And then your mother made me go and stare at him lying in that coffin, wearing the suit he hated and smelling of your dad's aftershave." Louise had trailed off, her anger turning into something else, something more desperate. "He looked so...nothing like Tom, he looked more like..." She'd stopped herself, her hand coming up to her mouth involuntarily.

"Me," Adam had finished quietly.

"I didn't mean that." Louise had reached out to him and touched his arm. "I'm sorry, Ad, I didn't mean..."

"It's okay." Adam had pulled her towards him and held her tightly. "I know what you meant."

And she'd felt safe again, in those arms. Listening to that voice. She could have stayed buried in Adam's chest forever, eyes closed, listening to his heart beating.

* * *

Louise knows she and Adam shared 'moments' even before Tom died, small things at first but with an ever-increasing significance. One night, while Louise was cooking dinner, Adam had leant against the wooden sideboard in the kitchen and watched her, a small smile on his face and she'd felt content in a way she never did with Tom. She'd been battling over a wok and singing to herself as steam rose into the fake extractor fan above her. Louise had no method, she was cooking the onion after the chicken, the garlic wasn't chopped yet and an unopened packet of lemon grass sat next to the chrome gas hob. She knew her lack of method annoyed Tom but she also knew Adam found it charming. As Louise had leant over to put a grubby plate into the dishwasher, she'd glanced at Adam and smiled.

"Don't tell Tom." She'd winked. It had been Tom's contention that dishwashers weren't for washing. Dishes had to be washed before they were placed in the appliance. A dishwasher, according to Tom, was for sterilising.

"You'd better hope I don't," Adam had laughed. "He'd dump you on the spot if he knew."

Without meaning to and without even realising it, Louise had created her own private relationship with both Tom and Adam. As twins, they were always in each other's company, which meant Adam was always in her company. And they each gave her something different. Before she knew it, she'd come to rely on both of them.

* * *

"I was standing in the garden having a cigarette earlier." Tom's DVD carries on, oblivious to her thoughts and memories. "The moon was a perfect half. As I turned around to study it I heard a large crack. Felt the pressure in my heel." Tom touches the back of his head. "Realised what I'd done."

Louise watches him motionless, poultry skin.

"Now you might say 'it's only a snail' but how do you measure that? When does something become 'only'? Have I made an imprint? I'd killed the snail. I thought about burying it, but you don't do that, do you. They sit exposed where you kill them."

You were still. Lying awkwardly, like an arm was broken, twisted under you. I knew when I put the key in the lock. Isn't that strange. Before I'd seen you, before...

"I've had some time to think," Tom sighs.

More than I had, Louise thinks as she pours herself a glass of the red wine from the package.

"It's the strangest thing. I don't feel like I'm dying."

Louise sits, dry-eyed. The emptiness of shock is giving way to something else.

"Well you did," she says. Her voice is no longer wavering.

"I can't feel this thing in my head." He isn't looking at Louise anymore, he's staring at the floor. She downs her drink and pours herself another glass. Red.

"And I doubt I'll see His face. God. And I doubt Death is gonna come swooping in on a black horse. It's more likely that I'll..." His voice constricts slightly. "Die. And that will be it, won't it. No more Tom. But you'll still be here, Lou. I know how much you've lost already, but you've got to live. You have to find a way to carry on and I think I know how." He pauses, staring directly at her, piercing eyes, beautiful, full lips. He's about to speak, then it seems like he's changed his mind. Eventually, he leans back again and says:

"Ceasing to be. That's what we can't handle, isn't it. But we don't have a choice..." he rubs the back of his head, "...not about anything."

"You had a choice, you could have told me. Prepared me," Louise says calmly, her chest rising and falling slowly, rhythmically.

"I can't die thinking you'll mourn me forever. I need you to promise me," Tom says. Louise doesn't move but her grip on her glass gets a little bit tighter. "However much I might want to share this with you, I can't. I won't have your pity, Lou. I don't want it."

She cracks. A scream slivers out through the rupture, slowly gaining force. Louder. Louder still. She's a whistling kettle left unattended.

You always thought of me last didn't you? Am I supposed to be grateful for this? A DVD goodbye that cheats me of the real thing? What do I get? I don't get to say goodbye, I don't get to dump my emotions on you. You died and took away my options, you selfish fuck. I don't care if you're dead YOU SHOULD HAVE TOLD ME.

My name is Louise. I never found Lou sweet. I always hated it. For six months I've been wondering what I could've done, why you couldn't open up to me – then you send me this. I don't want a DVD, I want you. You want me to forgive you?

And then another thought hits her, one she should have thought of before. Who did he trust to post the package? He didn't tell her and he didn't tell Adam. But he must have told somebody. But who?

For a few seconds, her body is rigid, before all her strength disappears and she collapses to the floor, statue to shredded rag doll.

Chapter Four

Adam has always lived slightly in his brother's shadow. He simply doesn't shine quite as brightly as Tom... Didn't shine quite as brightly. God, when will he stop thinking in the present tense? When will the past tense slip easily to mind, accepting what's happened?

Despite being identical, their parents had done a good job of fostering their individuality. Once, when he and Tom were little, his mum ordered him a book from Readers' Digest. Tom had gone to a party and Adam had feigned a bad tummy to get out of it, so he'd been in the back garden alone, holding a stick aloft.

"Playing Arthur again?" his mum had said softly, touching his arm to get his attention. "I've got something much better than that, little man. I've got a present for you."

In the hallway, between the cowboy swing doors of the kitchen and the glass door of the porch, his mum gave Adam his present: a small red leather book with gold trimming: *The Secret Garden* by Frances Hodgson Burnett. These were the moments that made Adam's childhood breathable. His mum didn't say another word; she simply left him staring at the book in his palms. He never asked her why she bought him it. He only knew that it was his special gift, something his brother didn't have. He read it that night, finishing it by torchlight well in to the early hours of the morning while Tom slept soundly on the bunk above him.

Adam had kept the book secret from Tom, hidden from him. This was his, something his brother wouldn't take over or take away. Adam had been enchanted by Mary Lennox's world and the space in the secret garden that she created, all of her own. After Tom died, this once-cherished memory, so beautiful and important, felt selfish. He wanted his brother back, he wanted to tell him about the book and what it had meant to him. He wishes he hadn't kept *The Secret Garden* secret at all. Adam could never have shone there alone. He now knows the world is too dark and lonely without Tom's reflected light.

* * *

On his way to Louise's, Adam has decided to take the bus to Victoria. He's now waiting in a long line, trailing out from the protection of the bus shelter and down the street. The sky is throwing water bombs, but everyone is trapped. Getting wet. They can't move under the shelter because nobody thinks of snaking the queue. Everyone has the same collective fear: losing their place. The clever ones have come prepared, with rain macs or umbrellas. Adam squeezes his jacket around him as the rain soaks through the woollen material. He blinks water and feels jealous of the lucky few underneath the shelter.

"Nasty day, isn't it, love?" the woman in front says, snuggling under her umbrella. "Young guy like you should be walking not taking the bus," she adds.

"All the way to Victoria? In this weather?"

"Aye. Young lad like you."

Adam mutters under his breath and turns away. The woman behind him looks like Jackie Onassis and is wearing a tight blue raincoat and enormous black sunglasses. Face fillers.

She starts signing "Waterloo" loudly. Adam can't help smiling and catching her eye as she grins back and they continue to crouch in the rain together, wondering when the bus will arrive. When it finally gets there, Adam goes upstairs and sits down, thinking again of Louise, wondering how he's going to open the conversation, how he's going to broach the subject with her. The woman dressed as Jackie O, the weird singing lady, sits down next to him and stares uncomfortably.

"Can I help you?" he says, turning to stare out of the window. It's a comment meant to shame her but seems to have the opposite effect.

"I doubt it," she replies.

Adam glances at her sunglasses-filled face for a moment and frowns.

"Why do you wear those? It's raining."

"Why do you care?"

"I don't, I don't even know you." Silence. Gentle rocking as the bus travels slowly. Eventually: "My brother died," Adam says. He has no idea why. Jackie studies him for a moment and gently touches his hand. Adam surprises himself by not flinching from it.

"But that's not it," she says quietly, taking her glasses off. Her brown eyes find his and hold them to her.

"No, it's not," he mutters. "I'm in love with his girlfriend."

* * *

Before they met Louise, Adam and Tom had moved to Brighton to go to university. The morning after one party or another, the twins stood in their boxer shorts in their kitchen preparing a breakfast of black coffee. Tom's girlfriend of the moment was silently smoking a joint and exhaling it in his direction, a subtle way of telling him to fuck off, Adam assumed. Other bodies littered the floor, along with empty cans and bottles.

"Are you going to work today?" Tom asked. Adam worked in a local record shop on Saturdays.

"Of course not," Adam replied, leaning over and taking the spliff out of whatsername's hand without looking at her. He'd never taken to any of Tom's girlfriends if he's honest. If you could call them girlfriends. Before Louise, they were nothing more than teen flings or conquests. But later that day, he and Tom had both gone to the newsagents to get fizzy drinks, hangover food and papers. And there she was: Louise.

Adam often wonders what would have happened if Louise

had seen him first instead of Tom. Adam had been standing by the magazine rack in the newsagents as Tom went to the counter to buy cigarettes, unloading an arm full of Lucozade and Irn Bru and crisps and chocolate onto the counter. Leaning down to pick up a paper, Adam glanced to his left and there she was, standing between the razor blades and the tampons. Her hair was tied back into a messy ponytail, her t-shirt and jumper self-consciously crumpled but somehow, it all worked. She was quite simply the most perfect thing he'd ever seen. Except she wasn't looking at him because she'd spotted Tom, his identical twin brother. She was staring, mouth slightly open, at Tom's back. Almost in slow motion, Adam saw Tom glance over his shoulder, as if sensing someone looking at him and their eyes met. Unlike the normal protocol, neither flinched or looked away, they held each other's gaze, too long, long enough to confirm they were both thinking – feeling – the same thing.

Adam wanted to cough, to knock something off the side, to do something to break the moment, to force her attention his way and away from his brother. But it was already too late, they were lost in each other. Adam had lost his brother and the girl of his dreams in one silent, unspoken moment.

* * *

"Maybe I've always loved her," Adam says to the strange singing lady on the bus. Jackie O smiles and places her hand on Adam's knee. The bus jolts before it starts moving again. "But she loves Tom," he continues.

"But he's dead."

"She misses him." Adam sits back in his wet jacket and pulls the damp scribbled note that arrived in the post this morning from his pocket. "I miss him."

He hands it to the Jackie. "I shouldn't be trying to step into his shoes."

"Is that what you're trying to do?" She reads the note and hands it back to Adam.

"No. I couldn't."

"So what's your problem?"

"She's Tom's girlfriend."

"Tom's dead."

"But she belongs to him."

"Belongs? Are you sure?" They sit in silence for a moment.

"Why do you sing?" Adam asks eventually, as the bus pulls in and the doors open. A couple of people get off, nobody gets on. Outside the rain slows but the sun still hides.

"Why not?"

"Because it's a strange thing to do."

"So?"

"So, people will think that you're odd. I did."

"And am I?"

"No, you seem nice."

"So does it matter what people think?"

"I'm not sure I understand."

"Yes you do." She smiles.

"But Tom only died six months ago."

"And do you still love him."

Adam doesn't answer – they both know he doesn't need to.

"And would he think you were being disloyal?" she continues. He knows where she's going with it. His heart is beating too quickly, his fear and denial giving way to something else. Hope? Adam glances at the note in his hand, reads his brother's scrawled handwriting.

"No," he says.

"So what's your problem?"

"What will she say? I can't just roll up and tell her that I love her."

"Why not?"

"She loves Tom."

"But does she love you, too?"

Adam shakes his head and wishes that his travelling companion hadn't put her large glasses back on. He wants to see her eyes.

"But she'll always love him," he says.

"And so will you."

"So I should support her, not complicate her life."

"But what if she cares for you?"

"She doesn't. And anyway, what will people think?" Adam says, turning away and looking out of the window. Jackie O shakes her head and sighs. Then she stands up and starts singing Abba songs.

When he gets off the bus, Adam lights a cigarette. He stopped smoking a couple of years ago with Tom, but after his brother's death, he doesn't see the point. It was a good excuse to start again, he supposes. He isn't proud of it but he does love it. There, he's said it, the thing ex-smokers are not supposed to say. He loves smoking. He inhales and shoves his lighter back into his pocket. He missed it so much when he didn't smoke and it wasn't like the feeling of loss ever went away, it was always there, in the background, day in, day out. There is only so much of that one person can take, he reasons with himself. He can't bring Tom back but he can damn well go and buy a packet of twenty Marlborough Lights.

Finally, he reaches the train station and buys a ticket, getting on board with about a million other people all squeezed in uncomfortably close. Adam stands and sweats, trying not to breathe in the smell of an overweight guy in a shell suit pressed up against him. Adam feels sure his moist jacket must be seeping the man's odour in. In front of him, also pressing into him, is a woman with a personal stereo, loudly playing thrash-metal music. Adam holds his breath and squeezes his eyes shut. Another hour and he'll be in Brighton. He'll be with Louise.

* * *

A week before Tom died, he and Louise had a Halloween party. When Adam arrived, Louise was still getting ready. Tom was dressed as the Grim Reaper.

"I'm a Munchkin," Adam said as Tom ushered him into the sitting room.

"So I see," Tom replied. "How is that Halloweeny? Besides, you're six-foot tall."

"Dunno. Was all they had left at the shop. And you're the prophet of doom?"

"Angel of Death,"

"Happy fucker."

"It's more 'Halloween' than a Munchkin." Tom smiled, ushering Adam into the flat.

"What's Louise coming as?"

"It's a surprise," Tom said, before being interrupted.

"The Good Witch of the North," Louise said, arriving in the doorway, ginger wig all skew whiff.

Even without the Grim Reaper outfit, Tom would have looked brooding. Adam should have known that something was up, but Louise was dazzling him. Her ginger wig and pink white netting dress was beautiful. It shouldn't have been and Adam suspects that on anyone else it wouldn't have been, but somehow Louise made it work.

Later, as other partygoers shimmered around them, not staying long enough to appear real, Adam noticed that Louise was watching him. When his eyes caught hers she didn't turn away and didn't blink. They recognised each other. The dark cloud breaking their gaze wore a cloak and white face paint.

Of course, this wasn't as romantic as it would have been in an American movie because Adam did what he always did in moments of stress and got shitfaced. He and Louise shouldn't have been looking at each other like that, she was his brother's girlfriend. It would be the biggest betrayal possible. So he avoided her all night and found whatever substance he could to numb any feeling he might be having, weed, whisky, wine, and a pill someone gave him. Anything not to think about Louise and the look she'd given him.

Later that evening, Adam went out on the balcony, walking a trace, head throbbing. The air outside was cold and his shoes were squeaking, making high pitches over his breathing. He shouldn't have had that last drink. Not after the last smoke. He was feeling the fear and his anxiety levels were through the roof. The roof terrace had dead flowers along its edge. Shouldn't someone have kept them alive? His head was throbbing and music was playing in circles, repetition again, again, again. He shouldn't have come, he shouldn't feel the way he does, he shouldn't...

Somewhere in the background he could hear party noises and conversations.

"Well, I walked into this large study room and there she was, sitting in a large leather chair wearing thigh-high PVC boots and nipple rings with chains dangling from them," a guy trying too hard to be cool was saying loudly, so the entire flat could hear. "There was a whip over her shoulder and this massive steel dildo in her hand. Well, can you imagine? I didn't know where to turn."

Repeated action, foot after foot after foot, green shoe met grey roof terrace, again, again, again. The trace he was making, his circular pace, curled like a millipede, stretching, getting thinner and thinner until, unable to take the strain, it split and Adam staggered, nearly fell. Was caught. By Louise, of course by Louise. Who else? Glinda the Good Witch of the North. She grabbed his arm, the skin of her palm clammy against his cold forearm.

"Adam, are you listening to me?"

He didn't think so. His jeans were blue, worn and pacing. His t-shirt felt tighter than it should have done, like it was too small for him. What was she saying?

"Adam." Her voice from somewhere. He glanced up, stopped his pacing to see Louise, Tom's Louise, the light from the room behind her carrying partygoers, dancing and shimmering around her. Someone was being sick in the corner. Adam's saliva seemed to have turned to paste in his mouth.

"I want to go," he said. He felt sick, he couldn't focus on her properly.

"Have you smoked too much again?" Louise said.

Silence.

"You haven't taken anything else, have you?"

He couldn't remember.

"Come on, I'll get Tom to take you home."

* * *

That all feels like a lifetime ago, now, but in reality it's less than a year. Adam's train pulls into Brighton and, still lost in his thoughts he begins to walk up the hill to Louise's flat. As he rounds the corner he stumbles into a woman selling lucky heather.

"Sorry," Adam mutters as memories continue to overwhelm him. His left fingers play with the note from his brother in his pocket. He's now less than five minutes away from her and he still doesn't know what he's going to do or how he's going to say what his brother wants him to say.

Chapter Five

"I keep imagining the blood travelling around my head," Tom says. "Like it's a river that's slowly becoming blocked. It won't be long.

"I'm noticing things, seeing how temporary everything is. I don't know what I'm supposed to do with that? How can I share this with you? This is mine." He taps his head with his index finger. "I don't want to share it."

Tom looks at the table in front of him and picks up various books. Louise, a crumpled figure on the floor, lifts her head and stares once more at the television.

I came home from work and you were dead in the kitchen. Have you got any idea how that felt? You were dead in our kitchen. On the floor and cold. You didn't have the decency to warn me. Left me lying on the floor with you.

"He asked questions," Tom carries on regardless, holding up one of the books. Louise squints: *The Last Days of Socrates*. "But alone, that didn't help. So he made people question themselves. Problem is, people fight you if you make them do that." He pauses for too long. "Death is the only thing that makes you question yourself. Reflect on your life. There's nowhere else, is there?" He leans forward in his chair and addresses Louise intimately. "Do you remember that room we had in that little Italian village? What was it called? Amalfi, wasn't it?" He sits back in his chair. "We had fun there, didn't we?"

* * *

Her fingers reach out and stroke the glass of the television set to touch his face. She's been dreaming of that holiday in Amalfi, their first together. But she never expected that Tom would remember it. It was small Italian village on the coast with a gargantuan church in its town square. She and Tom had happily wandered through a maze of narrow lanes and markets each day, the sun burning their pale skin. The room they were staying in had large windows that allowed the fresh, salty scent of the sea in, along with the smell of leather goods sold on the market, of chilli and freshly brewed coffee.

"Let's go to the church," she'd said one day, making a grab for Tom's arm to drag him up the ever-long staircase. As she stepped inside, she lost all sense of whether Tom was even with her or not. The intense heat from outside was sucked out of her as she stepped into shadow. Goose pimples argued for space on her flesh, the dominant ones finding the back of her neck and arms. Her eyes searched the vast space before her – the stone floor, the wooden pews, the impossibly high painted ceiling. She heard echoes, of nothing, of something? As she took one step further into the church the light changed and she blinked. The atmosphere, the air quality, got heavier. Her footsteps rippled, her breathing was alien and for the smallest of moments, she was immersed. She stood in the corridor between wooden pews and stained-glass windows, larger than even this church should have allowed. Tricks of multi-coloured light sparkled and moved as if governed by free will, searching for somewhere to rest. In the distance, there was a bang as the heavy wooden door slammed open. The echo rebounded off the walls and Louise had flinched, feeling the tension rising. The peace of was about to be broken as Tom shouted to her across the church.

"Jesus, how many steps were there, I'm knackered."

Louise had glanced around, searching the far of recesses of shaded enclaves, looking for somewhere to escape to and reclaim the calm of moments before.

"It's beautiful," Tom continued.

The church was lost. Louise ran back through the pew corridor and stumbled past Tom through the overlarge doorway into the heat, staring down the steps into the village.

* * *

"We should have known in Amalfi, Louise." Tom's smile disappears and she presses her fingers tightly to his cold, solid cheek. He swallows, glancing away from the camera. When his eyes find hers again they're darker.

"I'm dead," he says, "but you, you've got to start living again. See, I know you, Louise. I love you. But just because I'm dead, doesn't mean we were Romeo and Juliet. We weren't. You know that. But Adam," he pauses. "He loves you, Lou. He'd never shut you out like I have."

I can never say goodbye. My comfort died cold on cold tiles. You let me carry on getting bogged down in the little thing and I barely noticed you as you were dying. You should have given me the chance to mourn with you.

"Do you know what I dream of? Creating a world with only the two of us in. A replica of this world, a retreat, a world within our own that we can visit. A place where this," he rubs the back of his head, "doesn't matter. A world where my body can repair itself without killing me." He raises his glass.

"But do you know why we can't go to that world, Lou?" Tom pauses long enough for her to formulate her own answer. She can see their world, this place that Tom has created. She can see Tom smiling and she stands next to him and clutches his arm, warm breeze brushing through their hair. She stares through the market and to the steps of the enormous church. There's a man sitting at the bottom, turning towards her. It's not Tom, but she can't make out his features, doesn't want to make out his features, she's been trying to ignore him.

"Adam. You'd always be looking for Adam." Tom leans forward in his chair. Louise swallows and stares into his eyes in a way she never could when he lived.

"You see, the truth of the matter is this. You don't love me anymore, not like you used to." He leans forward in his seat.

"How can I tell you I'm dying knowing that?" He pauses again before sitting back. Louise is shivering as pushes herself fully onto the sofa and tucks her knees to her chin, like she used to do as a little girl listening to her parents argue.

"I've seen you and Adam together. I'm not stupid. Oh, my death will confuse you, it will make you pretend that you were still in love with me. You'll play the bereaved girlfriend." His tone softens. "I appreciate it, I do. But you can stop now. It's been six months if Mr. Carmichael delivers this DVD on time. It's time to get on with your life.

"I probably haven't got long left, Lou. And I do love you. Whatever we have or haven't got, you used to love me. But move on. We weren't the greatest love affair of all time. You needed someone after your dad, I get that, but don't build us up in to something we're not." He smiles slightly. "For the record I don't think you and Adam will go the distance either. But at least give it a go. For me?"

Rain punches the windows. Louise's heart punches her chest as she exhales chalk.

"Pour yourself some wine."

She glances at the near-empty bottle and smiles in spite of herself.

"A toast. To life. Your life, Lou. You and Adam." He raises his glass. "Good health."

* * *

She can feel the heat of the mosaic floor in the Amalfi square through her sandals as the small fountain with leaking cherubs sprays water towards a mother holding her son up to drink.

"For good health," the mother says. The son gurgles. Tom, sitting outside a café with Louise, sips his coffee and wears his happy face.

"Let's drink from the fountain," he says joyfully. Louise

scowls at him, staring past him to the small shop with large bunches of red chillies hanging outside like fiery grapes. Grandmothers and granddaughters sit in shop doorways stringing these strange attractions together on cotton.

"Lou. Did you hear me? It's supposed to give eternal health. Let's drink." Tom's voice irritates her. The future her would love to grab him and run to the fountain laughing. But she isn't her future self, so she refocuses on him and snaps.

"Oh shut up, Tom. It's tourist drivel."

"Don't be so miserable."

"Don't be such a tourist."

"We are tourists. What's up with you?"

"Nothing." She finishes her coffee in one gulp. "I want to go back to the room."

"Why? You have to spoil everything, don't you?"

* * *

In her sitting room, she cries as she watches Tom and wishes that she'd acted differently. She wishes he'd allowed her the opportunity.

"So that's it. I've run out of things to say. Or I haven't got enough time to say them. One or the other." Tom lifts his glass, drinks Rioja.

"So this is goodbye." He smiles at her and she knows that when he sips his drink, when he tastes his wine, the picture will fade. He'll say goodbye and go. Forever. He'll never say another word to her. She scrambles for the remote control and as his glass meets his lips, the wine touches his tongue, her finger finds the pause button. She breathes heavily and watches his face stammer, settle. Freeze.

I loved you. You can sit there and tell me I but it won't change the truth. Why didn't you give me the chance to tell you that? You were the only one for me. Adam's...I...I didn't love him then.

42

She jumps to her feet, knocking her wineglass over as she runs from the room, leaving Tom's paused face drinking. The stairs lead to her bedroom, her room leads to her bed. The sheets don't hold the comfort they promised as she sobs into them. They bristle. Sleep, when it comes, isn't restful.

In her dream, the walls are white. Heat rushes towards her face as she opens the large shuttered windows. She is high above the ground yet the church is still above her. Enormous stone steps rise from the square below up and up and up until they meet the church. She breathes but already the warm sea air tastes stale. This is the end of the dream, the part she dreads. She knows when she turns back Tom will be behind her, smiling. She knows that as she pulls the window shut and brushes her hair behind her ear, she'll start to turn. She'll search for Tom's face. Then she'll realise where she is and she'll feel the sheets beneath her and she'll wake. Alone.

So though she feels Tom behind her, this time she won't turn and she won't wake. She'll stay here and won't try to look at Tom – to do so is impossible. Maybe that was always the problem. Is that what the dream is telling her? She'll search the faces of the people in the square below her instead. The men and women scattered across the steps of the church. She already knows that a young man has been trying to get her attention. For months she's noticed him from the corner of her eye but today she'll see him. Today she'll look for his face and forsake Tom's. She leans forward and places her hands on the windowsill. The air is dry in her eyes and it takes all of her willpower not to turn around. One more glimpse. But it won't be allowed, she knows that, so this time, she searches the market stalls instead.

The sun is large and casts shadows of the church. And there he is. Beautiful. Patient. Sitting on the first layer of steps, somehow avoiding the shadow and catching the sunlight, making his dark hair seem lighter, more vibrant than she's ever seen it. She wants to shout his name, to wave and call to him but for a moment she drinks in his image. He's alive and he's waiting for her, she can see that now. All this time she's been trying to look backwards, trying to hold on to someone that no longer exists, but Adam does, he's the here and now. He's waiting on the steps, so calmly, so patiently. She opens her mouth to shout his name but a loud banging drags her away from the room. She flinches and arrives behind swollen eyes. It's him. She jumps up and runs down the stairs, beating. She stands behind the closed front door. Tom is still paused in the sitting room. Wine is still on the carpet. Makeup still smudges her eyes. But she thinks it's over. Nearly over. Can she restart now? Is that possible? Is it as sordid as it seems? Is it even him beyond the wooden barrier? She's smiling. It's him. She's going to live in real-time, not within a paused DVD. Not within an Italian holiday. She knows he can sense her here. He knows she's debating whether to answer the door.

She opens the door to see Mr Carmichael, trimming his roses after the rainstorm and offering one to Adam.

"Thank you," Adam says, taking the rose. Mr Carmichael smiles and continues gardening.

"I love you," Adam says. Mr Carmichael chuckles and Adam glances nervously at him before making eye contact with Louise again.

"I love you, Louise." Adam rubs his right eye and shifts uncomfortably. Louise stands in the open doorway staring at him. He scratches his cheek. Louise doesn't speak but stands aside to let him in. Mr Carmichael glances at Louise as she begins to shut the door.

"Spring leaves," he says.

"Thank you," she says quietly. She thinks she means it. Mr Carmichael bows his head slightly and continues clipping his roses. Louise shuts the door.

In the sitting room the television holds Tom's picture. Adam stands solid, eyes fixed on his brother. He hands Louise the letter he has been gripping, without looking away from the screen. She reads it. Strokes his hand. Doesn't speak.

"Do you miss him?" Adam says quietly. Louise reaches out and touches his cheek but they stand in silence.

"Always," she says eventually. He nods and sits down on the sofa and stares at his brother's flickering face. Louise looks from one brother to the other and can't help thinking of Tom's parting comment.

"For the record I don't think you and Adam will go the distance either. But at least give it a go. For me?"

Louise presses rewind.

Interlude

I got into the habit of reading Tom's *New Scientist* magazines after he died. I'd never been interested before, thought it was one of his weird things, but loss like that changes your perspective on the world. Some people turn to religion, I suppose, but I went the other way, into contemplating the universe and its unimaginable vastness, its inexplicable nature. It's a habit I never lost, I read it for years, right up until I...well, until now.

Memories are flooding over me like chilling, icy waves. The white wooden living-room windows of our flat were dirty around the edges. Had they ever been cleaned? I shouldn't think so. I suppose we could have paid someone else to do it but we never did, I'm not sure why. Middle-class guilt? We got over that once the kids were born, that's for sure, we took any help we could get once we become parents. So this memory must be from early on in our relationship. When we were happy, not that long after Tom died.

Outside, I can see Mr Carmichael's garden, always so perfect. There's the gnarled, arthritic oak tree opposite us that looks like an old woman stooping to pick up her shopping. I'd forgotten all about that, funny how you can forget things that are tucked away somewhere inside your brain. I stare intently from the window, studying people as they clean cars, walk dogs, interact: lives still being lived. Not like mine, rushing headlong towards its end.

"Wow, did you see that puff?" a little boy on the television exclaims. I glance backwards in my mind to see a little round plastic mushroom on an advert on the TV screen in our old flat, spraying clouds of perfume, chemically flowering the room with every spluttered exhalation. Shouldn't these thoughts be more...I don't know...important? Shouldn't these last memories be about something else, not just compressed knitted together streams of nothing? Or is that all life is in the end, moment after moment after moment of not much at all, punctuated by feelings of worthlessness?

No, that can't be true. I had children. If I did nothing else I did that. Our marriage may have not been perfect, but we had Maria and Matthew so my life wasn't meaningless. Why am I remembering this shit? I don't even know what's real anymore. I was filled with toxic worry, apparently. A magazine told me so it must be true. Of course it also told me if I popped butter beans out of their skins whilst still warm they'd make a groovy paste so perhaps it wasn't the most reliable source.

I don't want to think like this, I want something more positive, something tangible, something that will overpower my senses and stop the hurt getting in because I don't want to die hurting. I don't want to die at all. I just wanted to prove a point. I can't begin to tell you how ridiculous that feels now.

We're good swimmers for land mammals. I read that once in Tom's *New Scientist* magazine. "We cannot go long without a drink and seem to waste large amounts of fluid in sweat and urine," the article said. I forget who wrote it. "By wading upright, the ancestral primate would have kept its hands free for manipulating objects and climbing. This would have allowed the hands to evolve into a supremely dextrous tool-making appendage." Aquatic Apes the writer called us. She was convinced we'd spent a good part of our history living by the coast, wading in the water and catching food from the sea. Our babies have fat like the blubber whales have. Matthew was like that, a real porker as a baby. Other land mammals, even other primates, don't have this blubber. Not sure if that proves the writer's point or not. Probably not, things are always a lot more complicated than that. I'm a good swimmer. I won badges for it when I was at school. I doubt it will stand me in good stead now, though. I don't think people survive plunging off Beachy Head. Mostly they don't want to.

But *I* do. I want to go back. This has all been a terrible mistake.

* * *

In the past, in the beige neutrality of our flat with lawn mowers and televisions and scaffold poles and chirping seagulls outside, I swallow and open my eyes. Blink. My back aches because I've been sitting cross-legged on the living-room floor for what seems like an eternity.

"Are you meditating?" a voice says, but I'm not sure if it's taking the piss or not. That's the thing about marriage, after a while, you stop knowing when your spouse is serious or not, when they're joking or jibing. Next – and you don't remember when – you stop even caring. At least, that's how my marriage became. But not yet, not in this moment.

In this moment, I'm trying to remain centred and in the present, removing myself from all past and future concerns. I'm holding my palms face outwards, resting them on my knees.

"Shhh," I'm saying gently. "I'm concentrating."

"I've got something to tell you," the voice continues. I struggle to open my eyes and stand up but my legs are still crossed and twisted. The blood rushes past my eyes and I see a blur, like white rock and sky, spinning out of control. I can hear the sound of children wailing, but they're trapped inside white, feathered, seagull bodies. I see the sea, crashing waves, needle-sharp rocks.

"You okay?" The sunlight is filtering through our living-room windows and I am desperately trying to focus, to remain here, in the past, when we were happy and alive and our world was filled with possibility. Our lives were wonderful sometimes. Ordinary and humdrum and wonderful. I forgot that towards the end, but now I'm seeing it through dying eyes, I remember. It wasn't all bad – we both fucked up. But people do that all the time don't they. And there's always a way back if you want it hard enough.

"What?" I struggle to say, clinging to my memories desperately, like a child clutching a balloon in the wind.

"Doesn't matter," the voice says simply, disconnecting from me. Disconnecting permanently, maybe. My heart stops beating, just for a moment. I think it did matter, but I didn't notice until now. Too late, always too late. But it mattered. Listening to one another mattered.

Perhaps that's how all relationships end, not with a bang but with the accumulation of millions of tiny moments that matter, going unnoticed by one partner or the other because life gets in the way. And then one day you both stop trying to make the other one notice anymore. And that's it, the slow death is in motion. The rest is entropy.

We should have taken better care of each other – that's what we promised. It could have been either one of us dying right now. We both thought about it, for different reasons. I guess it was always going to be me though. Despite everything, I was never the survivor. The thing I find most heart-breaking is that the kids will think I left them and I wasn't coming back.

I can see things with such clarity now, such useless, blinding clarity. But what's the point in that now? Knowledge isn't always powerful. Sometimes, it's just heart-breaking.

Part Two: These Other Things

"You're nothing like your mother."

Chapter Six

Adam sits in his kitchen, staring through the window into the garden and listening to the next-door neighbours banging and hammering, trying to fix the legs on a broken chest of drawers. The sounds of suburbia, something he never thought he'd find comforting. They've been in this house for five years now and he's surprised how much he loves it.

"I don't know, Louise," he said when they'd first viewed it. "I grew up in suburbia, I don't know if I can do it. It just feels so…dead behind the eyes."

Louise flashed him a smile: "But look at the size of it," she said, her smile turning into an enormous grin. "We can't get anything this big in the city centre, nothing like it."

And she was right. At first, with just the two of them, it seemed massive in comparison with the flat, extravagant even. But now, with a four-year-old girl and a three-year-old boy haring about in it, it doesn't seem too big: it's just right. He loves it, it's a real family home, somewhere he thinks he can stay forever. He can't believe he's been this lucky, that out of the tragedy of Tom's loss, something so good could have happened. Louise, Matthew, Maria. His family. He leans back in his chair, a feeling of warm calm settling over him as his mobile phone starts buzzing on the table. He glances down to see 'Imogen' flashing.

"Hey, Imogen," he says, her name forming a question as he speaks. She's Louise's friend from antenatal classes. She never rings him.

"Adam, how are you getting on?" Imogen asks, her faux concern not even disguised.

"Oh, I'm fine, we're fine."

"Going off on a conference all week and leaving you all alone with two young children," Imogen continues, oblivious to his protestations. "I know she's my friend, Adam…"

"They're at school and nursery, it's fine, I don't need…"

"But honestly, I don't understand Louise sometimes." Imogen's voice is firm, she's not going to be persuaded out of her way of thinking.

"It's just a conference, Imogen, she must have told you about it."

"I'll come around, I've made a casserole," Imogen says. "Do you have food for the kids? Of course you do. Gavin can look after Timmy for a couple of hours. Not all dads are as hands on as you, you know, Adam. It'll do Gavin good, teach him parenting is every bit as hard as investment banking."

"No, honestly, Imogen, it's…"

"Scones," she says, pronouncing it sc-owns, not s-cons. He wants to interrupt, to tell her she's saying it wrong, that posh people – real posh people, would never say it like that, just like they'd never say dessert, they'd say pudding.

"I'll bring sc-owns. Do the kids like sc-owns? Of course they do, everyone likes sc-owns. Well, except Alice, she doesn't, but she's always on a diet isn't she, especially now she's met John. Did Louise tell you she'd met someone? I wish her all the happiness, Adam, I do, but I can't see it working."

"Imogen…" Adam interrupts. If she says 'sc-owns' one more time, he'll have to hang up, he can't bear it.

"So, I'll see you around eight," she says, and she hangs up before he can protest any more. The last thing he needs is Imogen coming over to try and help or, heaven forbid, to keep him company. He's never been fond of her at all and he's not sure that Louise is either. She's one of those friends that somehow hangs on, despite the fact nobody can stand them. It's odd that she wants to come over, though. She's never paid him that much attention before. He suspects in reality she's on a fact-finding mission, wondering if there's something going on. *Why has Louise gone away? Is there something going on I don't know about?*

* * *

Adam sits back in his kitchen and returns his mobile to the table. He can hear next door shouting and ranting at one another as the try to fix their chest of drawers. Not angry shouting; the type of banter and arguing that comes with being a family. Adam actually finds it quite comforting. Initially he liked the house simply because it wasn't Louise and Tom's flat. Now he loves it because it's where his children are growing up. It drinks in their memories, absorbing them into its walls so that its essence has become their essence.

Adam had never felt comfortable in the flat. Replacing Tom in his own home, with his own girlfriend seemed like it was a step too far, somehow. Not that either of them had cared what other people thought. Once they'd committed to each other, everything else became secondary. Their lives became a happy haze of…well, just a haze. Watching movies, smoking weed, drinking and eating and shagging. Wearing sunglasses when they went out so people wouldn't see how fucked up they were from their eyes. Or maybe in the early days, it was so they could avoid the stares from the neighbours with their gossip and thoughts and opinions.

Is that Tom? He looks like Tom? It can't be Tom, he died.

The word *died* would be whispered under their breaths Adam knew, because people couldn't bear to say it out loud for fear of bringing it – death – too close, close enough that it might attach itself to them, a tiny limpet on their skin that would grow and eventually turn into a boil, a tumour, devouring them and their loved ones from within. Better to whisper the word, almost so quietly as to not say it at all, just to be safe.

But death had no such power over Adam and Louise after Tom. Despite how raw they were from his loss, they'd been wildly happy. In some strange way, their experience had made them grab life and wring everything they could out of it. Having committed what seemed to many the ultimate taboo, Adam and

Louise didn't have to pretend to be anything. They'd blown their chance of 'fitting in' with society and its norms – and that was liberating for both of them.

At first, they had spent their days in the flat, floating about, making each other coffee and watching daytime TV. When they went out, the only neighbour who didn't double take was dear old Mr Carmichael, but so what? Being on the 'outside' of 'normal' suited both of them – in many ways it made them feel more alive, more able to live fully and completely. Things weren't perfect, of course. In death as in life, Tom cast a long shadow. Adam missed his brother continually. Pain is supposed to get more tolerable over time, but for Adam, it was something he learned to incorporate into his daily routine without showing the signs outwardly. Nobody was interested in long-term grief – most people had lost interest within a week of the funeral, let alone months and years.

It wasn't simple, however. He certainly wasn't without his insecurities where Louise and Tom were concerned.

"You're a better shag than Tom was," Louise had grinned once, when he'd been asking her if she was sure she loved him.

"You can't say that…"

"Tom's idea of foreplay was slapping my quim," she'd said.

"No," Adam had said, sticking his fingers in his ears. "Don't want to hear this." They'd stared at each other for a moment, both smiling until he couldn't resist saying: "Quim? Who uses words like quim?" He'd taken his fingers out of his ears. "He liked slapping it?"

Louise had nodded, chuckling to herself.

"What? Like…" Adam had paused, miming a slapping motion in the air with his left hand and making popping sounds with his lips.

"Uh huh." Louise's shoulders had been shaking with laughter.

"And did you like it?"

"Nope."

"Did you tell him?"

"No, it seemed rude."

"Giving you a red-raw quim seems a bit more rude." Adam had laughed, diving on top her and kissing her on the mouth.

"And," Louise had said, pushing his head downwards, "you're much better at oral than him."

Later, as she sat naked between his thighs, head leaning back comfortably into his chest, she'd said, "I'm putting the flat on the market."

Adam's heart had sped up, beating a little faster with utter, complete love. A place of their own, somewhere to create their own memories, away from memories of Tom. He kissed her head, inhaling deeply the scent of her cherry blossom shampoo. He hadn't spoken, he'd simply sat there holding her. Eventually they had to give in and move, to go about the business of life again, cooking dinner, putting the washing on and tidying up.

* * *

Adam double locks the front door behind him and glances up at the blue sky and sunshine, smiling to himself. Now they are parents, they don't have the freedom they had in the early years of their relationship, but Adam wouldn't change it for the world. Besides, they'd wrung everything out of single life back then.

Shortly after getting married, they'd gone to Spain, somewhere nobody knew them, where the whispers and nudging wouldn't touch them, somewhere they could drink in the sun, like there might be no tomorrow.

"Why is that girl licking herself all over like a cat?" Louise asked, sitting in a Spanish nightclub, sipping her cocktail through a straw and nodding her head towards a girl on the multi-coloured dance floor. Adam had taken a sip of his own cocktail, taking his eyes off his wife's cleavage for a moment to see what she was talking about.

A girl, maybe only eighteen years old, was sitting down on the dance floor, a fur coat (fake, he hoped it was fake) on the floor under her, wearing nothing but a bra and orange hot pants. And she was licking her forearm earnestly, like a cat preening itself, lapping and nuzzling as if it was the most normal thing in the world. Adam had burst out laughing, a throaty, full-bodied laugh he'd forgotten he was capable of.

"She's on something, right?" He'd laughed. "Jesus, I hope she's all right, how much shit has she taken?"

"Ha, Adam, you've changed. I remember a certain man dressed as a Munchkin taking everything he could get his hands on."

"Fuck, that was terrible," Adam had said, smiling and spinning around on his bar stool. Louise had stood up and grabbed his hand and dragged him onto the dance floor, laughing. Two days later, they'd hired a small car, purple, number plates half falling off. Cheap, probably not even road-worthy but they hadn't cared, it did the job. They'd driven up a tiny narrow potholed road, weaving around the cliff towards the small town of Comares in Andalucía and everything was perfect. Louise had been driving (she always had to drive) and Adam had stared from the window at the cliffs and valleys beneath them, not green like England's hills, they were drier, more barren, but beautiful. They'd jolted along the tiny, unsafe road, hitting pothole after pothole, sometimes getting uncomfortably close to the edge, near the crash barriers that would have been hard pushed to stop a Robin Reliant doing ten miles an hour from plummeting over the edge. And Adam had realised something alarming. For a brief moment, he had contemplated the car spinning out of control and smashing through the barrier and plummeting off the mountain and he'd calmly thought 'okay then'. He'd have been happy to carry on staring at the beauty of the Sierra Nevada mountains, waiting for his existence to cease as long as he was with Louise. He would have looked sideways at her, grasping her hand and neither of them would have screamed, they'd have grabbed each other and kissed and held each other tightly.

Adam's thought about that moment a lot. It wasn't that he wanted them die, far from it. But he'd realised in that moment that he was so happy, so complete that if their lives had ended there and then it would have been okay. It was nothing more than a transient thought, a fleeting emotion, but it affected Adam massively, made him realise that despite losing Tom, he was going to be okay. Louise had pulled the small car into a space in the small town of Comares and Adam had jumped out and held his head up, closing his eyes, feeling the breeze and the sun on his face. His nostrils had filled with the smell of olive oil and garlic from a café behind them an as he'd opened his eyes to survey the scene, he'd seen a maelstrom of knitted green yellow cacti on the mountainside with bulbous, red, sticky fruit ripening on them.

"Come on, I think it's this way," Louise said with growing excitement, smiling and grabbing his arm, dragging him along. She led them through some narrow, winding lanes to the town cemetery. It was not like an English cemetery; the dead were buried above ground here, not below – five bodies high, twenty or sometimes thirty rows across.

"Why did you bring us here?" Adam asked, actually quite fascinated but feeling it was a little morbid.

"Shame for the ones at the top," Louise said, ignoring him. "How can loved ones come and mourn and lay flowers all the way up there?"

"Maybe they've got step ladders?" Adam said, half joking, half serious.

"Silly sod." Louise flashed him a smile. "Look." She pointed to the end, where large iron steps on wheels stood beside one of the grave halls.

"Well, nearly a step ladder," he said, squinting to read the inscriptions in front of him. "Juan Perez, died 1920." The grave halls each had a small window, containing a tiny gravestone and flowers.

"You haven't got family here or something have you?" Adam asked, thinking there was a wider significance to their visit that he'd been too self-absorbed to notice.

"No, I just read about it in the guide book, it's cool isn't it."

The only similarity with British cemeteries and this place was the silence. Apart from a dramatic wind picking up through the cliff tops, rustling dry leaves and grasses in a slightly eerie sonata, there was nothing. No human interference, apart from Louise and Adam, tourists in a graveyard.

"Yeah," Adam had said, walking over and taking Louise's hand. "It's wonderful."

* * *

Adam walks down the road, heading to Maria's school, still thinking about the early years with Louise, before the children were born. He missed Tom, still does, with every fibre, but somehow being with Louise made him feel closer to him. Things had worked out okay, something he hadn't thought possible. Except there's something niggling him, something he's not letting in. Louise isn't coping, he knows she isn't. He thought she would be all right, that she'd get over things, but lately he's started to think it might not be that simple.

As he crosses the road, his mobile goes off again. This time, it's his mother.

"How you getting on?" Her voice is stern, like he's done something wrong. This is always how she speaks to him, always her opening tone. The assumption being he's done something wrong or there is something wrong or something needs to be fixed. Equilibrium doesn't exist for Janet Gaddis, only different shades of crisis.

"Mum, I'm fine. This is the third time you've called today. Louise's only away for a week."

"Well, I still think it's a little strange," his mother says. "Leaving her kids alone like that."

"They're not alone, Mum, they're with me."

"Still, a mother's place…"

"Mum." His tone has an air of finality; it's a conversation they've had many times before. Janet has never been able to accept that Adam is a stay-at-home parent and Louise goes out to work. Actually, she'd never been able to accept Louise full stop. If Janet can find a reason to have a go at Louise, she'll take it, no matter how big or small.

To say that his mum didn't take kindly to Adam's marriage would be an understatement. Janet has never apologised for anything in her life, but she makes a habit of finding inexcusable behaviour in others. When she feels she has someone bang to rights – that they've behaved so badly that everyone else in the world would agree with *her* – well, she'll hold that bit between her teeth until her gums bleed. So when Adam moved in with Louise, when he'd married her, when they had two children, it was quite high up on her list of unforgivable actions. One more thing on the long list of grievances his mother will never forgive him for, like when she caught Jason Atkins going down on him when they were fourteen years old. Or when Tom died instead of him, the son they both know she would much rather have lost.

In the early days, Adam and Louise had tried to get her onside and win her approval. Adam had invited them to the flat for dinner once, desperately trying to prove to them that their relationship wasn't as weird as they thought it was, trying to navigate a path back to some sort of *normality* for their family. Predictably, it had been a disaster – frosty, uncomfortable and filled with snipes and silences. Afterwards, as Adam had sat in bed watching Louise perform the bedtime rituals he loved so much, they had decided it was probably best not to do it again.

"I don't want her here anymore." Louise had stood in her knickers, smoothing face cream into her cheeks. "We invite her round for dinner and what do we get? Sour-faced old cow."

"Come on, Louise, she's my mum,"

"If I mash the potatoes, she tells me you like them roasted. If I roast them, I'm told they should be crispier. Even the soap I buy is wrong. Unhygienic, apparently. How can soap be unhygienic, Adam? It's bloody soap. And I like them soggy."

"What?"

"Potatoes, Adam. I like them soggy. The only one who doesn't like them a bit soggy is your mother."

"Actually," Adam had said, taking his life into his own hands, "Mum's right, everyone in the world except you prefers them crispy." He'd ducked in time to avoid the lid of Louise's face cream as it sailed towards him.

"You're such a sod," she'd said, running over and jumping on him, straddling him. "You wait." She'd leant in for a kiss but had withdrawn at the last moment and jumped off him.

"Unfair." He'd grinned.

"No quim for you tonight." She'd laughed.

While Adam had wanted to repair his relationship with his parents, he knew his mother well enough to know there wasn't much he could do about it. When she had her mind set, she rarely changed it based on other people's actions; she could always find something wrong if she wanted to. Instead, Adam decided not to waste any of his energy trying to appease her, he'd play the long game and get on with his life. She'd come around eventually.

The trouble this time is that Adam can't help feeling that his mother might be right – about one thing at least. Something isn't right with Louise, hasn't been for a while. It's like an open secret nobody mentions. After Maria was born, Louise suffered from post-natal depression. Having Matthew only fifteen months later didn't help. She'd thought she would somehow feel differently the second time, that she'd feel like a woman was *supposed to feel*. Her words, not his:

"I don't feel like I'm *supposed* to feel, Adam. Like a mother is supposed to feel. I see you with her and you're so natural, so…I don't know. I'm like my mother, aren't I? Not capable of loving her."

"You're nothing like your mother," Adam had tried to reassure her, "nothing like her at all." But as time went on, he began to privately, secretly (oh so far inside his head that he didn't even allow it conscious expression) suspect that she might be right. What if she was a little too like her mother?

Chapter Seven

Louise has been at a country hotel alone for nearly a week. She told Adam she had to attend a catering conference, that it was important to her café business. In reality, there is no catering conference. But as Adam and the children had buzzed around her, the invisible woman sitting on their family sofa, nothing more than an obstacle for them to climb over, she'd felt that feeling of panic growing, the whistling kettle inside again, bubbling away, desperate to scream, to vent, to escape. They'd be better off without her anyway. Because she's like her mother, inescapably, genetically, the same: selfish.

* * *

"You don't think she's jinxed, do you?" her mother is saying, a constant memory replaying in Louise's mind.

"Don't be stupid," her dad replies, exasperated to be having the same conversation yet again.

Louise, a small child, sitting crouched, knees hugged, staring into the glowing slit that reveals her parents' bedroom.

"I know, it's just...I don't know. I know it's awful to say about your own child, but she's different since it happened. She's got these dark little eyes."

"She's got green eyes, Jane, like you."

"Icy, then..."

"She saw Lucy die, it's bound to have affected her."

"She watched Lucy die, Pete. She didn't see it, she watched it. And that psychic woman said she was going to be involved in something terrible."

"She wasn't a psychic, Jane, she was char lady from Dagenham."

Louise had been five years old when Lucy, the suicide

babysitter, killed herself.

"Louise, I'm dizzy," Lucy had said, falling dramatically back onto the sofa. Louise had remained cross-legged on the floor, playing with her doll – called Sylvia – and a plastic Trog called Janette-Plantette. Louise hadn't paid much attention to her babysitter; she'd seen it all before. Whenever she babysat, Lucy would down some of the whisky from the drinks cabinet or smoke a cigarette or throw up in the kitchen sink. The pills didn't seem like anything new. Later in life, Louise realised Lucy had probably meant her to tell someone and get help. But Louise hadn't realised it wasn't a game until Lucy had stopped convulsing.

"But…" Louise's mum continues in the memory, still trying to convince Louise's dad there's something fundamentally wrong with their daughter.

"Look, can we stop talking about Lucy. Hasn't she caused enough harm?"

"Don't talk like that – she's dead. And in our house, why in our house? It was probably a cry for help, Pete. If only Louise had done something."

"It's not Louise's fault, Jane, stop blaming her."

"I'm saying, is all. It's a bit weird, isn't it? She just played with her dolls while Lucy was right next to her, dying."

"If we hadn't gone out that night…" her dad says quietly.

"Pete, we're allowed a life. It's not like we ever get to do much with Louise hanging off us all the time."

"But if we'd come home earlier. Or phoned to check how Louise was?"

"Louise was fine," Jane says coldly, "she was playing with her Sylvie doll, wasn't she."

"Jane, stop this. It wasn't Louise's fault."

"I'm just saying."

"You're always just saying. It has to stop. It's not fair on her, she's not stupid, she picks up on things."

"Other people must think it, " Jane continues. "What kind of kid watches her babysitter die?"

"How many kids' babysitters top themselves?" Louise's dad raises his voice a little, before tempering it back down to a whisper. "Enough, Jane."

"And you know she's got an imaginary brother now?" Jane carries on regardless. "Silas, she calls him. Silas, I mean where did she get that name from? It's creepy. There's something not right about her, I knew it the first time I held her."

Listening outside, little Louise chews her knees through her pyjamas.

"It wasn't your fault," Silas whispers in her ear, but she doesn't believe him. Why would she? Louise bites harder into the yellow fabric covering her small, soft knees. If she applies a reasonable amount of pressure, she knows she can leave tooth prints in her skin. She wants to mark herself there, to create a landmark that only she knows about, hiding beneath the surface. After a while, she stands up and creeps silently back to her bedroom where her dolls are strewn on her threadbare, waxy multi-coloured rug. Barbie lies car crash on top of Sylvie doll. Janette-Plantette the troll glowers over them menacingly. Silas loves Sylvie the rag doll with the stripy legs best. He says it reminds him of Jemima from *Play School*, even though it doesn't look anything like her. Louise hates *Play School* anyway. The girls at school say they like Hamble the best but try as she might, Louise can't understand that. Hamble is rubbish, how can they like her the most?

Calmly, Louise sits down in the centre of her room and rips Sylvie limb from limb. Once she's ripped the doll's head off, she finds it easy to pull the stuffing out and remove her stripy legs. Silas rocks in the corner of the room, crying for her to stop, but Louise doesn't care.

"Stop it, stop it, stop it," Silas sobs over and over.

"Get out," she whispers in response. She doesn't look up as he leaves; she doesn't want to see his face. It's only when she knows he's safely banished to the landing that she climbs into bed herself. When the tears come, they are throat-squeezing and silent.

* * *

These memories are still so current, so powerful, that Louise finds herself weeping as she sits on her hotel bar stool. What must she look like, her mascara will have run, she'll look like a bloody clown, she'll...

"Are you okay, madam?"

A hot waiter. Young, too young for her now, she supposes, he's probably ten years her junior.

"Yes, I'm fine, thanks. Just thinking." She tries to smile but knows she probably looks like a gargoyle. "Actually," she says as he nods and turns away, "can I have another glass of wine? Dry white. Actually, make it a bottle."

She stands up from her bar stool and takes a seat by the window again, a comfy armchair where she can see the view of green fields from the window. What is she even doing here? Why isn't she at home with her husband and her children? *Because they don't even want you*, the automatic response fires off in her mind.

She's been sitting nursing glass after glass of wine for days and she's not sure she's any farther forward in her thinking. She loves Adam, not like she did in the beginning, perhaps, but she loves him. Their early days are soft focus for Louise, fuzzy and warm around the edges. After the DVD, after Tom gave them permission to start replacing grief with love, they'd settled into this madly hedonistic phase of life together. Adam had made her laugh, he made her feel safe and he went down on her. And it wasn't the sloppy, misaimed tongue lappings she'd been used to. Adam hit the spot, oh God he hit the spot. Her toes had curled so much she was afraid they'd get stuck that way, twisted forever like some gnarled, arthritic punishment for having more than one orgasm in a single sitting.

That's how it used to be when they still had sex. But with two children, their sex life isn't what it was. But that's okay, she tells herself. She's still attractive. Adam is still attracted to her. At least, she thinks he is. How normal is it that the man goes off sex? Usually you hear about women, especially after having children, who go off sex, or are too tired. But it's the other way around for Louise, it's Adam who doesn't want it anymore.

Louise respects him as a father, envies him even. But his shift from husband and lover to father of her children seems irreversible, like something has cracked in their relationship and any move now shatters the crack a little more, sending invisible, spider-like splinters outwards, irreparably damaging the mesh that used to bind them. The completeness they used to feel together was overwhelming, like she'd felt with Tom before him, but he'd gone and died on her and now Adam is so focused on Matthew and Maria, she doesn't get a look in. Somehow, she always seems to end up alone.

Louise conceived Maria on a weekend in the New Forest. She'd been an accident – they weren't thinking about contraception. They were screwing and walking and drinking and smoking and enjoying being alive and together. Louise still had spare inheritance money from her dad, so they'd hired a convertible to drive there. Adam had pulled up outside with the roof down and the wind in his hair. They'd thrown their cases in the back, like they were in some romantic American movie. As Adam had sparked up a spliff and revved the engine, a newsreader on the radio said:

"...and a new survey suggests that as many as one in ten young people drive while under the influence of drugs."

Laughing and exhaling a cloud of smoke, Adam had pressed the accelerator and they'd driven away. Happy, happy days, almost too happy to be real. So far away now, like another life lived by somebody else. But there are consequences to living as there are consequences to avoiding life. Maria was one of them – and Louise doesn't regret her, she doesn't. She doesn't regret having Matthew 15 months later. But that doesn't mean motherhood comes easily, either. But she wants it to, she wants it to more than anything in the world. She doesn't want to be anything like her own mum, but as the years drip by, she can't help thinking about it more and more. *You're turning into her*, her mind whispers to her at night in the darkness. *One day, you'll have had enough and you'll up and leave, like your mum did.*

* * *

"I don't love you," Louise's mother said calmly. Louise had been in her normal position on the stairs with her knees scrunched up to her chin.

"Don't say that, Jane…" Her father had sounded desperate. "I know I've not been perfect," he carried on, sounding lost.

"I've met someone." Her mother had been calm, almost emotionless.

"What?" her father said, genuinely confused. "You can't…"

"I was too young, Pete. With you. With Louise. I had so much potential, I could have been anything…"

"She's your daughter…" Louise will never forget the tone of her father's voice at that moment, almost ethereal, not like her father at all, like he'd been possessed by someone else, something else. Not a nice something.

"Louise is not right," her mother had said. "I was too young, Pete. I should have got rid."

From her seat on the stairs, Louise hadn't seen her dad punch her mum but she heard it; full-fisted and bony. She'd heard her mother fall backwards, heard the clattering coffee table and the lung-breaking thud as she hit the floor.

"Shit, Jane, I'm sorry," her father's voice had warbled, softer now, desperate. "I'm sorry, fuck, I didn't mean... "

Louise had heard scrambling, then she'd seen her mother bolt out of the living room and flee through the front door.

"Mum," Louise had yelled, her small voice sounding feeble and useless. It was night, dark and cold. Where had her mother been going? She hadn't been leaving her, had she?

"Louise," her father had said, trying to grab her arm as she ran past him and out of the door after her mother. "Louise!" he'd shouted after her as she ran down the uneven slabs of the garden path to see her mother disappearing around the corner, a small bloody trail running from her nose. Small stones had pushed into the soles of Louise's iced feet and the night air had sucked the warmth from her lungs. She'd wanted her mum to stop running, to turn around, to scoop her up in her arms and hug her close and tell her it was going to be okay. She'd wanted to feel safe again.

She barely remembers her father finding her, or how she'd struggled and kicked and screamed as he'd tried to cuddle her, to tell her everything would be okay. In the days that followed, the house fell silent. Louise hadn't cried, she hadn't even asked if her mother was coming back. She'd simply played in her room and kept her bedroom door shut.

Louise now realises her mother's spectre is always there, trying to force its way back into her life. She's built her life on a bed of sand. Everything she is derives from the lonely little girl sitting with her knees tucked under her chin, listening through a crack in the darkness to her mum and dad arguing in their bedroom. Everything comes from the little girl abandoned, not good enough to be loved.

On her first day back at school after her mum left, Louise knew things were going to get harder for her there, too.

"I'll be your best friend for a month if you tell me," Narinda had said, her eagle eyes spotting something different about Louise – perhaps the un-ironed blouse.

"Promise not to tell?" Louise had whispered, knowing already it was a mistake. Narinda always told.

"You can have my rainbow rubber if you tell," Narinda had said solemnly. Less than twenty minutes later, Louise's whole class had known her dad had hit her mother, who had in turn run away – and somehow, it was like that had given everyone permission to bully her even more. It was little things at first; knocking her books onto the floor, spilling orange juice on her lap. Then Narinda and the other girls would stand in corners, whispering and laughing and pointing at Louise.

"Please, leave me alone," she'd said desperately to Narinda.

"Did you hear something?" Narinda said, looking through Louise at Sally.

"No, I don't think so. I can smell something, though," Sally said, making Narinda snigger.

"Narinda," Louise pleaded, clutching her schoolbag to her chest for fear they'd steal it again and empty it all over the playground.

"Come on, Sally," Narinda said, walking past Louise and knocking her out of the way as if she wasn't even there.

After school, Louise had waited outside the school gates for her dad to pick her up. She'd counted the leaves on the oak tree ahead of her and she'd spotted how many red cars she could number as they passed on the street. Anything to occupy her mind so she didn't have to listen to the taunts from Sally and Narinda.

"Pikey," Sally had shouted, "stinky pikey."

"No wonder her mum left her," Narinda had chimed in, "who'd want to look after that?"

Narinda and Sally hadn't always bullied Louise. They hadn't always stolen her things, or stamped on her crepe-paper lanterns or spat in her semolina. When Narinda had moved to the school, she and Louise had even been friends. Narinda had asked her to her birthday party and they'd played pass the parcel, sardines and hoola hoop. All the girls from school were there but Narinda had stayed by Louise's side all day.

"Best friends forever?" she'd whispered as they hid in the bath behind the shower curtain.

"Best friends forever," Louise had replied, her heart beating giddily with the thrill. Finally, she had a best friend, a real-life best friend that nobody could take from her.

"When's your party, then?" Narinda had asked coyly, peeking around the corner of the shower curtain as she heard Sally Duncan coming up the stairs, seeking them out. Louise hadn't had a party – her mum hadn't wanted the hassle of it. She'd had candles and cake with her mum and dad and hadn't told anyone at school that it even was her birthday. But she didn't want Narinda to know that. Narinda would think she was weird and wouldn't want to be her friend anymore.

"I've had it already," she said. As soon as she said it, she realised what she'd done. Narinda withdrew from her, pulling her hand away. She'd been upset, of course she'd been upset. She'd thought Louise, her new best friend, had held a party and not invited her.

"We're in here, Sally," Narinda had called, blowing their cover. As quickly as she'd found her, Louise had lost her new best friend and found a nemesis instead.

Getting through the school day became an ordeal for Louise. Each afternoon, when her father pulled up in his old Ford Escort, Louise's chest would thrash and punch in excitement as she ran towards safety.

"I can't do this every day, love," he'd said once, when she got in the car. "I've got work, I can't drop everything for you."

She'd looked at him in horror, her heart lodging in her throat, choking her into silence. It was only when she saw his gentle smirk that she'd realised he was joking.

"I can walk home on my own," Louise had said, big and brave.

"Don't be silly." He'd winked, turning the car over and listening to it wheeze, wheeze, wheeze before it finally growled into action. "I wouldn't miss this time with my little girl for anything in the world."

Louise always remembered what he'd done, though. She never forgot that he'd hit her mother. She'd always harboured some fear and resentment because of it. And deep down, she thinks he knew that. But in the end, Louise had forgiven her father for a simple reason. He'd stayed and her mother had left. He'd been the one that made her feel safe again.

Eventually, they found a new rhythm, they moved on. Every Friday after school, they went to the park and she sat on his lap by the pond, feeding the ducks. He'd gently rocked his knee and indicated a point in the water where he'd just thrown a pebble in.

"What do you see, little one?" he asked once, his voice warm and reassuring.

"Water," she replied.

"What else?" he said, smiling.

"Ripples," she said eventually, her soft brow furrowing. He smiled again and jiggled her up and down making her giggle.

"Better eyes, little one," he said.

"Sunlight," then more quietly, "bouncing off the water. And little rainbows, where it's shimmering."

He hugged her close and they sat for a while, content and silent. It had been a beautiful day, in a way that only remembered days can be.

"The world's always shimmering if you know where to look," he said sadly. "But sometimes we forget. Some people forget to look for years and years and years until it's too late. But you know what? It's important to remember, Louise. Better eyes, we've all got to use better eyes."

Chapter Eight

Pick up Maria from school, play in the park, pick up Matthew from nursery, go home for dinner, 'I didn't want pasta, I wanted chicken nuggets', 'I wanted the blue fork not the green one', 'You said I could have a yoghurt', 'I want ice cream', 'I didn't want that one, I wanted that one', run the bath, shampoo their hair, 'Do Matthew's hair first, you did my hair first last time', 'No you didn't, you always do mine first', 'I don't like that toothpaste, it's too spicy', 'I want the strawberry toothpaste that Grandma uses', 'I want *Gruffalo*', 'Matthew always has *Gruffalo* it's boring. I want *Princess and the Pea*, it's not too long, can you read that?' Story time, big cuddles and kisses, bring up an extra glass of water for Matthew, ask Maria if she needs another wee before she gets in bed, more cuddles, 'I love you Daddy', 'When's Mummy coming home?'

"Soon, sweetheart," Adam says, stroking Maria's forehead and kissing her again. "Just a couple more sleeps. Now lie down and get close your eyes. School in the morning."

Adam checks Matthew again on his way down – he's snuggled up with his massive stuffed toy dog in his arms.

"Nu-night daddy," Matthew mutters, already drifting on his way to sleep.

"Night, sweet boy," Adam says, kissing him gently on the forehead.

* * *

When Maria was born, it made sense for Adam to stay at home with her. He worked from home anyway and Louise had the café to run. So without much discussion, Adam did the night feeds so Louise was fresh enough to go to work. He could fit his freelance work and writing around the childcare.

Parenthood isn't easy, but Adam loves it. The shift from being an individual, a husband, a person who had reclaimed his life after the loss of his brother, to immediately becoming a sleep-deprived servant to his daughter and son has been challenging but Adam wouldn't change it for the world. The love he feels for Maria and Matthew is sometimes utterly overwhelming, like he has no space to feel anything else. He knows parenthood has changed things between him and Louise, he knows they don't have sex like they used to, they don't talk like they used to. But he doesn't mind, he knows these things will pass. It's the stage they're relationship is at with two young children. The love they have for each other is as strong as ever. At least his is.

Adam pours himself a glass of wine and puts the oven on. He assumes if Imogen is bringing a casserole, he'll be expected to eat it with her, despite the fact he can think of nothing he'd like to do less. He's never thought much of Imogen, she's always seemed such a mean-spirited woman, so much so that the whole casserole thing doesn't make any sense unless she has an ulterior motive.

Plonking himself down into an armchair in their living room, listening for sounds of movement upstairs in case one of the kids needs him, he thinks again about his wife, wondering again if this conference is all it seems. His mother seems to think something else is going on. Imogen seems to think something else is going on. He knows she finds the children difficult and that she feels pushed out sometimes, but she wouldn't run away, would she?

He can see how it hurts her when both kids continually say: 'No, I want Daddy to put my shoes on', 'No, I want Daddy to get me dressed', 'No, I don't want Mummy to do my seatbelt up, Daddy do it', 'No, Daddy needs to push the pram.' With Matthew, Adam is never sure if he means it or if he's copying his sister, but the end result is the same – Louise feels like an outsider, someone who can do nothing right for them. But to Adam this is normal. When he listens to Louise's friends from antenatal class talk about their own children, it's exactly the same in reverse:

"Oh, Gavin isn't allowed to do *anything* for Timmy, he wants me for everything, it's exhausting."

To Adam, the solution seems simple – time. He's the stay-at-home parent, the one they look to for their needs, the one they see more of. As they get older, things will adjust and they'll attach more to Louise. But he supposes this doesn't address the problem immediately enough for Louise. Part of him feels that she resents him for not putting her first like he'd always promised to, but he can't see a way to change things. They are parents now, things are different.

"Little tip when you're doing the shopping," Louise said a few weeks ago, screwing the lid back on the peanut butter and throwing it in the bin. "Don't buy the cheap crap, it's vegetable oil and salt. And it tastes like shit."

"But I nicked it from your café." Adam grabbed her from behind and tickled her, trying to make her laugh and offset the oncoming storm.

"It's all right for the punters," she said, shirking him off, "but I wouldn't give it to the kids. You've got to think about their meals a bit more carefully, Adam, it's important."

Adam knew why she was stressed; the kids had refused to let her bath them earlier, wanting Daddy to do it.

"They do love you, Louise," Adam said as his wife began scrubbing potatoes in the sink to within an inch of their lives before slamming them on the side.

"It came so easily to you, didn't it," she said, turning around and leaning on the counter. "Being a dad."

"No, babe, it didn't. I work at it. They drive me mad. Some days I'm staring at my watch from three pm onwards, watching the minutes tick by and waiting for bedtime. Some days I shout at them because they push me to my limits. Some days I just want to be able to have a shit in peace without a toddler trying to wipe my arse."

Louise smiled a little bit at that.

"You're depressed, Louise," Adam continued. "You've got to understand that. You're not a bad mum."

"I do love them, Adam," Louise said, "I know I'm not the greatest mum in the world…"

"You're a brilliant mum and they love you." Adam put one hand on each of Louise's shoulders and looked her in the eye. "Stop beating yourself up."

"It's hard, Ad. They want you for everything… I feel like they wouldn't notice if I never came home from work."

"Are you mad? They love story time with you before bed. They love their Saturday mornings with you."

"Yeah, but…"

"But nothing. Try and clear some more time, spend a morning or two with them and you'll see. That's all it is, time. You're their *mum*, Louise. They love you. Okay?"

"Okay," Louise said. Adam smiled at her and refused to break eye contact until she smiled back.

"Now," he said, stepping back from his wife, "can you stop bitching at me about peanut butter? It's not my fault the kids think I'm best, is it." He laughed and ducked as Louise threw a potato at him and chased him out of the kitchen. When she caught him in the hallway they kissed and held each other for a little while, no longer speaking. Eventually:

"We're doing all right with them aren't we?" Louise asked quietly.

"Yeah, I think we are," Adam replied.

* * *

It's all quiet upstairs, both children have gone to sleep relatively quickly. After ironing Maria's school uniform and packing her and Matthew's bags for the morning, he pours himself another glass of wine and stares from the front window, missing Louise, wishing she was here to speak to. He spoke to her this morning, a quick call as she'd been distracted, saying there was a seminar she needed to attend or something and couldn't talk. They've always found time to talk to one another, but now he's starting to worry that he's missed something, that she's struggling more than he'd realised.

There hadn't been any sign that Louise would struggle with motherhood the way she has. In fact, throughout her pregnancy, it'd been the other way around, Adam had been the one who wasn't making adjustments to their new reality. In the early days of their relationship, it wasn't only hedonism that made him drink and smoke all of the time, it was the fact he didn't know any other way to stop feeling. He and Louise were grieving, but they were also young so neither of them thought much of their overindulgences. They told themselves they were getting on with life, getting through it – they both knew life could be short and they wanted to wring everything out of it. But then Louise got pregnant and had to stop smoking and drinking. But Adam took a little longer to adjust. If he wasn't drunk or stoned or both, he would start thinking about Tom. And he didn't want to do that.

With overuse, weed also brought anxiety, stress and paranoia along for the ride. So as Louise's pregnancy progressed, Adam had to make sure he had no weed in the house and no dealers would tempt him. He was still drinking, but he wouldn't begin his day with wine, beer or vodka like he used to with weed, so it was a start.

Is there any difference between addictions, Adam wonders? Too much of anything is bad, after all. Maybe everyone is an 'oholic' in some way or another. Maybe that's the true human condition. Addicted to money, power, chocolate, soap operas, caffeine, sex, nicotine, exercise, alcohol, cakes, quilted toilet paper, desire, pleasure, pain, stress, masturbation, daytime television. All escapes from thinking, from the real world, from reality.

As her pregnancy progressed, Adam still smoked weed, but he took to hiding it from Louise because she wasn't so accommodating of him being quite so fundamentally fucked all day long as she had previously been. He understood that, he didn't resent her for it. Actually, he thought she'd been remarkably tolerant and he loved her all the more for it.

"I can't drive," he'd said one day as she'd held the car keys out to him.

"Why not?" Louise had been standing in the doorway, jacket half on, heavily pregnant, staring at him quizzically.

"I haven't got my glasses," he'd mumbled in reply.

"They're on the side behind you."

"What are?"

"Your glasses."

"Look, I don't want to drive. You drive, will you?"

"You're stoned, aren't you?" she'd asked, not angry, more exasperated.

"A little bit, I just had a small pipe before I showered, that's all."

"Adam, you're gonna be a dad. What if I went into labour and you had to drive me to hospital? You've got to grow up."

For the entire pregnancy, Adam had been *terrified* of being a father, absolutely mind-numbingly terrified. Louise, on the other hand, had been calm and in control. She'd been looking forward to being a mother, to righting the wrongs of her mother before her. But the moment the nurse handed Maria to him, the moment he saw her screwed-up, beautiful little face, everything had changed. He'd fallen in love. He had purpose, a new life depending on him. But Adam realises now that those emotions, the ones flooding through Adam, weren't flooding through Louise as she'd expected, not immediately anyway. And he supposes she couldn't handle that – maybe she still can't, he doesn't know because they can't talk about it because she's at this bloody conference.

He sips his wine thoughtfully, staring from his front window and watching Imogen turn into their road, waving to him in her summer dress and low heels. She's pretty, Adam thinks, good for her age. But on the inside? Not so much. She's always ready with a barbed comment or unnecessary put down.

A couple of weeks ago, she'd popped by for a coffee with Louise.

"Hello," she'd said, air kissing both of his cheeks as he'd let her in. "Is Louise home?"

"Yes, she's expecting you, she's in the kitchen."

"Thanks, darling," she'd said, breezing past him, looking over her shoulder as she went, saying, "I suppose you're taking care of the kids again? You're so good, Adam, not many men would put with what you do. Not real men, anyway." She'd winked, as if she'd said something nice or something amusing and made her way into the kitchen to chat to Louise. Adam stood in the hallway for a moment, not sure how to feel. Maybe she had been joking?

Imogen isn't the only person that makes comments about Adam being a stay-at-home dad. He doesn't think it's that unusual, certainly not in Brighton, but sometimes other people say things that give him an insight into how they see him, bringing their situation sharply into focus. Like when he'd taken Maria and Matthew to the library after Matthew was born so Maria could play in the children's area. He'd prepared a bottle before he left the house, making it hot enough so that it would cool down by the time he got the library so he could feed Matthew. They'd arrived and Maria, sixteen months herself and still overexcited with the use of her legs, had hared off to play with the toddler toys while Adam parked the pram next to six or seven other prams in the corner and found a comfy seat to sit in, a couple of feet away from Maria.

Matthew hadn't even woken as he'd taken him out of the pram and cradled him in his arms and sat back. Adam knew Louise was finding things difficult so he'd left her at home in bed, knowing she needed the space. She'd get through it, he was sure. Look at what they'd made, after all, these two wonderful, perfect little beings. He'd stared at Matthew's scrunched-up little face and a wave of utter euphoria came over him. Maria had been giggling, finding herself a little friend to play with around the wooden blocks – they were building a tower. Matthew was stirring, opening his sticky little eyes and gurgling. Adam leant down to his change bag of many pockets and found the bottle of milk he'd made before leaving the house. Putting Matthew's little bib on, Adam had tested the temperature of the milk on his wrist and offered his son the bottle teat, which he took greedily.

"There you go." He'd smiled down at his son, one eye glancing at Maria every few seconds to make sure she was still in sight and nearby.

"Isn't Mum breastfeeding?" a woman's voice had asked. Adam had glanced up to see a woman in her early thirties who he'd never seen before, smiling at him.

"I'm sorry?" he'd said, averting her gaze and looking back into his son's eyes.

"Mum, isn't she breastfeeding?" The woman was still smiling and she'd sat down next to Adam, leaning over and moving the blanket away from Matthew's face so she could see him more clearly. "He's adorable," she'd carried on seamlessly. "How old is he?"

"Two weeks," Adam had replied.

"Two weeks? And you're out with him alone – you're brave," she'd said.

Would you have said that if I were a woman? Adam had thought but not said. What was brave about a father being out with his children?

"We're not alone, we're with his sister," Adam had said

instead, nodding over to Maria, who was squealing with delight, playing with another little boy, trying and failing to spin a spinning top.

"You *are* brave," the woman had said in something like admiration.

Would you have this much admiration if I were a woman? Adam had thought again. *Isn't it entirely normal for a parent to be out with their children?*

"Are you mixing then?"

"Mixing?" Adam had said, still drinking in his son's face as he devoured his milk greedily.

"Bottle and breast," the woman had said, "or has Mum expressed?"

"I'm sorry, I'm not sure what you..." Adam started.

"Because there's nothing like breast milk for them."

Adam had tried to hold back the irritation he felt, without success.

"Hello, by the way," he'd said without looking up.

"Oh, yes, hi," the woman had replied.

"Because you didn't say hello," Adam had continued, raising his head to meet her gaze. "You didn't say hi, didn't introduce yourself, you opened with 'Is Mum breastfeeding?'."

"I'm...I..." the woman had stuttered.

"For reference, that's pretty rude. There are women all over who can't breastfeed for one reason or another, have you ever thought about how you make them feel?"

"I just meant that..."

"I am well aware what you meant."

"I didn't...I mean." The woman had lapsed into silence and Adam had returned his gaze to his son. Maybe Adam had been hard on the woman, she'd probably only been making conversation. Except conversation is always laden with meaning and hidden truths and politics. Somehow, she'd made him feel like his being out with his children was political rather than utterly normal.

* * *

"Hello, darling," Imogen says, standing on the front door, all fluttering dress and casserole and Tupperware filled with homemade scones.

"Are those scones homemade?" he asks incredulously, making an effort to loudly and clearly say s-cons, so she picks up on the pronunciation. Who has time to make homemade scones, anyway?

"Of course," she replies, stepping in and kissing him hello on the cheek. Not an air kiss, a real kiss, lingering a little too long.

"Now, I can't stay long, Adam," she says, as if he's asked her to come over and it's a slight inconvenience. She walks through into the kitchen despite not being invited to and Adam follows behind.

"I just wanted to come and see how you are," she continues, "make sure you're eating properly."

"I'm fine, Imogen. Louise is only away for a few days and…"

"Go on then, I'll have glass of wine," she says. "Then I must get off, I can't stay too long, I've left Timmy alone with Gavin; who knows what mess I'll go home to. Gavin isn't like *you*, Adam."

Adam pours her a glass of wine and as she goes into the living room, he puts the casserole in the oven. Joining her in the other room, Adam sits on the sofa next to her, back straight, legs crossed.

"So, are you *really* okay, Adam?" she says again, leaning over to touch his knee sympathetically.

"It's just a catering conference, Imogen. I appreciate the concern, but we're all fine, honestly."

"It's…well, I'm only saying this because I'm your friend, Adam, you know that don't you. But I don't know if you've googled the conference she says she's attending, but…" She trails off, leaving the rest to Adam's imagination.

"Honestly, there's…" he starts.

"It's just… There *is no conference.*" Imogen's body relaxes slightly as she says this, clearly over the moon to be 'helping' Adam by imparting this information about her friend. Adam sits quietly, processing what she's told him. He hasn't googled the conference, why would he? He hasn't ever felt the need to check up on his wife, they are a unit, a team. So why would she lie to him?

"Adam, do you think Louise is having an affair?" Imogen says bluntly. "I'm just saying it as a friend." Imogen leans over and touches his knee again. "We all know she's not herself."

Chapter Nine

When she first found out she was pregnant with Maria, she and Adam had still been in the first flushes of love and infatuation…and the fact he was Tom's twin brother made it…sexier, somehow. Forbidden fruit. And when she found out about Maria, it felt like she'd finally have something that was hers that nobody could take away from her. After so much loss, this pregnancy felt right. Real. Her first attempts to tell Adam weren't overly successful. After she'd done the first home test, she'd run into the living room to tell him, only to find him stoned and muttering about seagulls and shopping bags, so she'd left him to it, waiting for another moment. Her next attempt hadn't been any more successful.

"Adam," Louise had said, touching his arm. His fingers found hers and clasped them tightly, but his attention didn't waver from the television. Defeated, she turned her gaze to *This Morning* and noticed the cooking segment was over and had been replaced by a medical segment. A woman was lying on an operating table with a surgeon standing above her with a tiny hammer.

"Oh my God, he's got a hammer," Louise had half laughed, half screamed, clutching Adam's arm a little tighter. He'd turned to her grinning, blowing smoke in her face and clutching her hand tighter. She breathed out heavily, turning her face away, aware for the first time that she was breathing for someone else now, someone who shouldn't have a lungful of marijuana and tobacco smoke.

"Nose job," Adam had said, quickly turning back to the horror show in case he missed anything. The surgeon had produced a small, chisel-like object and had inserted it in the woman's nose.

"Oh my God, they can't show this. It's morning television. Oh my God." Louise had snatched for a cushion, but couldn't help watching from behind it. Even Adam had been flinching and looking at the television sideways, as if this would somehow make the woman's surgery less explicit.

"Oh my God, he's hammering in her nose." Blood was being suctioned from beneath her nose in a frothy mess. "Oh my God. I can't believe they're showing this."

"Oh my God," Adam shouted, grabbing Louise close to him. "He's pulling a piece of bone out. He's pulling a fucking piece of bone out. I don't believe it."

Third time lucky: "I'm pregnant," she'd said, lying in bed beside Adam. He'd been asleep, so hadn't replied. She'd propped herself up on one elbow and stared into his face, handsome but unremarkable. Not like Tom's at all, but everything like his at the same time. How strange – all and nothing all at once.

Tom had only been dead a few years. He was still fresh in her mind; she could still picture him. Adam had rolled over with his back to her and Louise had lain motionless, staring at the mole on his right shoulder blade. Had Tom had a mole there?

Lying next to Adam, hoping he'd wake and hear her, Louise had realised that her memory of Tom was slipping away, becoming homogenised with that of his brother. What traits were Tom's and what were Adam's? They were so alike, yet so different – how could she have been merging them so quickly? She'd known Tom's memory would fade, that it would become something different, something intangible, but she hadn't realised it would happen in a matter of years. Lying there next to Adam, she'd felt a surge or desperation, an intense need to keep something of Tom alive.

"I'm pregnant," she'd said again, loudly this time, begging Adam to hear her. And he had, and he'd rolled over and grinned and spluttered in abject excitement and positivity. And she'd frozen, scared to feel, because once she'd let the thought in, she hadn't been able to let it go. A piece of Tom, through his brother, was growing inside her. This wasn't Adam's baby, not for Louise, it was Tom's: something she could keep hold of. Such a terrible, destructive thought, but pervasive:

This child will have Tom's DNA. His exact DNA. It's like I'm having his child.

Louise had recoiled back, knocking the bedside table and spilling her glass of water onto the floor. Adam had frowned, slightly confused, slightly concerned.

"It's okay," he'd said. "This is great...we'll be great."

But throughout her pregnancy, Louise couldn't let go of that thought: she was having Tom's genetic child. And she felt excited, like she couldn't wait to meet it and to hold it and to hug it, this little miracle, this piece of Tom that shouldn't and couldn't exist. Which made it all the more puzzling that when the nurse put Maria's purple little body into Louise's arms, wailing, genitals all swollen and...alien, Louise hadn't felt the immediate, overwhelming love she'd expected. The love everyone said she was supposed to feel was absent. She'd stared at her daughter and saw nothing of Tom in her, nothing of Adam, even. She saw herself. And her own mother. She hadn't expected that at all. Hadn't expected it and didn't want it. Her baby hadn't felt connected to the cherished thing she'd been carrying for the past nine months and her feelings – or lack of them – confused Louise. Exhausted and emotional, she'd done the only thing she could – pretended she felt all the things she was supposed to. Smiled in the right places while her brain screamed and bled within.

* * *

Watching Adam holding Maria after nine hours of labour was one of the most difficult things Louise had ever done. Every inch of him glowed as he cuddled his newborn. The pride burst out of him like a halo on a church mural as he handed her to his parents to hold. Even Adam's mum Janet seemed to be genuinely taken with this new little bundle of joy. So why did Louise feel so...not empty, that's not the right word, she was filled with emotions, filled to explosive capacity in fact. Was she scared? Not that either. None of the emotions were how she'd expected to feel. Not how her friends with children had described it to her. Not how anyone describes it. Are there even words for it? Desolate? Removed from reality? A banshee trapped inside skin too tight for her body, like it might split open at any moment.

She'd read about how amazing breastfeeding was supposed to be, how it made you feel at one with your child, nourishing them. She'd read that it releases hormones in both mother and child that relax and assist with bonding. In Louise's experience, it hurt. As Maria nestled into her chest, searching desperately for a breast to feed on, Louise had to grit her teeth.

"Don't worry, it gets easier," the nurse said, after Maria's first breastfeed. But it hadn't. A yeast infection followed, inflammation of both nipples as well as Maria's mouth. Before she'd even left the hospital, Louise had decided breastfeeding wasn't for her. Besides, if she bottle fed, Adam would be able to help her out.

And he had. Before she knew it, Maria and Adam were a tight unit and Louise felt like some woman who lived with them. An outsider incapable of feeling the things she was supposed to. The things a mother was supposed to.

When Matthew was born fifteen months later, he was poorly. If Louise strains hard, she can clearly smell the antiseptic smell of incubators and shock of all the tubes down Matthew's nose and the needles in his arms. He'd swallowed some meconium and the doctors were worried he'd got an infection. When Louise could finally hold him, his puffy hands and feet thrashed about, trying to escape from the hard blue hospital blanket, and his wrist-tag was tightly digging into his whale-fat newborn flesh. His tiny arm was still bandaged, securing a needle firmly in his vein so the doctors could deliver precautionary antibiotics.

"This is your brother," Adam had said, cuddling Maria and leaning over so she could see her newborn playmate more clearly. Louise had held him close in case Maria tried to touch him or hurt him.

"Adam, not so close," she'd said, staring down into her son's face.

"Do you think he looks like Daddy?" Adam had asked Maria, tickling her sides and making her giggle.

"He's handsome, like you," Louise had said, reaching out to squeeze her husband's hand. "I love you. You know that, don't you?"

"Of course I do," Adam had replied, jiggling Maria up and down on his knees. "And we love Mummy, don't we."

Matthew's arrival hadn't lifted the fog in the way Louise had hoped, though. Somehow, in the midst of all the dark feelings, she'd thought it would be better second time around. But in fact, once Matthew had come along, with her husband channelling everything he had into both of them, she'd ended up even further removed, somewhere on the sidelines, looking in on her own life and family without being able to fully partake.

And it wasn't his fault – what was he supposed to do if she wasn't capable? But shouldn't that have been her role? If she'd been a *real* woman, she'd have been the one who emotionally invested everything into her children, even to the exclusion of her husband. This version of perfect motherhood, the soft-voiced, bottomless well of patience and love... It didn't seem real to Louise. Motherhood was hard, much harder than anyone let on. And it didn't come naturally to her, not one little bit. Everyone makes out the feelings are there from day one, and you just *feel* it, but Louise didn't and she doesn't know what to do about it. The spectre of her mother weighs heavily around her neck. That's how her mother had felt about her, she now realises. And in the end, she'd left, incapable of dealing with it any longer. And now here she is, repeating the same pattern with her own children, with her own husband. Sitting staring from the window at the green fields, not caring about her smudged makeup and snotty nose, Louise hates what she's becoming. But she doesn't know how to feel anything else, she doesn't know how to make things better. She is unable to connect with her own children. Here she sits, silently in her hotel bar, the bar and hotel she's lied to her husband to visit, leaving him at home being Super-dad, like her dad was to her.

"Who are you, Louise?" she whispers to herself. She's always felt so sure of herself; even in the midst of grief, she's had an inner strength, an ability to stand up and carry on. But the helplessness she feels as a mother is crippling, it's attacking her from the inside, making her doubt everything. Her self-confidence, the only thing she's had to rely on at some points in her life, is gone. Maybe it had only ever been an illusion anyway. Either way, it had helped her, propped her up and enabled her to carry on going after so much loss. But now? What is she doing here? Why isn't she at home with her children? The honest answer is because if she'd stayed at home with Adam and the kids for one more second, she'd have stood in the hallways and started screaming and screaming and she doesn't think she'd ever have been able to stop. So she ran away, like her mother had before her. And she kept running until she'd arrived here, a nameless hotel in a nameless English town. Where even is she? The Midlands somewhere? The landscape is flat and non-descript enough. She twirls her glass, white fingers, pale pink nail paint. Her hands are still young, she still has so much life ahead of her. But she's the same age her own mother was when she left and that terrifies her beyond belief. But is she leaving? Are they splitting up? She doesn't think they're even doing that, they're just...coasting along, side by side. Two people who share a life without actually sharing each other's lives any more.

It's not fair to blame Adam for it, but she keeps thinking back to their beginning and the thing she can't get out of her head is this: she pressed rewind on Tom's DVD the day Adam arrived to profess his love. Not stop, not pause. Rewind. Like she wanted to re-live Tom over and over again, so she'd never have to let him go, never have to forget him or move on. She's watched his DVD a million times, mostly when Adam is in bed. Maybe she'll never be able to let him go?

Until the children arrived, she hadn't questioned her relationship with Adam at all, they'd been so happy, she's sure of it. But recently, a new thought has occurred to her, and now the idea has taken hold it is hard to shake: *she only wanted him because he looked like Tom*. Is that how she sees Adam? As a poor copy of his brother? A replacement? If Tom had been alive, would she ever have chosen Adam? Some days, Louise feels like she married some sort of grotesque doppelganger, an imperfect mirror of the man she truly loved. Tom would have understood how she was feeling, he'd have found a way to fix things, to make her feel the way she was supposed to about her children. But Tom's not here, Adam is. And he barely seems to have noticed she's struggling at all.

And now, the real truth is this: Adam has begun to irritate her. The little things, things she used to find funny or sweet or interesting just…annoy. For example:

"Why do you bother?" Adam asked her one day, laying down on the sofa and putting his head on her lap as she painted her nails.

"What?" Louise replied, squinting at the television as the sun shone onto the screen, obscuring her view slightly.

"Painting your nails with clear nail varnish?"

"It protects them."

"From what?" he asked, stroking her leg lightly.

"Chipping, breaking, that kind of thing," she said impatiently, more concerned with the fact she couldn't see the TV properly.

"You broke one last week," he said, stroking her thigh lightly, his fingers teasing under her skirt.

"So," she'd said, shifting her leg away from his hand.

"So… It doesn't work," he'd said, sitting back up.

"It does, it's good," she'd replied, blowing on her fingers to speed the drying process and holding her hand out in front of her, surveying them.

"It doesn't. You broke one last week so it clearly doesn't work."

"Oh fuck off, Adam," she'd snapped.

Once upon a time she'd had understood he was being playful. Not anymore. Nowadays she resents him so much, she can barely see or feel anything else.

* * *

Louise doesn't even know why she lied to Adam about the conference. She's not up to anything underhand, she's using the time to step outside of her life and switch off. No business, no children, no husband. Just to be herself for a few days with no dependents, with nothing pulling her this way and that. But there is something fundamentally wrong with her marriage, Louise knows. If things were okay, she'd be able to tell him she fancies a few days away on her own to reflect, to recharge. But she doesn't feel she can tell him that. Why? Probably because she can't offer him same thing in return. The idea of a week alone with the kids, in sole charge of them terrifies her. Adam does most of the childcare. He did all of the night feeds when they were babies and now he still manages to fit in freelance writing work and novel writing around the edges. She's running the café, helping out with Maria and Matthew where she can. Some days, she thinks nothing gives her any pleasure of any kind – not work, not Maria, not Matthew and not Adam. Her life seems…bleak. And it shouldn't feel like that.

Everything her marriage once was, she no longer feels. At some point, they stopped noticing each other like they used to. Maybe when Adam's first novel was published. Maybe when Louise bought the café to run. They are growing, changing, becoming different people. But they are moving apart, not together. Of course, Louise is lying to herself, like always, not wanting to admit the truth. She knows exactly when it started to happen. They both know, but neither wants to acknowledge it: it was the day Maria was born.

How can she be a good mother if she doesn't feel what she should? The weight of expectation doesn't help. She can see the way people look at her, the way Adam's mum looks at her. Everyone expects a mother to love their babies, look after them, hold down a job, smile, lose the baby weight, fit into that dress again, paint some lipstick on, look amazing and enjoy every moment of it, even if she hasn't slept for three months. But it isn't like that for Louise. When her daughter was born, she could lose hours sitting staring at the wall, holding Maria in her arms and hating herself, wondering what was wrong with her, what had died inside that made her so emotionless?

She quickly became adept at smiling in the right places, laughing and chatting, painting a picture of happiness and contentment. But mostly, she felt alone. No, not alone, segregated. Separate from Adam and Maria, like they existed on some parallel plane. She could see them and interact with them but she couldn't quite touch them or feel.

Gradually, without them even discussing it, Adam had taken over fully with Maria and she'd gone back to work. At first, it was only supposed to be a temporary measure. Adam had wanted her to see a doctor, to get help. He'd been trying to help, to be a supportive husband.

"I know you're feeling down," Adam said to her shortly after Matthew was born. "Just go and talk to someone, Louise," he'd say. "Lots of women feel like you, you're aren't alone."

If she'd been a violent person, she'd have punched him in the mouth.

"What would you know about being a woman!" she'd have screamed at him. "What the fuck would you know about what

I'm feeling!" As it was, she'd waved him off, refusing to engage with it, retreating from him further, unwilling or unable to accept his support. So she'd gone back to running her little café and had thrown herself into that, leaving Adam to become her children's mother and father. His lack of understanding was almost the hardest thing to bear. When he asks her if she's okay, she doesn't ever say "desolate", she doesn't say "I'm worried I don't connect with my children" and she doesn't say "I'm drowning here, I need some support, I need to feel like part of this family". Instead, she says: "I'm fine" because she knows that in reality, that's what he wants to hear. But deep down, she'd love it if he noticed, if he pushed through the surface to find the woman he used to love hiding underneath, knees tucked to her chin and crying.

Chapter Ten

It upsets Adam that Louise doesn't feel she can tell him she needs some space, that she's finding life hard and she needs a bit of time out – God knows he'd love that himself. He respects her need for space and he'd never have stood in her way. So why has she lied to him?

The way he sees it, Louise's 'catering conference' is, at best, a euphemism for 'I'm taking a break because I might want to leave you'. At worst, she's having an affair and it's a dirty week away. Neither version leaves Adam knowing what to do next. Sitting with Imogen in his living room as the sun fades outside, flicking its dim fingers through the window at him, time slows down for Adam. What if Louise is not going to come back at all? What will he and the kids do then? If she does come back, how is he going to handle it? What's the best approach? Say nothing and wait for her to talk to him? Confront her and ask what's going on?

"Adam, are you listening?" Imogen's voice, grating on him, breaking through once more. She's enjoying the drama a little bit too much.

"She needed some space, Imogen," he finds himself saying. "You know what it's like having children, it's so full on. And since she bought the café, she doesn't get a minute to herself."

"So you *knew*?" Imogen says, her hand leaving his knee. "Oh, Adam, that is a relief. I was so worried about the two of you, I didn't know *what* to do for the best."

"Honestly, we're fine. But thanks for your concern, you're a good friend."

"I would have asked Louise myself, but she's not answering her phone," Imogen says. "And then I thought to myself, there must be a simple explanation. But why," Imogen says, leaning back into the sofa for the first time and sipping her wine, "did she tell all of us she was going to a catering conference."

"Oh, you know Louise, she didn't want people worrying," Adam answers, desperate for Imogen to finish her wine and leave, his stomach is churning.

"But are you sure that—"

"Imogen," Adam says firmly. "It's fine. She needed a break and didn't want everyone to know about it."

"I should call her," Imogen says. "See how she is. Except I tried and she's not answering her phone."

"Really, I think it's best if you leave it," Adam says, closing his eyes tightly for a moment. "Now," he says, opening them again, "are you sure you won't stay for some of your casserole, it'll be done shortly?"

"Oh no, I've got to get back. Heaven knows what state Gavin and Timmy are in by now. I bet he won't be sleeping soundly in bed like your two, Adam. You *are* good, you know. Most men wouldn't put up with what you do." Imogen stands and puts her glass on the coffee table. "Well, maybe another glass of wine. Is it a Pinot? I prefer something with more body myself, but I don't mind if that's all you've got."

Adam stands up, ignoring her comments, and takes her glass, scuffing his feet along the hallway carpet as he walks to the kitchen.

* * *

Adam, Louise and the children went on a day trip to London once and found a hidden little garden with a fountain and a restaurant in to have lunch. He and Louise both ordered a luscious baguette with ham, cheese and salad with fries on the side. The kids' lunch consisted of a floppy, soggy cheese-and-onion roll, with no actual onion in it, a biscuit and a yoghurt, but they both seemed happy. After eating, the kids had run around a small fountain in the courtyard. It consisted of a small stone tablet, circular and about two feet in diameter. Water jetted from the centre of the circle.

"Some things have a centre," Louise said, her voice wavering a little. The water ran down over the stone tablet creating a small waterfall, falling a short distance to a pool filled with pebbles.

"What are you on about?" Adam smiled.

"Nothing," she replied, toying with her baguette thoughtfully for a moment. Adam sat back, contentedly watching the children laugh and play chase, round and round in circles. Their endless energy was both inspirational and exhausting to watch.

"I've got to go away for a few days," Louise said abruptly.

"Oh yeah?" Adam replied.

"Yeah, just a catering conference, but I think it'll be really useful."

"Okay, cool," Adam said. "When's that?"

"Oh I can't remember; a couple of weeks' time, I think."

"No problem," Adam said. "Me and the kids will be fine."

"I know you will," she said quietly.

"You okay?" Adam asked, sensing something was troubling her.

"Me? Yeah, I'm fine." Louise smiled at him. "Just a bit tired, that's all."

And stupidly, he believed her.

* * *

Adam pours both himself and Imogen another glass of wine, lost in his memories. How much has he been not picking up on? Are there other signs he's missed? Has Louise been crying out for attention or help and he hasn't noticed? He glances at the oven timer, seeing that in a couple of minutes, it'll beep and tell him Imogen's casserole is warm enough to eat.

"You sure you don't want any of your casserole?" he shouts through. She doesn't reply and for a second he thinks she hasn't heard, but then she appears in the doorway, arms back, chest thrust slightly outwards.

"Don't shout down the corridor like that," she says. "I hate it when Gavin does that. Why can't he just walk in the other room?"

"Sorry," Adam says in spite of himself, his Britishness coming through with an apology when in reality he wants to tell her to stop being rude.

"I'm glad things are okay with you two," Imogen says, leaning against the doorframe and twirling her hair in her fingers. If Adam wasn't so out of practice, he'd swear she's flirting with him.

"We're fine, Imogen," Adam starts, and then, "Why, has she said something to you?"

Shit. He's let his guard down, shown the Louise and Adam united front he's been presenting now has a chink in it.

"No," Imogen says, stepping forward. "She only ever has good things to say about you."

She *is* flirting. It's not that Adam isn't flattered, but Imogen? She's such a...well...he'd never thought of her *that* way on account of her being so...abrasive.

"And you and Gavin?" Adam asks awkwardly, stepping back a little. It's a genuine question, not one designed to upset her, but designed to remind her she has a husband. Immediately, he sees a change in her demeanour. Looking slightly unsettled, she steps back again, any trace of potential seductress disappearing in an instant.

"Actually, I won't have that glass of wine," she says. "Best get back. Gavin will be wondering why I'm so long." She puts her bag on her shoulder and leans in to give Adam another kiss on the cheek. "Tell Louise I'm looking forward to dinner in a couple of weeks."

"Will do." Adam nods as the oven timer goes off. "You sure you won't stay for some? You're welcome."

"No, it's fine. I need to sort Timmy out, I'm sure he won't be in bed yet with Gavin in charge."

"Okay," Adam says, feeling a little bit sorry for her in spite of himself. "Thanks for the casserole, Imogen, I appreciate the thought."

* * *

Once upon a time, Adam would have had a friend to call and talk things through with. He used to have friends, real friends. Or maybe that was just Tom, maybe Tom had friends and Adam went along for the ride. Whatever the truth, now he only has couple friends, which mostly means they aren't friends at all: they certainly aren't people he could talk this through with, they're all too close to Louise. It strikes him all of a sudden that none of their mates are his friends primarily. When did that happen? When did he lose himself to being the other half this entity 'Louise and Adam'? He supposes that's always been his role, when he thinks about it. Before marrying, he was half of 'Tom and Adam'. He's always been part of a two, second in command. He's never just been Adam – he wouldn't know how to be if he tried. But right now, he'd do anything to have Tom back, someone that was there for him entirely, someone who'd offer him advice on Louise based on no other agenda than helping his brother out, just like Adam had always done for him.

He remembers the day after they'd both met Louise in the café – two brothers, sitting on Brighton's pebbled beach. Adam's mind had been filled with this impossibly perfect girl in the newsagent shop, a girl who had noticed his brother, not him. Both brothers had closed their eyes against the autumn sun, enjoying an unexpected reprise of summer, both picturing nothing but her face. Adam remembers the gentle waves underneath the music that played behind them, coming from one of the seafront bars. Earlier that day, Tom had insisted on going swimming in the sea.

"Come on, Ad, what's wrong with you?"

"It's probably full of sewage. No way," Adam had replied. Tom had ignored him, running down the pebble beach letting out tiny yelps as the pebbles pressed into his heels and the balls of his feet. Adam sat alone, remembering Louise's face in the newsagents, replaying that moment of connection she'd had with Tom over and over again. Why couldn't it have been him?

After his swim, Tom had said, "What if I never see her again?" He'd leant up on one shoulder and looked down at Adam's face. Adam had opened his eyes, letting his own thoughts dissipate, forcing Louise from his mind, knowing that his brother had already made 'contact', that he had to stop thinking about her. She belonged to Tom already, not him, he had to give up on the idea of her for his brother's sake.

"Brighton's not such a big place, you're bound to see her again," Adam had said.

"She might not even live here," Tom had moaned, lying back down and sighing heavily.

"Oh for fuck sake, Tom, it's too late to worry now anyway, you didn't get her number. Stop going on about it."

"Thanks for the sympathy."

"Just go and get us a pint, will you. And stop moaning."

"You go and get it, I always have to go."

"You're better at getting served quickly than me," Adam had said, leaning up on his own elbow. "Go on...you never know, maybe she'll be in the pub, just waiting for you."

She wasn't, of course, it had been nearly two weeks before Tom had met Louise again. After that, they'd barely been apart until his death. And then Adam had swooped in, all knight in shining armour, not thinking of the consequences, sure he could make her happy. But now he's questioning everything he's ever believed.

Chapter Eleven

Louise is drunk now, enough to be eyeing up the hot-but-too-young-for-her wine waiter in his tight black trousers. Maybe that's why she lied to Adam after all. He'd probably think she was having an affair or something if she told him the truth – and while she has had affairs – a few, in fact – that's not what this week is about for her. It's about space to breathe, not sex.

She does feel guilty about sleeping with other men – she'd never even contemplated being unfaithful to Tom, but who knows what would have happened if he'd lived. They hadn't had a family like she and Adam have. The first time was about a year ago. It was a guy called Alan, the married delivery man at the café – it amounted to nothing more than a rushed fumble in the store room every now and then, but it made her feel that little bit more alive. The sex wasn't good and she had no interest in Alan at all. But someone wanted her, someone saw her as an object and for a few grunting moments, she felt like a woman again, not a failed wife and mother.

Weirdly, she never equated it with her marriage or family life. It was something she did in her own time that had nothing to do with them. It was something she needed and actually, she felt like it made her more able to love them.

Alan was replaced by an electrician called Steve, was replaced by a handyman called Noah, was replaced by a student called Toby. It didn't matter who, if she was honest. It was a transaction; they got something they wanted, she felt something she needed to feel. She does love her husband, that isn't the point. But he is so…sexless nowadays. She's lucky if she gets a quick grope on her birthday, let alone any other time.

Louise can't remember the last time she and Adam had sex. It's not fair to blame him, life is different now they have children. But she can't help feeling that somewhere along the way, they lost their mojo and they can't get it back. Somehow, Adam became a father to her children, not a lover anymore.

"I'm sorry, love, I'm knackered. I was up all night with Matthew last night, he's got an ear infection, bless him," or, "D'you mind getting yourself off tonight, I'm shattered. Had to make Maria's nativity outfit for her school play – she's an angel. Took me half the bloody night and I've got the publisher pushing me on my next book and I've got no idea…"

There's always an excuse. A reason. They all sound plausible but all Louise hears is, "I'm not interested in you anymore. I don't find you attractive; you've put on weight since the kids; your tits are saggy." Sometimes, she wakes in the middle of the night and realises he's lying next to her wanking. He isn't too tired for that, apparently.

So sometimes she goes elsewhere for it and after an initial period of guilt, she has reconciled herself to it. Why shouldn't she get what she needs? She's a lot happier and that means the family is a lot happier. But this week isn't about sex. She isn't going to make a play for the wine waiter. This week isn't about anyone else. She's here to reflect on things and help clear her head.

* * *

Louise and her father visited her mum once, in her new house with her new boyfriend. Louise had cried and clung to her father in the hallway, terrified and not sure why they were there, worried he was going to leave her there with her mum and this strange man.

"You've turned her against me," she remembers her mother screaming. "I'm young enough to have more, you know. I don't need her."

Her dad had bundled her up and cuddled her and they'd left, climbing silently back into their car on the suburban street.

"Just you and me, little one," he'd said quietly as they drove away. "That okay?"

"I love you, Daddy," she'd replied, swallowing and burying her feelings deeper and deeper and deeper until she didn't even know they were there anymore – something she became proficient at. She wasn't even eight years old and she'd learnt not to feel. Sometimes that was the only way to cope with life.

Louise has a lot of happy memories from childhood, it wasn't all bad. In many ways, it wasn't bad at all. One warm spring day, for example, her dad told her that while the chips were in the oven, she was allowed to play in the back garden. It was a magical, messy, overgrown playground for a child. Before her mum had left, it had been pruned and planted, cared for and beautiful, cherished and adored. Louise's dad used to harvest runner beans and in summer, they ate them with every meal. One of the things Louise remembers about her mum was that she loved runner beans and chicken in breadcrumbs. But the garden had become a tangle of ragged weeds and bushes after she'd gone. Grass pushed up through cracks in the paving stones, creating an uneven walkway for anyone unlucky enough to transverse it.

This particular day was about two years after her mother had left and life had actually been pretty good. Even Narinda had stopped bullying her a bit after Louise had won the long jump in the school sports day. Louise had been pottering around the back garden, picking long blades of grass from the edges of the lawn to create a grass bouquet when she saw the new next-door neighbour over the fence. She must have been in her 80s, a dandelion glow of a woman with enormous topless breasts sagging over shining yellow bikini bottoms. As the woman pottered around, watering plants and singing, she was smiling quietly to herself. Eventually, she looked across the garden fence to Louise.

"Hello, little one," she'd said.

"Hello," Louise had replied, staring down at her feet.

"Here," the topless old lady had said softly, holding her arm out and offering her a small purple flower. Louise leant over the fence and took it, smelling it like she'd been shown to do.

"A beautiful flower for a beautiful girl," the old lady said. And Louise's heart had smiled a little.

Louise spent a lot of time talking to the old lady in the back garden. She was so relaxed and happy, like nothing in the world worried her. That was something Louise had never experienced before. Her dad was always pre-occupied, always slightly absent, like there was a part of him that should be elsewhere. He loved her, she knew that, but there was something missing in him, something that caused him pain and she didn't understand what it was. And her mother…well, her mother wasn't there. And Louise herself was never quite relaxed. If she wasn't worrying about her dad, she was worrying that Narinda would start a bullying campaign again, or she was remembering Lucy the suicide babysitter, wondering if it was her fault, like her mother said it was. Louise was always slightly edgy and jittery inside. It became part of who she was – but she hid it well. On the outside she was composed and calm. But the old lady next door seemed to exist in the moment, like nothing outside of her garden mattered – her calmness seemed like it was real and it fascinated Louise.

"Why so troubled, little one?" she said one day, still wearing only a skimpy pair of bikini bottoms and a hair clip.

"I'm not troubled," Louise had said defiantly. She'd wanted to seem relaxed and happy, too.

"That's good then." The old lady had smiled. "Someone your age shouldn't have troubles."

These are the years Louise remembers fondly. She had her dad and Mrs Harris the next-door neighbour to talk to. She didn't necessarily have close friends at school, but she didn't have enemies either as the bullies had moved on to other targets.

And then, when she was 16, everything changed. Thinking back, Louise should have known something was up when her dad got home that day. She'd wanted to tell him about her exam, but he'd seemed distracted and disinterested, so she'd rushed round the side into the back garden so she could tell Mrs Harris instead. It was like slow motion as he ushered her back in the house and sat down at the kitchen table, offering her a glass of acidic orange juice.

"I've got cancer," he said simply. In less than ten weeks, he was gone. Louise was alone again, completely, utterly alone. No time to process it all, no time to grieve, nobody to care for her.

* * *

Louise walks down the corridor from the hotel bar towards the ladies' toilets. As she starts to push the door open, she sees the wine waiter coming towards her, carrying a tray with snacks on for some guest or other. He's blonde, blonde in a way not many adult men actually are but it looks natural, not dyed.

"You okay, madam?" he asks, a wide smile on his face.

"Yes, yes I'm fine thank you."

"I'll bring you over some bar snacks if you like," he says, leaning momentarily on the wall as he speaks to her, balancing his tray on his right hand, hips pushed slightly forward. *Is he flirting with me?*

"Right," she says, a little flustered. He smiles, seeing her embarrassment but not moving. She pushes the door open fully and goes into the toilet, ignoring the smell of bleach and heading straight into a stall. After she's been, she washes her hands and fixes her face in the mirror, wiping the smudges of makeup where she's been crying away and studying her face.

Why shouldn't he flirt with me? I'm all right. I'm not ancient, it's not like I'm over the hill. It's not like I'm untouchable, is it? Why shouldn't he find me attractive?

The toilet door opens behind her and she glances around, expecting to see one of the other women from the hotel bar; maybe one of the girls on a work conference or the older lady, away from a weekend with her husband. Instead, she sees the wine waiter. At first, he doesn't come in; he opens the door slightly, enough so that she can see it's him. He waits a few seconds, perhaps to see if she's going to be indignant or that she's going to complain but she does none of these things; she stands quietly, unmoving, heart beating furiously.

"You're beautiful," he says, still not stepping into the toilet. Still she doesn't say anything, doesn't move. She stares at him, at his youth. How old can he be? Twenty, maybe? If that. She's not sure if he'll be handsome when he's older, he's got a look about him that suggests he might not age well, but he's young and somehow that makes him intensely appealing to her. That's the other thing about having children she hadn't expected – they make you feel old overnight. She's still young but she feels older than she should. And yet here's this young guy, showing some interest in her, telling her she's beautiful and all of a sudden she needs that, she needs it more than anything else in the world.

He pushes the door open a little wider, glancing behind him as he steps inside.

"Is this okay?" he asks, as he takes the first step. She nods and doesn't say anything, she's not sure she could, her heart is racing so hard, she's not sure she could say anything sensible anyway. And then he's on her, lips, tongue, hand, straight up her dress, no niceties, no hanging around, just up there, tongue in her mouth, finger inside her. As one unit, they shuffle across the toilet and into the cubicle and he slams the door behind her, unbuttoning his trousers to release himself. She doesn't even see what his cock looks like, but she feels it, short and wide, as he enters her, as she wraps her legs around him, her back hurting as it pushes up and down against the wall of the cubicle. As he thrusts, she turns her head sideways, staring at the white china toilet, at the toilet brush, probably flecked with the faeces of numerous guests. What is she doing? Why is she doing this? It'll only make things worse. He finishes quickly, before she can even think about changing her mind and stopping it herself. Before she knows it he's doing his trousers back up and she's wiping herself with tissue, pulling her knickers up and leaving some tissue in there in case of leakage and straightening her dress out. She walks back over to the sink as he moves towards the toilet door.

"You're on the pill, right?" he asks, as he steps back out. She nods. "Okay, great," he says, flashing her a smile. "I'll bring those snacks over in a minute." As he shuts the door and leaves she starts to cry, the sobs coming from somewhere deep inside, their waves encompassing her entire body.

* * *

Louise heads back upstairs to her room, unable to stop sobbing, filled with self-loathing. She showers, cleaning herself and calming herself before standing naked in her hotel bedroom mirror, cupping her breasts. She didn't even breastfeed and they still look like tennis balls shoved into a pair of old tights. She's still young, her body shouldn't look like this. So...lived in. But she's still desirable, she's got to convince Adam of that again. She shouldn't be looking elsewhere, she should be concentrating on him, trying to work out how to get the spark back with him. She's been sitting in this hotel room, or the hotel bar, or walking along country lanes, thinking and pondering for nearly a week now and she's been missing the point entirely. She envies the people who seem to clearly know what they want and how they feel. For her, life's never been like that, her interior life is a mix of emotions all bundled up together like entwined balls of wool – she has no idea where any of them come from or where they lead to or which ball of yarn dissects another. There's no cohesion to her emotions, no right or wrong, no clarity. But now she knows what she has to do. She has to try and get the spark back, she has to at least try. Because Adam has always been there for her, even before Tom died. She confides in Adam in a way she never did with Tom. He knew all about how she'd behaved after her dad died in a way Tom never had. She's always been able to open up to him. Why shouldn't she now?

* * *

Louise's dad left her a decent inheritance. She was at A-level college but she was alone. Casual sex filled the void for a while, and she quickly built a reputation for herself at college – one she knows she'd never have had if she'd been male. But so what? She needed those moments where she felt someone was with her, that someone needed her. They helped her and she didn't care what people thought. At least, that's what she told herself, but then, as the despair and loneliness threatened to end her, to push her to a place she hadn't imagined she was capable of, she'd bumped into a beautiful guy in the local newsagents, with his t-shirt riding up slightly, revealing a tiny bit of his midriff. And she'd been immediately transfixed. In no time, Tom had moved in and she had a new life, something to live for. For a while, anyway. But she'd never been able to share everything with him, never been able to tell him about her past, about the guys she'd slept with. Tom had only slept with three girls before her, so she matched him, told him that she'd only slept with three guys as well. Even Stevens.

"We're not Romeo and Juliet," Tom had said in his DVD, and he'd been right, even if she didn't want to admit it. The things she couldn't explain to Tom, she could explain to Adam, his twin. They'd stay up late one night, talking about the loss of her dad, while Tom snoozed drunkenly on the sofa. She'd told Adam of the loss she felt, how it had changed her in ways she didn't understand. About the hole she had inside somewhere, that she couldn't fill. She told him how she'd lost all sense of security and she'd tried to find it in other places. She told him how she'd lost her virginity and began looking for love and affection in all the wrong places – in the sloppy affection of the boys at school. She told him of the reputation she'd earned and that she now understood the short-lived intimacy sex gave her wasn't a replacement for real love or affection. She knew that the boys had pretended to like her and had pretended to be interested in her. She knew once she'd given them what they wanted, they were gone – usually to tell their friends what a dirty slag she was.

"She gave me my brown wings, lads. You don't have to ask, just slip it in, she loves it."

As Adam listened, nodding, not offering advice, not judging, Louise had continued. She had money, her dad's insurance and the sale of the house have left her well enough off not to worry about her finances. She had a flat and she was smart. But she was young and alone, with few friends and a reputation. And meeting Tom saved her from destruction. Adam had flinched slightly when she'd said that, she remembers. But she'd leant forward and touched his hand.

"Oh, Adam, when I think of the path I could have gone down...drink, drugs, nameless fucking. Anything to take the edge off life, anything not to feel. But Tom saved me. I saw him in that newsagents and I knew he could fix me. Isn't that weird, there and then in the newsagents, I knew. And not in a needy, negative way, but because we fit. We work together."

Adam had smiled and looked over at his sleeping brother.

"What does Tom think of all this?" he asked. Louise remained quiet, shaking her head.

"I'm too ashamed to tell him any of this," she said.

"Oh, Louise, you've got nothing to be ashamed of. Some of the guys you mentioned – they've got things to be ashamed of, but you? Never."

Louise forgets these things too often. She forgets what Adam gives her, that he can often say the right thing when she needs him to. Yes, she and Tom were comfortable and easy, but Adam has always been genuinely interested in her. He asks what she thinks about things, what she feels. He encourages her to talk about her dad, her mum, Tom. Everything, even Narinda and the bullying, because he knows it left scars, left her mistrustful of friendships with other women, even her friends Imogen and Alice. Adam is happy to talk about how she used sex to make herself feel better. He doesn't care about any of that, he doesn't think she was a slag. And actually, thinking about it now, she never discussed half of that with Tom. And Tom certainly never discussed anything with her, he was a closed book. Did Tom support her in the way she remembers he did? All this time, Louise has been putting Adam up against the impossibly perfect spectre of his brother, but actually, who was the better brother? The better partner? The one who knew he was dying and wouldn't even tell her, or the one who stayed and helped pick up the pieces? The one who'd given her two children, who had done what few men would do and become a stay-at-home dad to them because she wasn't up to the task?

She might not be everything she hoped to be, but she's something. She's a business owner and a mother. She's a wife. She forgets that sometimes. Often, even. After throwing her clothes into her suitcase, Louise lies down on her bed. First thing in the morning, she's going home. It's time to leave it behind. She can't keep lying to Adam, she has to accept her life as it is now, not for the thing she thought it once might be.

I'm going to make this marriage work, she thinks as she lies back, naked on top of her bed sheets and closes her eyes. *I'm going to be a good wife and mother, whatever it takes. I will not be like her. I'll never be like her.*

Chapter Twelve

The children can always tell if Adam is stressed or distracted. It's the morning after Imogen's visit and they're taking advantage of his lack of control. He feels stupid, like the biggest idiot that's ever lived. Do café owners even have conferences? What would they talk about, how to steam milk and serve a Victoria sponge on top of a serviette effectively? He's trying to get Maria to dress for school and he needs to get Matthew ready for nursery. Instead, both are currently climbing on the windowsills and neither will even contemplate sitting still for breakfast. First thing this morning, Maria found some aftershave and emptied it all over the bedroom floor, ruining the carpet, and Matthew managed to find the poster paints and palm them all over the walls. Adam had shouted at Matthew then, telling him he had to listen to Daddy, that he couldn't go around doing whatever he liked when he liked.

"Daddy, you're shouting," Maria said. He hates it when he's too pre-occupied to do his best for the children, when he loses his temper and shouts. They had forgotten about it in seconds, of course, but he remains feeling guilty, like he's a terrible father. Just yesterday, he'd been feeling so happy and content, looking forward to Louise's return, enjoying the time he was having with the children. Now he doesn't know how to think or feel, it's like his marriage is in turmoil and it's blindsided him, he hadn't seen it coming. Maybe he is too wrapped up in himself and the children and hasn't paid Louise enough attention? But it's been a good few years for both of them, he doesn't feel like they've been struggling. Louise bought the café and she's making it a real success. He started writing again and actually managed to get a novel published. They have had two children together. Okay, so Louise struggles with motherhood a bit, but it's not like she's a bad mum, far from it. She doesn't stay at home with them, but so what?

* * *

Adam's first novel, *It feels like I can still smile*, was published before Maria was born. He's always loved to write. It was one of things that differentiated him from Tom. His brother loved books, like Adam, but he never felt compelled to write them. Not so with Adam, who wrote his first attempt at a book when he was twelve on an electric typewriter his parents got him for his birthday. At first, after Tom died, Adam found it increasingly difficult to put pen to paper – or more factually, fingers to keyboard. He was consumed by the enormity of losing his twin, so he channelled his emotions into Louise and looking after her and helping her through everything. She'd already lost her parents – losing her lover on top of that before she was even out of her twenties? It was so cruel. And helping her helped him, if he's honest. It gave him something to focus on, to concentrate on. It allowed him to bury his grief and incorporate the loss and aching sadness into his skin, his veins, his internal organs, making it part of him everywhere he could as long as it wasn't inside his mind. He couldn't have it in his head, couldn't think about it, couldn't deal with it that way. Some pain can't be consciously endured.

With Louise, he could avoid thinking about losing Tom by supporting her loss. It suited him. He got to listen to someone talk about his brother without having to lay himself bare about it. Louise rarely asked much about his feelings, so he didn't feel uncomfortable. Everyone gained something from the relationship – but he realised his writing had suffered. For the first time in his adult life, he wasn't a writer. It wasn't even like he was ignoring the constant itch, the manic *need* to create something of his own with words – he hadn't even thought about it. He knew why, even if he didn't want to admit it to himself. It was because the story that kept appearing in his head, the one his deep inner self wanted to write, was about Tom. And his conscious self wanted to avoid that. Adam couldn't bear to tell it. He didn't want to explore those feelings in reality or on paper. He knew if he let that pain out through his fingers it would make it real in a way he could never cope with. But the calling was so strong, every time he sat down in front of the keyboard, he found himself thinking about it, wondering if he should explore his brother's last months and how it must have felt to be the keeper of such a secret. But he would never do that, he'd never let himself enter that headspace, he couldn't. He'd never recover from it. So he stopped writing completely, almost overnight.

Tom used to say Adam was a good listener, but Adam knew it was more than that. It was an avoidance tactic. It meant he didn't have to answer questions about himself or his thoughts or feelings. He was the man who nodded his head with his neck tilted to an angle while talking to you. He was the man who listened and nodded in agreement, who offered advice, who helped you to open up a little. He was the man who laughed or joked, but he didn't offer any of himself in return, not the real Adam. He knew all about keeping people at a distance and he'd never thought it would cause him too many problems.

It was Louise who had changed things, made him open up. And she'd known how important his writing was to him, known how it drove him.

"Why don't you do an MA in Creative Writing?" she'd said casually one day. "I've still got enough money from Dad's inheritance to keep us going. Why don't you do it? Might help the writer's block."

And that was it. He hadn't thought about it, hadn't questioned it, he'd applied for it and done it. And weirdly, it hadn't been as hard as he'd imagined it would be. The writing workshops started small – write sixty-six words about the beach or write a scene of dialogue where nobody says more than three words at a time. None of which lent itself to Tom or his death. And then, all of a sudden, Adam realised that Tom's death wasn't rearing its head begging for attention, and he was writing again and enjoying it. And he and Louise were enjoying each other and not spending all of their time poring over Tom and how he'd kept them in the dark and how the world felt empty without him. They were slowly becoming Adam and Louise, a couple with a life of their own, not a painful shared history.

Within a few months of starting his MA, he wasn't writing small dribs and drabs, but reams and reams of material, real words with real meaning. His output became nothing short of prolific and before he knew it, he had written a novel: *It feels like I can still smile*.

When he looks back at that time, he knows the feelings that flowed through him were like gold dust for a writer, rich emotions and characters with lives more vibrant than half the people he knew in real life. Friends, of a sort, happy for his attention and waiting for their stories to be written. Not directly related to Tom or what Adam was going through but influenced by it, informed by it in a way he'd never have been able to write before.

Adam hasn't been succeeding at Louise's expense, though, far from it. She bought a café and has turned it around and made it a success. They've got two wonderful children. Things are good, aren't they? He can't understand why she's lied to him or what she's doing. It's true that he doesn't have the time for Louise he once had, but that's the same vice versa. She has the café and they have two young kids. He's trying to write a second novel, juggling that with childcare and the odd freelance writing job. Life is hectic, but that's the nature of having a family and both having a career, isn't it? And they are always there for each other when it matters.

One day, shortly after *It feels like I can still smile* was published,

Louise had sat on the edge of the sofa and asked Adam why he wrote.

"I don't have a choice," he answered quietly, sure she'd understand. And she had. She'd sat with him, stroking his arm and not speaking. But now he has to acknowledge that things have changed, and he's not entirely sure why.

* * *

Adam has done the school and nursery run and is now sitting in the sunshine at a café in the local park, stirring his coffee despite the fact he doesn't take milk or sugar and there's nothing to stir. Staring blankly at the patchy grass and weeds beneath his feet, he can't work out what to do for the best. Should he call Louise now? Confront her, tell her he knows there's no conference and demand the truth. Or should he wait for her to come home, wait for her to tell him what's going on?

He knows that sometimes, Louise feels he's stolen the kids' affection from her, she's said as much. Maybe it's that? Maybe she's right, in a way. Before Maria and Matthew were born, he remembers people – parents – smugly saying it was something you couldn't understand until you were a parent yourself. He'd hated those people and would happily have told them to their faces they were up their own arses. But now he's become that person. The love, the physical pain that comes with worrying about Maria and Matthew, the joy when they give him a smile or a cuddle, these things make him feel complete in a way he hasn't felt since Tom died. His kids are a part of him, like Tom had been. Maybe Louise *is* on the outside of that? But he'd needed to step in, because Louise was struggling to cope.

And then it hits Adam, a revelation so horrible he doesn't want to admit it. He's been so caught up in the day to day, in being a father and trying to write his second novel, he hasn't noticed that she needs his help and attention. Louise is an outsider in her own family, standing outside, looking in, desperately trying to find a way to be part of her children's lives.

He sips his coffee, jolting slightly as his mobile starts ringing, buzzing and vibrating on the table in front of him, a little dance of nerves and anticipation. *Louise.* He sits still for a moment, contemplating whether to answer it or not.

"I'm on my way home," Louise says, when he finally picks up the handset. "I'll pick Maria up from school, take her to the park for a while. Then I'll get Matthew from nursery."

"Okay," Adam replies, cradling the phone in his neck. She sounds happy enough. She sounds like everything is completely normal. "So you'll be back about five?"

"Bit before." she pauses. "My train leaves in an hour or so, I'll grab some lunch on the way. You okay?"

"Yeah," he says breezily, "I'm fine. We've had a good few days." He pauses, taking a breath and holding it, trying to calm his beating heart. "How was the conference? Useful?"

"Oh, you know," she says nonchalantly, "boring stuff, but might have found some new suppliers. I'm looking forward to seeing you all, though. I've missed you."

"Missed you too," Adam says. And at that moment he knows what he's going to do and say: absolutely nothing. When she says she's missed him, she sounds like she means it and that's enough for him. If she wants to tell him what she's been doing she can, but if not, he can wait. And he can start listening to her, trying to understand what's going on with her. He owes it to her to be the husband she always wanted him to be, not someone so caught up in his own career and being a parent that he doesn't notice her. He doesn't think he'd gain anything from forcing her into a conversation about where she's been or what she's been doing. She's coming back, that's the main thing. If she's worked through whatever she needed to, then great. All he can do is try to be the best husband he can be.

With a rush of something like excitement, he decides to go

home to have another shower and a shave. Then he'll get some clean clothes on, tidy the house up to make their home look presentable. Maybe he'll prepare a nice meal for when the kids have gone to bed, Persian chicken or a Thai green curry? Yes. No point sitting about thinking what ifs and maybes, he's got to do his bit to get things back on track, to notice the things he hasn't been noticing.

* * *

When Louise gets home that afternoon with both kids in tow, she seems perfectly normal. The children are happy to have their mum back and are racing around and laughing and the house feels filled with energy and excitement again. She smiles and kisses him and they do the kids' story times together and he starts to think he should never have listened to Imogen or his mother in the first place. Louise is fine, there's nothing wrong at all. Later, lying in bed next to one another, getting their post-coital breath back, Louise says, "The fog's lifted."

"I should think so," Adam grins, leaning up on one elbow and stroking her cheek. "I put a lot of effort into that."

"I'm serious, I feel…I don't know. Things will be okay."

"I'm always here for you," Adam says, "you know that, right?"

"Of course I do," she says, grabbing his hand and squeezing it.

"That conference did you good," he says, "you should go every year." It takes every ounce of willpower for him not to add, *"Where were you really, Louise? Talk to me, let me in."*

"Maybe I will," Louise replies, and Adam's heart somersaults, like it's hit an unexpected speed bump in the road and momentarily stopped dead in its tracks. He waits for something else, for an elaboration that doesn't come.

"I love you," he says eventually.

"You too," she says, pulling the sheets back over her and turning her back on him.

Interlude

When I was a kid, I used to think death would be like some kind of holding space, like the blinding white-red light you see when you close your eyes against the summer sun. Now I'm worried there will be nothing. What if when I finally hit the rocks and water the neurons in my brain stop firing and there's nothing beyond? No darkness, no light, no lost loved ones to greet me. Nothing? Where's the comfort in that?

If I tell you I'm scared, don't believe me. I'll admit the initial shock was terrifying, but now? It actually feels quite peaceful. If you have ever done a parachute jump, you'll know what I mean. Getting out of the plane is the heart-stopping moment but once you've jumped, a weird calm descends. When you're in free-fall, there's nothing else to do but enjoy the ride. Of course, this time I didn't jump. And I haven't got a parachute.

It's odd how quickly calm took hold – one minute I was standing on the edge, grasping for clarity, realising there was a chance for us after all and the next I was falling, heart thumping, lungs aching, eyes streaming. It can't have been more than a second before my brain locked down and accepted everything, started savouring every last moment of the flight: the air, needle-sharp, salty and fresh; the rocks below, mountains with teeth, worn down and sharp from the sea's buffeting; the waves, gnarled, frothing monsters, hungry for me. My screams are alien, like they're coming from somewhere else, appealing against someone else's death.

A lot can happen in an instant. If you don't believe me, ask your dreaming mind. Maybe an instant can be an eternity in the right circumstances. Perhaps this is what people talk about when they say life flashes before their eyes when they're about to die. Maybe I'm locked forever in that last millisecond before death because time seems endless and my brain is firing a million memories at me, not all of them good. But I suppose if they were, I wouldn't be in this situation.

It wasn't planned, you see, none of this was planned. I needed to get out, to get away, to run screaming from reality, lungs blazing. Guess I got my wish. Reality recedes. Lungs blaze.

Maybe I knew death was coming. Maybe I've been waiting for it, like it's been woven into the fabric of my being for years. Maybe I've heard the murmur, felt the vibration ever since Tom died. But I held on to the illusion, the belief that I was allowed life, that I could have something of my own, that I deserved something. But eventually, reality floods back in, filling my lungs so fully that I can no longer speak, like waves of salt water, choking me. Maybe it had to happen this way but I still thought in the midst of all our pain, we could find a new spark, a new direction, a way out of this. I couldn't forgive you, you couldn't forgive yourself. But there was nothing to forgive. If only we'd talked to each other we'd have known that. But we ran away from each other and now I can't ever come back.

I am my own narrator. Memory is an artist, an impressionist. She adds colour, sound, smell and emotion to events at her whim. She adds, subtracts and embellishes until the event she started documenting is quite unrecognisable to the others who also experienced it, but at the same time, is more truthful to the owner of the memory. There is no reality. There are only impressions of past events, made by a million selves, all interacting with each other, vying for superiority. Reality doesn't exist, perhaps in the end, that's my only truth.

I am my mother, my father, my brother. I am the plastic toy I buried in the sand when I was five, I am our first and only cat Lily, I am the green and white swirled lino in my gran's kitchen, I am a runny-yolked egg pierced with a fork, I am my over made-up, white-faced primary-school teacher Mrs Jones, I'm the shop assistant who wore too much lipstick, I am Mr Rynne the 70s throwback music teacher with sideburns who told me I was pitch perfect, I am my mediocre GCSE results, I am words spoken, thoughts thought, I am the cut on my left palm from the potato peeler, I am the woman I comforted because she was crying on the steps outside the pub, I am the commuting man I saw yesterday with the infectious smile, I am the dreams I'll never fulfil, I am cold, I am a painted whirlwind, escaping reality. That word again. Reality.

Every atom that makes up our body was forged in some distant star. That's madness isn't it? And here's another fact to blow your mind: so far humans have only identified 4% of the universe. That's it, 4%. This covers *all* the matter we know of: humans, beetles, dogs, dirt, wood, plastic, your fingernails, the Earth, the planets, the Sun, the solar system, galaxies, the elements, comets, meteors, space dust, pot noodles, stars, everything.

What about everything else – the whopping other 96% of the universe? That's Dark Energy and Dark Matter, apparently. Nobody knows what either is, though. We can't prove they're real – they just have to be real in order to make everything else make sense. That's an awful lot of ignorance by anyone's standards – not the sturdiest platform to build reality on, if you ask me. But then nobody is asking me. Why would they, I'm plummeting to my death.

Funny. Or not funny. Have you noticed how we say that? We say something is funny when we really mean it's disturbing or uncomfortable. We know so little. At this stage of my life – or should I say death – I don't know if that's comforting or not.

It's weird how long a second or two can stretch out inside your own mind. Millions of thoughts, all attacking me at once, creating an endless moment, like a dream where days pass but you've only been asleep for a moment. Is that my fate? Will I hover here above the rocks, locked in a timeless mind explosion for all eternity?

I am soon to be past tense. 'I am' becoming 'I was'. What used to seem important seems altogether trivial now. And tomorrow? Double 'r' one 'm' – flashes of grey plastic tables and small wooden chairs. Spelling tests? There is no tomorrow. Not for me, not now. A word-association game, you mustn't pause, you mustn't hesitate otherwise you get a bash on the head like this, or like this.

I shouldn't have come here. Shouldn't, couldn't, wouldn't – all so distinct from each other, not even related, really. Related. Reality. There's no connection there, right? No reason for the similarity in those words?

There was a documentary about Prince Philip on the other week. Is he the most misunderstood man in the British Monarchy? In other news, by 2020, over two million people a year will be killed in road accidents. How do they know? Most victims are pedestrians, cyclists and the users of public transport, apparently. Again, how do they know how these future people are going to die? Seems like a ridiculous study to me. Apparently, treating their injuries is a going to be a huge drain on poor countries. Should human life always come down to money? That's not right, surely?

Human life, so complicated and difficult – yet everyone paints a mask on and tries to pretend it's not. Underneath their smiles, beneath their public 'I'm all right' grins, most people's lips are all chewed and cracked and bloody. Mine certainly were, towards the end anyway. Maybe ever since Tom died, if I think about it. I lived a borrowed life. I stole things, a marriage, a family. Maybe I never deserved love or happiness. But that's not true, I know it's not true. My kids still love me.

Loved me. Soon to be past tense.

Part Three: Interested Others

"She doesn't watch him all the time. She's not weird."

Chapter Thirteen

Her café is called Louise, not Louise's café, not café at all: just Louise. Standing behind the counter, coffee pot in hand, it's not hard to see why. The café is her. It's how she fills her days, how she concentrates her efforts. She spends all day, every day in Louise. She's there early in the morning to take the bread delivery. She's there last thing at night scrubbing tables and cleaning out fridges. Louise takes her mind off things. It stops her thinking about her life and her marriage. The café is her lifeblood, her validation, something she's got right.

By the time she got home after her 'conference', she'd actually been excited to see Adam. The kids had been overjoyed to see her, both running into her arms screaming "Mummy" and in that moment she'd realised there was no better feeling in the world. Her family. At home, the kids had run into the living room, demanding some telly before dinner and Adam had stood in the hall, smiling, clean shaven, slim and handsome and she'd run into his arms and they'd held each other close, tightly, and she'd known, she'd known that things would be okay, that they could sort things out. He'd prepared a meal for her, Thai, and they'd sat by candlelight and eaten and polished off a bottle of wine and chatted and laughed. And it was like old times and then, oh God then, the sex, they had sex and she's missed sex with him; when he's on form, Adam is superb, better than youthful waiters or married delivery men or the students or the electricians who pummel her like she's a blow-up doll or a hollowed-out melon or something. It was a perfect evening in soft focus. A Vaseline-smeared lens of an evening.

The next morning, she'd got up and done her bit with the kids before coming to the café to catch up with Bella and see how things had been while she was away. Everything felt like it was going to be okay.

"Take the day off, Bella," she'd said, smiling. "I can handle it, doesn't look too busy today." And she'd whistled and hummed to herself and served and smiled and wiped and...she felt contented in a way she hadn't for ages.

And then, later that day, everything changed again, in an instant.

"Put the TV on," a man had said, rushing into the café from the street, his blue overalls unbuttoned, revealing a greasy white t-shirt beneath. "I just heard on the radio."

"Heard what?" Louise had asked, but he'd ignored her and waved his hand at the television screen. Intrigued, she'd clicked it on. As the news sank in, Louise dropped her coffee pot. Nobody understood what they were seeing. Nobody understood the enormity of it. A young guy froze coming out of the café toilet, eyes locked onto the TV screen in the corner. The builder who'd ordered coffee simply stared, rubbing his hand over his beer belly and muttering "fuck me" over and over. At the back of the room, a teenage girl sat at a table with a Coke and an unread magazine in front of her.

"What...?" she'd mouthed, her eyes not wavering from the TV screen.

The café was still, like a screen on pause, juddering, waiting for action. Orange plastic chairs sat silently around collapsible grey tables. Steaming coffee breathed mist from white china. Faces reflected the silver amber lights dancing from the TV screen.

"What's happened?" Louise had whispered to nobody in particular. Then other noises had infiltrated the room: ripples of 'Oh my Gods' from the TV, a newsreader speaking in staccato, repeating himself, slightly stunned as if he was talking about something that couldn't have happened.

"Jesus fuck." A woman's voice this time, from inside the café.

And then, as if from another place: "You're spilling it." His voice was gentle. He leant over the counter and stood up the coffee pot Louise had dropped on its side.

"Oh," was all Louise could manage, "thanks."

"No worries," he replied, touching her arm gently and turning his attention back to the TV. But Louise wasn't looking at the television anymore. She wasn't looking at the coffee as it dripped off the side of the counter to create a pool on the tiled floor. She was looking at the man in the blue overalls and white t-shirt.

"I'm Jarvis, by the way," he said, flicking her a smile.

"I'm Louise Gaddis," she replied, grey cheeks turning pink. The briefest second followed where nothing happened at all. Then mayhem sprang from the TV screen and Louise's moment was lost, swallowed by an event with infinitely more importance than anything her life could produce.

That night, she and Adam had sex again, the best they'd had in years, better even than the night she'd got home from the 'conference'. Except this time, someone else was filling her mind as her toes curled. Jarvis. From that moment, she hasn't been able to stop thinking about him. She can barely think about anything else anymore: Jarvis with the smile, Jarvis who lightly brushed her arm as he spoke. Jarvis, Jarvis, Jarvis.

* * *

Take today. It's quieter than normal for this time on a Thursday, so Louise has nothing to do other than stare languidly at the door. She has nothing to distract her from the fact that she knows Jarvis is working on the woman from the bakery's car this afternoon – she overheard him talking to his accountant when he bought his coffee this morning.

"I've got an emergency this morning, Harry, woman from the bakery down the road. Her Metro won't start."

"We need to talk about your year end," the accountant replied, rubbing his sweating forehead with a napkin and smiling half-heartedly at Louise.

"This afternoon," Jarvis said, grabbing his coffee and winking at Louise before turning his back and leaving the café.

"I'll have a number one, please. With an extra sausage and fried egg," the accountant muttered to Louise, shaking his head in disapproval. If she could, Louise would close up and go to Jarvis's garage but she knows that's not feasible. Besides, she doesn't want to seem obsessed. Watching him all day wouldn't be normal, she has to keep things in perspective. She knows she's the only woman for him, she knows it's only a matter of time before they are together.

Preparing a coffee for herself, Louise imagines Jarvis grabbing Sandra and pushing her passionately up against the side of her grubby Metro, ripping her shirt open, unable to contain his passion for her big, bouncing bosoms any longer. Unconsciously, she cups one of her own breasts with her free hand, weighing it up as if to judge it against Sandra's. *Pull yourself together, Louise. It's you he wants.*

She is sure he feels the same. It's like a thousand events in both their lives have resulted in their meeting and now their worlds have collided and converged into one, instantaneous, finger-flicking moment that neither one of them can deny.

* * *

She started watching him shortly after she met him. Not stalking him, she's not weird or anything. But he's living in the flat above the garage opposite the café and she can see so much. And he never seems to draw his curtains. Not fully anyway. He doesn't eat badly for a man living alone: some ready meals, but just as much fresh veg and fish (she's 'bumped' into him in the super-market). He likes beans on toast (he eats it on his lap on his leather sofa in front of the TV), a few takeaways – fish and chips occasionally, a curry most Fridays. Despite this, he's still quite thin, but he does a lot of running.

She doesn't watch him all the time. She's not weird. She's not obsessed or anything.

When Jarvis is at home, he often wears just a t-shirt and his boxer shorts. He scratches his balls absently while he watches TV. She thinks he draws the curtains when he masturbates, like he knows someone might be watching through the window. This morning, before opening the café, she crept upstairs hid behind the curtain of her store room, filled with broken chairs, tables and old china cups and saucers. She could see him pulling on his jeans through the crack in his curtains. She wishes she could see into his bathroom, as she's sure he must have just had a shower. She can't see the kitchen, either, that must be at the back of his flat. It doesn't matter. He never eats in there, he always eats on his lap in the living room. His kitchen is probably not big enough for a table.

Some days, she feels she's been watching him a little too often. But he's so friendly, so...demonstrative. She's sure he's feeling the same as her, she's certain of it. He comes into the café most days and he's always chatting to her, asking about her life.

She does feel bad that she's started watching him. She didn't mean to do it, it happened by accident. She was putting a broken chair into the storage room upstairs and happened to glance out of the window at his garage opposite. And there he was, in the first-floor window, pouring himself a beer and sitting back into his sofa. Without his top on. Her heart had nearly jumped out of her chest. This first time, she stayed looking at him a little longer than she should have done, hidden behind her curtain, peeking as her chest threatened to burst open with excitement.

But that was only the start. Once she'd started, she didn't know how to stop. She began working that bit later, so she could see him up there after he'd closed the garage. Then she started going in early, to see what she could see of his morning routine.

Maybe he wants me to see him? Maybe he knows I'm watching him?

Some thoughts can't be un-thought. Of course that was it.

How could he not know? He *likes* it. He likes that she watches him. He gets off on it as much as she does. As soon as Louise had let this reasoning in, she'd opened the floodgates. Whenever the guilt or doubt crept in, she'd remind herself that this is his flirtation as much as hers. Why would he be so interested in her otherwise, why would they feel so connected?

What would it be like to actually touch him? To run her hands over his chest, to stroke the back of his neck? In the café, whenever he pays for his coffee or sandwich, she tries to take the opportunity to brush lightly against his skin when she gives him his change. It makes her tingle all day long and she finds herself caressing her own fingers where they touched him, as if this makes her closer to him somehow.

She's not obsessed. This is real, she knows it is. She hasn't felt anything like it before, not with Tom, not with Adam. The voyeuristic nature of their relationship only adds to the excitement of it all. They have a private arrangement that nobody else could ever understand.

* * *

The bell above the door tinkles, jolting Louise from her thoughts. She hasn't had a customer for about half an hour and as she glances up, she gasps slightly. It's him.

"Hey, Louise." He smiles, followed by, "You okay?"

He's noticed her gasp, he's noticed that she can barely breathe when she's around him.

"Jarvis, hi," she says, nonchalance itself. If it wouldn't seem weird, she'd skip across the room to show how nonchalant and happy and carefree she is.

"Good good," he says. "Such a lovely day, makes you want go to the pub, doesn't it. But I'll make do with a latte, please."

"Semi-skimmed?"

"Yeah," he says, smiling at her again. Oh, that smile.

"Anything else?" She thinks she's blushing. Christ, she's a grown woman.

"No, thanks."

Louise stops short of continuing with a conversational piece, something like 'How was the Metro emergency?' or 'Did you fuck Sandra with the big bouncing tits then?' Instead, she says, "I'll bring it over," waving him towards the empty tables so he doesn't see her reddening cheeks.

As she makes his coffee, she thinks back to that first day.

"I'm Louise," she'd said as she served him his coffee.

"Jarvis." That smile again, always the smile. "Nice to meet you properly, I was in earlier, you probably don't remember, what with the attack."

"Of course I remember," Louise had replied, a little too quickly. A little too girlishly.

That was weeks ago, they've had loads of chats since then. Loads of flirtations.

"Looks quiet," he says as she places his latte in front of him. "Fancy joining me?"

Louise smiles and pulls a chair out, sitting down next to Jarvis, feeling…relaxed. Like she's with someone she can talk to, about anything she likes. It's been so long since she's felt that. Marriage is all about duties and the everyday – sometimes it feels like everything she does is burdened with baggage and expectation so she can't even speak anymore without it having twenty deeper meanings. But sometimes there isn't anything deeper going on. Sometimes, she wants to relax into a comfortable silence.

A few minutes later, the clock ticking on the wall: "Have you just moved here? To Brighton, I mean?" Louise asks.

"Yeah, saw the garage opposite for sale and thought why not?"

"What made you choose Brighton?"

"Seemed as good a place as any," he says, licking his index

finger and sticking it in the air, "but so far, I like it."

They sit comfortably, not talking but not feeling the need to either. It's the most relaxing and wonderful and ordinary feeling Louise has had in ages. When she and Adam sit together there's a massive weight of expectation and baggage and…things to sort out, shopping to do, washing to hang, bills to pay. But with Jarvis, it's…comfortable. Louise is so happy, she feels like her heart might burst in her chest, all warm and gooey and deadly. Soon, the damage will soak through her white blouse and her cover will be blown, he'll know she'd do anything for him. To him.

Eventually: "My middle name is Tiberius," Jarvis says.

"Ha," snorts Louise, a genuine laugh. "Like Captain Kirk. Christ, your parents must have hated you."

"Nah, they love *Star Trek*, at least my dad does."

Gentle silence again, then: "I don't have one myself," Louise says. "A middle name, I mean. I'm just plain old Louise Gaddis."

Jarvis looks into her eyes and for a second Louise feels like a teenager again, like she did that first moment in the newsagents with Tom. She's missed this feeling, this excitement. The unknown, the beginning of something.

"I doubt there's anything plain about you, Louise," Jarvis says perfectly. For a moment Louise waits for the clarification that undermines the compliment, for the rug to be pulled from under her. A moment more silence and she realises Jarvis has finished speaking.

"Thank you," she says quietly. Jarvis nods and looks back down at his mug. Louise would give anything in the world for Jarvis to lean over and put his hand on her thigh and move it gently upwards so he could feel how hot she is right now and how much she wants to feel his fingers exploring her, inside her, probing, gently, firmly, deeply. But the café door tinkles again, an irritation beyond her wildest imaginings, made even worse by the fact that it's Adam walking in. He's wearing jeans and a short-sleeve shirt and he's skinny again, too skinny. Not that he ever gets fat, but sometimes he looks too thin – she's often envied him for it, his ability to not put on weight, his ability to not worry about it. But next to Jarvis, who clearly works out, Adam looks scrawny, less manly.

"Hey." He smiles, raising a hand. Jarvis glances back over his shoulder, then stands up, pointing towards the toilet as he walks away without speaking. Adam comes over, leans down and kisses her on the cheek – a brother's peck, not that of a lover, not like the kiss Jarvis would give her.

"Who's that?" Adam asks breezily.

"The guy who bought the garage across the road – you remember, Alan sold it after his wife got that nursing job up north?"

"Oh yeah," Adam says. "What's he like, nice guy?"

"Yeah, nice."

"Oh right," Adam says, checking his phone for the time. "Just thought I'd pop in, see if you fancied knocking off early. I've got us a babysitter, one of the girls from the nursery. Thought we could go for a beer?" He moves behind Louise and crouches, putting his arms around her waist. "Come on, how long since we got pissed and enjoyed ourselves." He wiggles his hips suggestively, but it's slightly awkward with her still sitting in her chair. "No chat about bills or work or the kids, let's have a laugh and see where the night takes us."

"Do you think he's all right in there?" Louise says, shirking him off and staring at the toilet door.

"Who?" Adam says.

"The new mechanic – Jarvis. He's in the loo."

"He's only just gone in there," Adam says, clearly perplexed. Louise walks over to the toilet and taps lightly on the door.

"Are you okay in there?" Silence. "Jarvis, are you okay?" Louise calls again.

"I'm fine."

"Are you sure?" Louise perseveres. "We're going to the pub if you fancy it?"

"What?" Adam whispers. "I meant us, Louise. Some quality time, you and me?"

Louise waves him off without looking back at him. "He's just moved here, Adam. It'll be nice for him to get out and make new friends. It'll be nice." She fingers the rings of bone between her neck and breasts, glancing at Adam almost nervously. "Go in and see if he's all right, will you."

"Louise, let the man take a piss, for Christ's sake," Adam starts, but Louise glares at him in the manner of a woman who won't be denied.

"For fuck sake," Adam says, shaking his head and going into the toilets after him.

Chapter Fourteen

Adam sees the man standing clutching either side of the sink, head bowed, hair hanging over his eyes so Adam can't make out his face or reflection.

"You okay, mate?" he asks, walking over to the sink next to the guy and – for want of something else to do – washing his hands.

"Yeah, yeah, am good, thanks." The guy lifts his head and grabs a paper towel from the dispenser to dry his face off.

"It's Jarvis, right? I'm Adam, Louise's husband."

"Oh right, yeah." Jarvis smiles and extends a hand. "Good to meet you."

"Fancy a pint then?" Adam asks. "I mean, don't feel you have to, sometimes Louise gets all carried away and…"

"No, a pint would be nice, thanks."

"Great," Adam says, drying his hands on a paper towel and patting Jarvis on the back. "You sure you're all right? You look a bit pale?"

"Yeah, honestly," says Jarvis. "I felt a little bit sick for a minute, but I'm good."

"Okay." Adam grins. "As long as it wasn't the wife's coffee."

Adam leaves the toilet and sits back down at one of Louise's tables while Louise tidies up and readies to close. He fingers the teaspoon in front of him and stares down at the tablecloth, feeling nervous. He glances up at Louise, wishing for a moment it could be like the old days, that he'll catch her glancing at him, sneaking a peek like she used to, slightly coy, blushing, like she's been caught checking him out. But Louise isn't even looking at him, she's so intent on cleaning and wiping, he's not sure she even remembers he's in the café.

"Is he okay?" Louise asks, taking her pinny off.

"Yeah, he's fine," Adam says, "why wouldn't he be?"

"All right, I was just asking…"

"You're being weird, what's up?" He's a bit irritated, so his tone isn't one that will elicit a response, he knows. But it's all incidental anyway as Jarvis has emerged from the toilet, looking more relaxed and less stressed out than before.

"I see you met Adam," Louise says, walking over to the mechanic and touching him lightly on the arm. "It'll be nice to go for a drink tonight, help you settle in. It's horrible when you don't know anyone, isn't it?"

"Only if you're sure, I don't want to intrude?" Jarvis says, glancing at Adam.

"Of course it's fine," Adam replies. *He's her type*, Adam thinks, studying Louise and she fixates on the new mechanic. *But don't start getting paranoid, nobody likes a jealous neurotic. She's only being friendly. The fact he's good looking is completely incidental.*

"Okay," Jarvis smiles for an infectious moment, "I'm in."

* * *

The pub that Adam, Louise and Jarvis go to is old-fashioned, a proper boozer, not a wine bar, not swanky.

"So, how long have you been married?" Jarvis asks, smiling at Louise and taking a sip of his pint. The pub garden is already busy around them – Brighton in the sun seems to magically create a city of people able to leave work early to drink out of doors. It's one of the things Adam loves about the place; the sound of chatter and chinking glasses always form a comforting background noise, signifying happiness and a priority for living.

"God, a few years, I lose count." Adam laughs.

"Don't you even know?" Louise says, fingering a bar mat. "We married two years after Tom died. Not to the day, but—"

"Tom?" Jarvis asks, glancing at them both, sensing a slight change in mood. Adam purses his lips and smiles, trying to cover up his discomfort, but only manages to manufacture a terrible fake grin, like he's got fishing lines attached to his face, turning him into some disconcerting caricature.

"Enough about us, how about you?" Adam says, trying to move on.

"Me? Not much to tell," Jarvis says, ripping open a packet of salted peanuts and emptying some into the palm of his hand.

"I'm sure that's not true," Louise says, twirling her hair around and stroking her collar bone lightly. All the tell-tale signs of Louise in flirt mode. Adam begins nervously picking the skin from around his nails. He can see Louise glancing at him, irritated, as she talks. His nervous tics are like nails down a blackboard to her – he can see in her eyes that she wants to lean over and smack him one. Instead, she says quietly, "Adam, stop picking," and she touches his hand without breaking eye contact with Jarvis.

As the night progresses, Adam loses track of everything that's being said. Jarvis recently ran a half marathon and is training for a full one. At one point Louise offers him up to go running training with Jarvis, which is clearly a terrible idea as Adam couldn't run one mile, let alone 26. The evening drifts on and conversations flit back and forth. They all get more drunk and more raucous and then something curious happens. Adam starts to feel glad Jarvis came. They're having fun, the three of them. It's nice to be out and have company. They've moved inside now and Jarvis is leaning on the bar, chatting to the barmaid and ordering another round of drinks. He picks up a beer mat and flips it between his fingers. Adam looks from him to his wife and sees that she's relaxed, too.

"You all right, love?" he asks, seeing Louise looking at him.

"Yeah, yeah I'm good. Having a nice night?"

"Yeah, I am," he says, leaning over and giving her a kiss on the lips. "I love you," he says.

"You too," Louise replies, and for a second it sounds like she means it.

"Ah, come on you two, get a room," Jarvis jokes, putting

another round of drinks down on the table.

"Do you know what," Adam says, slapping the table. "Fuck it, I will go running with you. You might have to be patient, though, my fitness isn't what it was."

"What did it used to be?" Louise laughs.

"Deal." Jarvis grins.

"I'll tell you what," Louise says, "I'll cook us all dinner at the weekend after your first run, how about that?"

"Deal again," Jarvis repeats.

* * *

Two days later and Adam is nervously waiting in the hallway in his running shorts, realising that going running with someone who is clearly incredibly fit is a terrible, terrible idea. How did he let Louise talk him into this? Besides, Jarvis is coming and calling for him at eight am – way too early, in Adam's opinion, especially on a weekend when Saturday is his lie-in day, the day Louise gets up with the kids so he can get some sleep. But Louise was determined that he should go and wouldn't cop out.

"Come on, Adam, you've got to look after yourself," she'd said. "You're not getting any younger, are you."

"I'm not ancient either, thank you."

But here he is, in his running shorts and t-shirt and trainers with padded soles (all bought lunchtime yesterday – he didn't want to look like a dick by not having the gear, obviously). As Adam opens the front door, he sees Jarvis bent over in their front garden, stretching his hamstrings. Whereas all of the potted plants and hanging baskets Adam had planted earlier in the summer are now dead through lack of water, this man is in complete juxtaposition. He is alive in every sense you could use the word. Not only his physical fitness, or the way he manages to make his running gear look good (Adam looks like a pot-bellied dad playing at being a runner) but Jarvis's demeanour, every word, every gesture and every movement suggest a man who wrings the most out of life, who isn't prepared to let life pass him by – he is going to go out there and grab life and squeeze it so hard its balls bleed. Adam is simultaneously terrified and exhilarated. If he can absorb the tiniest fraction of Jarvis's positive energy it could be an amazing friendship, reminiscent of something he lost, not a replacement for Tom, never that...but something else. Something he didn't realise he needed until now: a friend of his own.

"How long since you last ran?" Jarvis asks, grabbing his arm and pulling him out of the house.

"Never," Adam says. "Or not since school, I guess."

"Ha, bloody hell. Okay. We'll start gently. Let's do a mile and see how you get on."

* * *

Not well, it turns out. It isn't his laboured breathing or the sweating, it's his legs, they ache and his shins feel like the bones have shattered and sharp points are digging into his flesh from the inside out. And all with only a mile's run. Panting, leaning on a fence at the bottom of a South Downs pathway, he urges Jarvis to go on without him.

"I can't...I'm sorry," he says. Jarvis puts his hand on his back and laughs.

"Good first run, now go home. I'm gonna do another five miles, then I'm going to sort you out a training plan this afternoon before I come over for dinner tonight. We'll have you running a 10K before you know it, trust me."

And with that, he runs off without looking back. Jarvis makes it look so easy, he's barely even broken a sweat and Adam feels like his lungs are having a barbeque. Eventually, he stands upright again and turns around to lean on the fence, taking a moment to bathe in the beauty of the South Downs, its rolling hills and green fields with views of villages and woodland. It's beautiful where they live – sometimes day-to-day life means he forgets to appreciate the little things. He doesn't come up here as often as he should, it always has a calming effect on him, makes him feel that little bit more…at home in his own skin. They could live in a concrete jungle or urban sprawl, but they don't, they live in Brighton – sandwiched between the grey-green sea and the rolling green Downs. There are worse places to be. Smiling broadly, he pushes his sweaty hair out of his eyes and starts to walk slowly back home.

Despite the fact he only ran a short distance and it felt like it was going to kill him, he's now experiencing something he hadn't expected at all. A kind of happiness and calm, filled with those endorphins people always talk about. He strolls home, enjoying the moment and taking in his surroundings – familiar, but somehow not – he feels calm and content. *So that's why people run,* he thinks to himself. He arrives back at his front door – he's been out for less than forty-five minutes, but it feels like he's had an afternoon away. As he puts the key in the lock he can hear Louise in the hallway.

"Hey, love," he says, expecting she'll ask about his run.

"Why didn't you tell me Jarvis had come for you? You should have called me, I didn't even say hello," she says instead.

"Sorry, I didn't even know you were up, it's still early and the kids weren't awake so…"

"It was rude," Louise says, turning her back on him and pulling her dressing gown around her tightly. "I should have at least said good morning to him."

"All right." Adam sits on the bottom step, picking at the square of carpet Matthew pulled up and frayed the other day. "It's not a big deal, Louise, I don't think Jarvis minded." He pulls his running shoes off and walks into the kitchen, putting his arms around her waist from behind as she puts the kettle on, listening to the sound of the kids playing happily in the living room.

"Aren't you going to ask me how it was?" he says.

"How was it?" she says.

Adam presses himself up against her and squeezes her buttocks. "Awful," he says, thrusting into her. "And good. I dunno, I'm unfit, but I think I'll give it a go. Might sign up for a 10K or something – if I've got something to aim for?" He hates himself for phrasing that as a question and not telling her that's what he's going to do. He still can't break the insecurity growing inside him, he's still waiting for her to explain where she's been, why she went away to a 'conference' they both know didn't exist.

"No," he says, breaking away from their embrace. "I *am* going to sign up for a race. And I'm going to train for it. Jarvis said he'd write me a plan and I'm going to take him up on it."

"Okay," Louise says, turning around again to finish making her coffee. "I think it's a good idea, I'm pleased. Now you'd better go and have a shower, you're all sweaty."

When Adam gets out of the shower, he can hear Louise and the kids laughing downstairs. Nothing normally makes her laugh out loud like that, not even the children. He hasn't heard her so happy in years – not since before the kids were born if he's honest. Wherever she went on her 'conference', it did her good and that's enough for Adam.

"All right, I'd better go, Louise," he hears another voice say. "Tell Adam well done."

Oh, she's not laughing with the kids. She's laughing with Jarvis.

"Jarvis?" Adam calls down the stairs, putting his towel around his waist and tucking it in to keep it up. "You've got nerve. I can hardly walk up here."

Adam walks halfway down the stairs and leans over the bannister.

"Oh shut up." Jarvis walks out through the kitchen door where he's been standing chatting to Louise. "You barely ran a mile."

"Got to start somewhere, haven't I," Adam replies.

"So you still up for it then?"

"Yeah, yeah I am," he says. "And thanks. I really appreciate it."

"No worries," Jarvis says, Louise hovering behind him, looking at Adam as if she's a bit irritated he's interrupted them. "I've never had a running buddy before, it'll be fun."

"Right," Adam says, glancing down at his half-naked body. "I'd better get dressed. See you later on for dinner, yeah?"

"Yup," Jarvis says, heading towards the front door.

"You don't have to go," Adam hears Louise say, following after him.

"No, things to do before tonight," he says. "Bye, Matthew, bye, Maria," he calls into the living room. Adam walks back upstairs and back into the bathroom to shave and brush his teeth. As he stares at himself in the bathroom mirror, he analyses his face, trying to be as objective as possible. Okay, he could go to the dentist more often, but his teeth aren't terrible. He probably should have had a brace when he was younger, but they aren't too crooked. His nose isn't big, isn't small. Average, he supposes. That's how he always feels about himself in general – he's average. Middle of the road. Dull, even. But he doesn't think he's alone, that's the lot of many people isn't it? The proletariat, the 2.2's, the 'everyman'. But he's never wanted that for himself. As he examines the bags under his eyes, he wonders what he does want for himself. It's been so long since he thought about it, he doesn't have a clue but now he's excited, he sees it as a challenge. *What does he want?*

He grins in the mirror, a proper, can't hold it back, spontaneous grin. He's excited by the prospect of finding out what he wants and then working out how to achieve it. Why not? You only get one life, if Tom taught him anything it was that. He hears the door slam downstairs and shouts down to Louise.

"That Jarvis going?"

"Yeah," she calls back up. "He'll be back round about half seven. You want a coffee?"

"Yeah, ta," he shouts down. "Just going to have a shave, won't be a minute."

"Okay," Louise says comfortably, like she feels happy and relaxed as well. "I thought later I might pop into town, get some new clothes and the food for tonight."

"Yeah," he says, still studying his face intently in the mirror as he smears shaving cream onto his cheeks. Somewhere in the back of his mind, hidden deeply and expertly and irretrievably, a dark thought lurks. He's not stupid, he sees how Louise looks at Jarvis. And now she wants new clothes before he comes over for dinner. But fancying someone isn't a crime, is it? And Adam feels Jarvis is a positive force in their lives. Everything feels like it's turning around since they met him. Louise is happier and more engaged with their marriage and whatever was going on with her seems to be in the past. Things are going to be okay, he's sure. Whatever darkness was appearing in their marriage is lifting and maybe that's down to Jarvis. Adam can see a whole new lease of life waiting for them, like a new skin, glinting in the sunlight, pale and unblemished, waiting for them to grab it and try it on and run with it, bursting with light.

Chapter Fifteen

For years their bedroom has been shrouded in darkness – the curtains are always drawn and the room has been in constant shadow, a navy-blue hue of depression. It's only now that Louise wonders why they never let any light into their bedroom. Is it a subconscious manifestation of their growing marital unease? Do their permanently closed curtains belie a sickness in their relationship?

She walks over and pulls the cord to open the curtains wide, squinting as the sunlight hits painted walls that have forgotten how to shine. She refuses to accept that anything is inevitable. She and Adam have been having sex again, good sex, like it was years ago before they got so jaded with each other. Okay, so it's fuelled by her growing obsess...her growing interest in Jarvis. But so what? Women are allowed fantasies. It's not like she's doing anything about it, she's not doing anything wrong, apart from thinking about him while squatting over the power shower head or pleasuring herself as she watches him from the upstairs window in the café.

The point is, she hasn't done anything with Jarvis and things are already better with Adam. So why shouldn't she have a crush? Why shouldn't she feel like an excitable teenager again? She's allowed some happiness, after all. She's allowed to *feel* isn't she? Life isn't all about being something for someone else, she's allowed feelings of her own, she's allowed to explore her own emotional landscape.

She smiles as she walks out of their bedroom, the sunlight on her back. *Things are going to be okay*, she thinks to herself. Adam's parents have got the kids for the night; they picked them up earlier and mercifully only stayed for a cup of tea before taking the kids off with them. Adam is now downstairs watching some sport or other on the TV – she often thinks he doesn't even care what sport it is, he'll watch anything. Today, she doesn't begrudge him it. After all, he went running with Jarvis this morning and Jarvis is coming over for dinner tonight. Jarvis. Jarvis, Jarvis, Jarvis. He seems to get her, to be interested in her. He's always asking about her life, who she is, her past, her family. He cares about what's made her *her*. How often do you meet a friend like that? Friend. Sometimes, she can even lie to herself that it's all she wants from him, that she's not craving anything else. Except her body tells a different story. The warmness, the washing machine in her womb, the heat she has for him, the literal, body encompassing heat… God, she can't remember the last time someone's mere presence made her feel like that.

Louise walks downstairs and grabs her handbag and some bags for life from under the stairs cupboard.

"Will you stop bringing bags for life home," Adam said to her once, only half joking. "We won't be able to get in the cupboard for them soon. You're supposed to take them with you when you go shopping, not buy new ones each time you go to fill the house with." He wasn't wrong, of course. Louise definitely has a 'bag for life' problem. She's surprised there aren't help groups for it – people who forget to take theirs to the supermarket but are too middle-class and British and embarrassed to use the normal supermarket ones, so they buy a whole new set every time they shop.

My name's Louise and I'm a bag-for-life-o-holic. This week, I bought 17 bags for life. We can't use the back room downstairs anymore because it's full of 'bags for life'.

"I'm going to town to get food for tonight," she calls to Adam as she opens the front door. "Maybe a new outfit. Shouldn't be too long."

"Okay, love," he calls after her absently. Louise stands on the doorstep and stares at the sky, the trees, the sunshine. Grinning to herself, she can't help feeling life is pretty good at the moment – it's been a long time since she has felt this content.

* * *

As Louise arrives at the high street, she begins to walk towards Waitrose. Tonight feels like a Waitrose kind of evening. Not Sainsbury's, not Tesco and heaven forbid she ever set foot in an Asda. Jarvis's first meal at the Gaddis house has Waitrose written all over it. She might even use a papaya in her dessert, although she doesn't know what to do with papayas at all. If she's honest, she doesn't even know what one looks like. As she walks towards the entrance, she hears a couple of familiar voices.

"Oh, Alice," Imogen is saying, "your dad worked in a factory, he was hardly devout."

"But," Alice replies, "I'm worried he'll think I'm losing my faith..." Alice starts.

"Oh, he thinks God is a vaguely attractive concept at best, stop worrying. Nobody who is C of E cares anymore..."

Alice is about to respond when she sees Louise and shouts, "Louise, oh Louise," and grabs Louise's arm. "Imogen and I were saying how much we are looking forward to tonight."

A jolt of horrific realisation runs through Louise's system. *Imogen and Alice are coming to dinner tonight – how could I have forgotten, how could I possibly have forgotten?*

* * *

Imogen isn't a 'healthy' friend for Louise to have, but that's a pattern Louise seems determined to repeat time and again. At school, after years of bullying, she'd still desperately wanted to fit in, to belong somewhere. She'd wanted to be liked. At school, the girl everyone wanted to be friends with was Narinda Kildare, the girl Louise had made an enemy of by not inviting her to her non-existent birthday party. But as they reached their teenage years, Louise had been invited to join the 'gang' led by Narinda, hanging around on the corner of the high street. They smoked, they wore too much makeup and they contemplated what they might try to steal.

That first night, with butterflies in her stomach, Louise had stood on the cold high street and wondered what on earth she was doing there. Why was she still so desperate to be friends with this girl she couldn't stand? These were the girls that had made her school life hell. They'd stolen her lunch, covered her in ketchup and told everyone she'd let Adam Granger finger her by the beech tree outside School Hut Three even though she hadn't.

Every time Narinda spoke, Louise wanted to lash out and slap her. Yet still she wanted inclusion. Still she wanted to be liked and accepted by them and they'd asked her to come and join them. She had to be friends with them, it would have been social suicide to refuse. Besides, there was only space in the gang because Susie Freeman got kicked out for talking to Andrea Barton, who Narinda didn't like. Louise had spent the next two years hanging around the Narinda's gang, constantly in fear of the next put down or, worse, being told she couldn't hang around with them anymore.

* * *

Years later, Louise is making the same mistake, becoming friends with a woman like Imogen. It's almost as if Louise cut off Narinda's head and it grew back with Imogen's face on it. And now she's coming to dinner with Jarvis.

God, Louise, why does this shit happen to you?

Because you deserve it, her inner self replies before she can supress it. She hasn't listened to that voice for a long, long time. The negative one, the one that tells her it was her fault her babysitter killed herself or that her mother left or her father and Tom died. Intellectually, she knows none of these things are her fault, but emotionally, she finds it harder to believe. Humans like to find patterns in things, no matter how random or unconnected.

And she's the pattern behind everything; she's the common link, the survivor, the one left behind. But she's grown stronger over the years – she's married, has two children. She runs her own business, she's a strong, successful woman and she's never depended on anyone. Not even Adam. She's not sure she's ever acknowledged that before. She doesn't rely on Adam for anything, not emotionally, not financially, not physically even, not anymore. He's just there, living alongside her. She relies on him to help bring the kids up, she supposes. But the point is, she's strong. She can cope with anything, even this. It's just a dinner party.

"Alice is worried her dad won't like her new boyfriend because he's an atheist," Imogen is saying, ignoring anything Alice says and pursing her lips.

It's a dinner party, it's nothing, calm down, Louise. Breathe.

"Where did you get this from?" Imogen continues seamlessly, touching Louise's blouse sleeve. She isn't being supportive, it's not like she's asking because she wants to go and get one herself. It's more of a dismissive comment. What she's saying is it's too cheap or it's last season or something substandard in one way or another. It's a comment designed to create a hierarchy with Imogen firmly at the top, like everything that comes out of her mouth.

Louise hates women who say they don't get on with other women. Like: "Women are always moaning and bitching about each other, I haven't got time for that. I like being around blokes, they're easier, what you see is what you get," or, "Women don't like me. I don't know if they're jealous of they think their boyfriends are going to fancy me, but..." or, worse, "I'm a man's woman, I like to flirt, I like to feel wanted. I don't want to sit there and talk about babies and shopping and who's going to win *America's Next Top Model*."

To Louise, it seems these women have a weird sort of misogynistic tendency, like they hate their own sex so much they can't bear to be around it. It's like these women don't understand they're women too – that women, like men, come in all shapes and sizes, each with their own personalities, baggage and ways of dealing with the world. How can a woman happily band all the rest of her own gender into one simple, sweeping, non-statement so easily? That said, when she's in Imogen's company, Louise understands it. And in all honesty, she does more naturally gravitate towards male company, she can't deny it, but she doesn't dislike women. She does, however, dislike her 'friend' Imogen. They've been friends – frenemies, she supposes – for years now, not just Imogen, but a gang of them, once ten strong, are now down to Imogen, Alice and Louise who stayed in touch after their children were born. They'd started doing dinner parties at each other's houses once a month on a rotation, and meeting for lunch at least once every couple of weeks. The trouble is, Imogen reminds Louise too much of the Narinda Kildares and Sally Duncans at school. Bullies, inflating their own self-worth by diminishing that of those around them. But given her confidence in other areas, she can't explain why she lacks the willpower to tell her what she thinks. Instead, she's ended up in this faux friendship that makes her feel bad about herself.

Imogen is the kind of person who preys on the things that are nice about people and does everything in her power to make them feel bad and insecure. It's like that's the only way Imogen herself can feel happy. Like a slow poison, she plants an observation here, a 'helpful' comment there, a bit of advice, quietly delivered so nobody else can hear…until the person in question begins to doubt everything about who they are and how they do things and then they try to alter their behaviour accordingly, damaging the things people love about them in the process.

For example, when Alice met her new boyfriend in the café the other week:

"I'm so glad we're friends, Louise," Imogen said, looking over Louise's shoulder, studying Alice, who was chatting to a good-looking stranger she'd bumped into. Louise knew Imogen was already bristling and jealous, despite the fact she was happily married. Alice was a single mum and was desperate to meet someone. For once, shy Alice hadn't flinched away as a seemingly eligible guy had struck up a conversation with her as she ordered a coffee after lunch. Louise had glanced over and smiled, trying to offer Alice some confidence and affirmation. Imogen, on the other hand, had scoured the scene, picking it apart, cataloguing Alice and the man's behaviour so she could give her friend some 'friendly advice' later on.

"You're glad we're friends?" Louise had said, slightly taken aback.

"Yes." Imogen smiled, flicking her eye contact for a moment. "Although, you're too nice, Louise. I always say it. I mean, look at you with Alice, giving her encouraging glances, but it's not what a true friend would do."

"I'm not sure I understand you? He looks nice, she could do with some luck."

"Oh, Louise, you're not a people person are you, you don't pick up on the signals. He's clearly a control freak, there's no way a nice guy would be interested in Alice. She's got no confidence, has she? Nobody could put up with that, not in the long run. I'm not being horrible, you know how much I love Alice. But she can be so...I don't know, insipid sometimes, can't she?"

And now here Imogen is, in the high street, telling Louise how much she's looking forward to dinner tonight. Except Louise has asked Jarvis over tonight and she can't have them over, not at the same time. She can't put Imogen in the same room as Jarvis, it'll be hellish. She'll have to cancel it. Tell them she's sorry and something's come up and can they do next week instead...

"I can't wait," Louise says instead. "You all eat salmon, don't you? I was going to cook herb-encrusted salmon." Somehow, Imogen's mere presence makes her feel weak, like the schoolgirl listening to Narinda and Sally call her a smelly pikey, asking why her mummy doesn't want her anymore.

"Alice wanted to ask you," Imogen says, all white teeth and red lipstick and malicious intent. "She wanted to know…"

"I just wondered if I could bring John along," Alice jumps in, desperate to ask herself, trying with every ounce of confidence not to be marginalised.

"Don't interrupt like that Alice," Imogen says. "You know how I hate that."

"Sorry," Alice says quietly. Louise wants to slap Imogen, or at the very least, she wants to say something, wants to tell Imogen not to be such a bitch. But of course she doesn't say anything, she says: "Of course you can bring him, Alice," and she smiles, trying to make sure Alice knows she's sincere, that it isn't something she's going to go home and worry about. "And what about you, Imogen, are you bringing Gavin along?"

"Oh God no." Imogen laughs. "I see enough of him already."

"Okay." Louise nods. "I'd better get off, lots to prepare. See you later on, usual time? Seven-thirty?"

She wants to cry. Her intimate dinner with Jarvis and Adam is now a meal with Adam, Jarvis, Imogen, Alice and her new boyfriend John. A meal for six wasn't the fantasy evening she'd had in mind if she's honest, a threesome had been the way she'd hoped it would go.

Louise stands in the doorway of Waitrose and curses Imogen under her breath. This is what happens – she sees her for no more than a couple of minutes and Louise regresses into being someone else, an obsolete version of herself she no longer wants to recognise, one who finds problems where problems don't exist, one who questions everything and tries to find solutions even if none need to be found.

Everything is fine, she thinks to herself, walking into the supermarket and grabbing a trolley. *Everything is absolutely fine. As long as fine means not okay at all.*

Chapter Sixteen

Adam has spent the day looking forward to the dinner party, even after Louise came home and told him Imogen, Alice and her new man John were coming along as well as Jarvis. After Imogen's visit while Louise was away, her presence should have sent him into a panic in case she made another veiled pass at him. But knowing Jarvis is coming has made him feel a little more comfortable somehow. Things seem easier with him around, like there won't be any problems or if there are, they won't matter. And Louise is so much happier when Jarvis is present. He's like a relationship magician, making everything shine a little brighter.

Earlier, while Louise was out shopping, he watched some sport, had a wank and pottered around the house. Not thinking, just pottering, enjoying the moment, no kids, no work. How long since he's done that? Just enjoyed being in the moment he's in, not thinking about the future, the past, anything? It was a great feeling, one he longs to keep hold of.

Happily, he helps Louise prepare the dinner, peeling, chopping and getting out of her way when the stress gets too much for her, to avoid an argument. Then he drinks a glass of wine or two and stares from the window, waiting.

Shortly, the guests arrive and Louise is all smiles and nervous pleasure. Imogen is there first, wearing an over-the-top black dinner dress and carrying a bottle of champagne, as if she's attending a black-tie event.

"I know Alice likes to bring cava," she says to Louise, thrusting the bottle at her and sweeping past into the living room and embracing Adam warmly, an embrace he returns out of politeness, despite how awkward it makes him feel. "But you can't beat the real thing, can you, Adam," she says, thrusting her chest towards him and grinning.

"I doubt there's anything real about those, Imogen," Adam says smiling and turning away from her. Adam doesn't think Louise would even notice Imogen flirting with him, anyway, she's so wrapped up in the evening. The doorbell rings and Louise bolts to answer it, her giddy laugh and lightness of tone telling Adam it's Jarvis before he sees or hears him.

"I've got another couple of friends around for dinner," Louise is explaining as she shows him into the living room. "We met at antenatal, didn't we, Imogen." She holds her hand out to Imogen, indicating that Jarvis should approach her.

"This is Jarvis, Imogen," Louise continues at a rate of knots. "He recently bought the car garage opposite the café, he lives upstairs from it. He's lovely. He doesn't know many people here yet, so we thought it would be nice..." She tails off. "Well, we thought it would be nice, didn't we, Jarvis."

Adam smiles – he can almost hear Louise's interior voice telling her to shut up, to slow down. She's so nervous, bless her, she wants this dinner party to be a success.

"Would you like a drink, Jarvis," Adam interrupts, walking over and grabbing Jarvis by the hand to shake it. Firm grip, that's good. Adam can't stand a wet handshake.

"What's on offer?" Jarvis says, smiling and glancing at Imogen.

"*Hello*, Jarvis," Imogen says, stepping forward, arms pushed back, breasts thrusting forward. "Lovely to meet you."

And like that, Adam knows he's off the hook for the evening. Imogen has some new sport, fresh blood in the form of a motor mechanic with a firm handshake.

"Why couldn't your husband make it tonight?" Louise says instantly. Jarvis takes Imogen's hand and leans in to kiss her cheek, saying, "Pleased to meet you Imogen," then the room descends into silence.

"Drink," Adam bursts out eventually. "What would you both like to drink? Red wine, white wine, gin and tonic, maybe? Or a beer, we've got lager and ale and bitter if you're a bitter drinker."

Now he's at it, jabbering away.

"I'd love a glass of champagne," Imogen says.

"Of course," Louise says. "Jarvis, champagne? Then you can tell Imogen all about your running."

* * *

The night continues – Alice and her new boyfriend John arrive. He seems nice to Adam in a non-descript kind of way. Not offensive, not particularly interesting but nice enough in an unmemorable way. Alice seems happy though, and that's lovely to see. Adam thinks she's been unhappy for a long time, even before her boyfriend left, if he's honest. She's one of life's meek people who tend to get bullied around a bit by everything and everyone – and having a friend like Imogen does nothing for her self-esteem.

Adam is leaning against the living-room wall while Jarvis, in simple jeans and a white t-shirt, sits on the sofa next to Imogen in her black party dress. Alice is sitting in John's lap on the armchair, which seems odd to Adam, like they're too old for such things, but as he quietly surveys the room, he tells himself off for such observations. Why shouldn't they be tactile and in love and happy and comfortable in their togetherness?

Louise is in the kitchen, putting the finishing touches to the starters before they all sit down to eat, and Adam isn't engaging with anybody in particular, he's comfortably monitoring the room, analysing people's behaviour and mannerisms. Alice and John are so early on in their relationship, they are still self-contained and happy to be touching and speaking to each other – every movement a masked desire. If they could, they'd stay at home fucking all day long. Dinner parties are an inconvenience to them.

Imogen and Jarvis are fascinating. Or rather, Imogen is. Adam can see from Jarvis's body language that her wiles aren't working on him yet, but Imogen clearly hasn't picked up on this herself. If she's touched his knee once, she's touched it twenty times. She's playing with her hair and laughing a lot, despite the fact that, as far as Adam can tell, Jarvis isn't saying anything funny at all. And her legs are slightly apart and every now and again, she kind of flaps them and Adam doesn't know whether to laugh or to be embarrassed for her. He settles on laughing quietly to himself. For a moment, Adam zones in on the conversation, to see what Imogen is saying, to ascertain how she's trying to reel him in, apart from the leg flapping and breast thrusting.

"And before you knew it," Imogen is saying earnestly, "Gavin was buying Chinese magazines and *People's Daily*. I mean, can you believe it? He's an investment banker, for Christ's sake."

Adam turns his attention to Jarvis, to see how he's coping with it all. He doesn't seem stressed or anxious like Adam would be in the same situation. In fact, he seems relaxed and he's taking it all in his stride...

"There was this strange man on the train today, Imogen," Alice pipes up, wiggling her behind into John's lap as she speaks, glancing at Adam to include him as she does so. "He was wearing a suit and these enormous headphones – have you noticed, all the teenagers wear massive headphones nowadays – and anyway, he was darning a nasty blue sock. A man, in a suit, darning a sock on a train."

She pauses for effect, so everyone can take in the details of the picture she's painted.

"Oh, Alice, really," Imogen says. "I'm telling Jarvis about Gavin and his new politics, do you *have* to interrupt?"

Dutifully, Alice shrinks back into herself a little and looks to the floor.

"It *is* a bit strange," Jarvis says to Alice, seeing the change in her demeanour. "A man in a suit, darning a sock in massive headphones." He smiles at her, trying desperately to undo some of Imogen's poison, recognising within an hour of meeting them the dynamic between the two.

"Okay, starters are ready," Louise says breezily, breaking the tension as she comes into the living room. "If you can all move to the dining room, I'll serve." They all stand and start filing out.

"Thank God for that," Jarvis whispers to Adam as they move rooms, grinning from ear to ear. "I thought it was about to turn into a full-on fight."

* * *

Of course, the starter wasn't quite up to Imogen's standards. It was 'nice', but probably could have done with more cayenne. Imogen knows a wonderful place that sells spices wholesale, down near the Taj on Western Road, she'll show Louise it before her next dinner party, because she's a caring friend like that. Main course fared a little worse – John, it turned out, doesn't eat fish and Jarvis isn't massively keen on salmon, although he was polite enough to eat it, although Adam could see he wasn't enjoying it. But Louise seems to be okay. She seems to be enjoying herself despite the criticism and this makes Adam happy. He likes seeing his wife smile – sometimes it feels like it's a long time between smiles for her.

"Would anybody like coffee or dessert?" Louise asks breezily.

"Oh, I'd love a latte," Imogen replies pretentiously without looking at Louise. And she pronounces it lar-tay. It takes all of Adam's willpower not to say 'It's lat-ay, you know it's actually pronounced lat-ay right?'

"That's why evolution created air conditioning," Jarvis says to Alice, as Adam zones in on a conversation he hasn't been paying attention to. "I can't stand being too hot. I could never live in a hot country, I like our climate, weird and unpredictable as it is."

"I've got this quote I love," Imogen says, leaning over and touching Jarvis's hand, not remotely in response to anything he or anyone else was saying. "But I can't remember who said it or where it's from, but it's really thought provoking." Imogen is almost shouting, she's grandstanding, keeping the attention of the entire room, especially vying for Jarvis's eye. "Do you know, I think it's one of my favourite quotes."

"What is it?" Alice says, smiling and grabbing John's hand for support as she does so.

"Haven't you read it? I emailed it to you the other week. Honestly, Alice, you don't take much interest in your friends do you."

"Imogen, I did read it," Alice stutters. "I can't remember it. But it's a lovely quote."

"What was it?" Louise asks, a false lightness in her tone that only Adam would pick up on. She's trying to avoid a confrontation between Imogen and Alice – or more properly, between Imogen and Alice's new boyfriend John, who is glaring at Imogen like he wants to say something to her but doesn't know the group well enough yet to butt in.

"The past increases in proportion as the future diminishes, until the future is entirely absorbed and the whole becomes the past," Imogen says dramatically. "I think it's so…meaningful."

"I don't understand it," Jarvis starts.

"Oh, I'm so glad you said that," Louise says, blushing and smiling. "I don't either."

"It was Saint Augustine," Adam says quietly. "It's a quote from his *Confessions*." He notices both Louise and Jarvis glance at him from across the table – he thinks they're both a little impressed. If Louise ever asks him, he'll never tell her he only knows because *St. Augustine's Confessions* was one of the books Tom was reading before he died – and that Adam had gathered all of his books together and made it his mission to read them all, to know what was making his brother tick in those final months. And weirdly, Tom had underlined that sentence, like it has some deeper meaning for him that Adam had never been able to ascertain. Why would an atheist be reading *St Augustine's Confessions* anyway?

"Is there a particular reason," John says – it's the first time Adam even remembers hearing him speak and the entire room waits as John pauses, sure he's going to add something pertinent to the conversation and the meaning of the quote, "that you feel the need to be such a cunt towards Alice all the time, Imogen?" His tone isn't aggressive, not even angry. It's conversational, except for the content but as he speaks, it's like a body blow to Imogen's stomach. John lifts his glass of wine to his lips and smiles at Imogen, who is momentarily winded and dumbstruck. Adam, without knowing he's even doing it, begins to laugh. And laugh. And laugh. The more he tries to stifle it, aware that it's totally inappropriate to laugh at such an insult, that the PC liberal in him knows calling a woman a cunt is the lowest of the low and isn't at all appropriate and...

Accurate, if he's totally honest. Now, Adam knows all of the arguments against such language; he's a writer, words are his stock in trade. He knows that demonising a woman's sex, giving it such an aggressive and offensive name and making that the ultimate swear word makes its use misogynistic at best...but sometimes, Adam also feels that's exactly why the word has the power it has – precisely *because* it's so unacceptable. And sometimes...most of the time, Imogen can be such a terrible...

"Nobody speaks to me like that," Imogen finally replies.

"I just did," John says bluntly. Alice starts stroking John nervously, muttering that it doesn't matter and it's what Imogen is like and it doesn't matter and please can everyone not fight and...

Jarvis is quietly smiling, as if he would have liked to say something similar although Adam can't imagine he'd have used the C word, because it's pretty strong and you've got to hate women to use that word haven't you? Or you've got to hate Imogen. And John clearly already hates Imogen already and

Adam can't blame him for it. Would bitch have been better than cunt? Probably not. Can you call a woman a dick or a prick? That seems weird.

Jesus, Adam, stop being such a linguist. A cunning linguist. James Bond joke. Keep it together, Louise will never forgive you if you laugh again… Get out of the room before…

He starts sniggering again and Louise stands up, jabbering away about making desserts and coffee and as she starts clearing the plates, clearly embarrassed, clearly unsure what to do next. Adam stands up to start to help her, trying desperately to put a face on that suggests he too is horrified and that it isn't the best thing that's happened to him for ages and he's sure he's trying to mutter something about helping her with the things into the kitchen, so he can make her see the funny side and realise that overall the night is going well and it's just that people have had a bit to drink and Imogen is…well, Imogen.

"No, sit down, Adam, I'll help," Jarvis says, touching him lightly on the back of the hand that's picking a plate up.

"Oh, right. Okay, thanks," Adam says, sitting back down as it would be impolite to do otherwise, but feeling intensely uncomfortable. Not only does he not want to sit in at the dining table with John and Imogen glaring at each other, he also doesn't want Louise and Jarvis alone and chatting in the kitchen over the dishes and dessert bowls. He doesn't want him to comfort her. He doesn't want them sharing a *moment*. He feels jealous. An intense, stomach-churning jealously that makes it difficult for him to concentrate on anything else.

Chapter Seventeen

Louise walks into the kitchen and puts the pile of dirty plates she's holding on the side and squeezes her eyes shut.

"Hey," Jarvis says, coming into the kitchen behind her. "Don't worry, it'll blow over."

"Bloody John," Louise says as Jarvis puts his arm around her shoulder, squeezing her to his chest. She looks up at Jarvis's face, almost close enough to kiss.

"He *was* rude," Jarvis says. "I'm not saying he went about it the right way…"

"You can say that again." Louise snorts a nervous laugh.

"But she's a bloody nightmare, isn't she? Why are you friends with her?"

"She's not that bad," Louise starts, but Jarvis frowns comically and she can't help but burst out laughing. "All right, she is that bad, but I think…I think she's… Oh I don't know. Bloody awful, I suppose." And she laughs again, more relaxed already. He knows what to say and do all the time. Knows how to see the funny side. Not like Adam.

"That's better," Jarvis says, leaning down and kissing her on the forehead. "Now." He claps his hands together. "Let me help you in here. Where's the bin and the dishwasher, I'll stack it while you sort out coffees and desserts."

Louise is lost in his face. Grey-green eyes, like hers. A few lines on his brow – smile lines, giving him a mischievous air. His hair is dark brown, almost black with no signs of greying, but he's younger than Louise. Too young for her. Why would he be interested in her, she's probably like a middle-aged woman to him. But love doesn't work that way, does it. You meet people and you click and it works. You just get on.

She loves everything about him, the way he dresses, the way he stands, the way he's so tactile, always touching her arm or putting his arm around her. The way he's always looking out for her, like now. It's Jarvis who's followed her to check she's okay, not her husband. Her dinner party is degenerating into swearing and insults and Adam's downing wine, watching from the corner. But Jarvis understands how stressful it is, he understands that she needs someone to help her through it. Already, she can't imagine her life without him.

"So, tell me again why you're friends with Imogen?" Jarvis says, smiling as he opens the dishwasher and picks up a couple of plates, scraping the leftovers into the kitchen bin before putting them into the bottom shelf.

"I'm friends with her, but I don't like her. Do you have friends like that? You get stuck with people sometimes, you know what I mean?" Louise says, getting the cream and raspberries from the fridge, then going to the larder cupboard to get the meringues out.

"Oh, fuck that," Jarvis says. "Life's too short to spend time with people who make you unhappy, Louise." Does he mean Imogen or is there a deeper meaning? Is he telling her to leave Adam? To be with him? She fingers the rings of bone between her neck and breasts, standing with her back to him, her heart racing.

"She's not a nice person," he continues. "I mean I'm sure she's got her reasons, her baggage, everyone does. I'm sure she's insecure, I'm sure she needs someone to look deeper. But that doesn't mean you need to be around her. Let someone else fix her, if she needs it."

He does mean Imogen then. Don't read too much into it, Louise, he's chatting, it's just chit-chat as we potter around the kitchen preparing coffee and dessert.

"You're worth more," Jarvis says, putting his arm around her shoulder again and waiting until she looks around at him before he continues to speak. "The only person who doesn't think that is you." He squeezes her again, then grabs some cutlery for the dishwasher. *Oh God, he does feel it. He does.* This isn't how a man behaves with a woman he hasn't known for long. A married woman. It's like he can see into her soul.

"I just…so much shit has happened to me, I don't always feel that good about myself," Louise says, surprising herself. She never talks about this stuff, she doesn't even think it when she's alone with her own thoughts. She has to be strong, she has to be capable and independent and not rely on anyone. If she thinks about it all – her childhood, her losses – she'll crumble. She's grown used to being emotionally frugal, locking everything away somewhere she can't access it. But here's Jarvis, opening her up and accessing parts of her she'd forgotten were there.

"You're amazing, why wouldn't you feel good about yourself?" he says gently, his hand on the small of her back again, his gaze one of concern and…love. She's sure it's love.

"My mum left when I was young," she says, as if she's known him for years, as if he's a confidante, a lover. "And then my dad, well, he died when I was a teenager. Cancer." Louise shrugs, trying to pass off the information she's imparted as trivial, as if it requires no discussion.

"Oh… I'm sorry. I'm…"

"It's fine, long time ago. That's life, right, full of surprises, bad shit, good shit."

"Yeah," Jarvis says. "You're right, there's good shit too. Like us meeting each other."

And she's telling him everything, more about her father's death, and how alone she felt. She tells him about being bullied at school and how Narinda and her cronies made her feel worthless and unlovable. She tells him about Lucy the suicide babysitter and how meeting Tom saved her. How he made her feel special and loved and whole again after she'd started using sex with the boys at school to make her feel loved and close to someone. And she tells him about Tom dying and how she and Adam got together.

It feels like that night with Adam, while Tom slumbered on

the sofa and Louise opened up, told Adam things she could never tell Tom. And here she is again, with this man she's barely met and he's interested and listening and attentive and she thinks she's falling in love.

She tells him how the hole of not knowing her mother engulfs her sometimes, that she feels something is missing, that she has a hunger that can never be satiated. She tells him how she can't shake the feeling that it's her fault her mum left and didn't want her. She never came back, never asked about her, even after her dad died. It's like her mother had written her off and Louise can't understand why but somewhere deep inside she feels like bad things are supposed to happen to her, that she's not worthy somehow. Normally, the subject of her mother would be off limits, even to Adam, it's a gaping wound she can't clean, can't dress, can't heal. So she covers it up and does her best to pretend it's not there at all. Yet here she is, telling Jarvis things she's never even told her husband or his brother before him. Maybe it's her time away in the hotel, maybe she's learning to deal with things, to talk about them like Adam's always wanted. Or maybe it's Jarvis. Maybe he's special.

"I'm sure she thought about you," Jarvis says, taking a tissue and wiping the tears from her cheeks. She's crying, she didn't realise she was crying. She doesn't cry, not in company, she can't let herself.

"She can't have done, can she?" she finds herself saying, leaning into Jarvis's chest so he can wrap his arms around her. "What kind of woman leaves in the night and never comes back?"

"She probably had her reasons," Jarvis says, but she knows he's reaching for something, trying to find a positive where there isn't one. She leans away from him, grabbing a tissue and wiping her own face.

"Sorry," she says, not wanting to continue this conversation after all, not wanting to appear weak, a victim. She's not a victim, never has been never will be. "I didn't mean to get all maudlin. I don't know where that all came from."

"It's fine," Jarvis says. "I like hearing about your life, you can always talk to me, whenever you need to. Nobody is all bad. Maybe your mum thought it was the best thing for you?"

"To abandon me?"

"Sorry, I didn't mean to…"

"No, no it's not your fault," Louise says, turning back around to finish making the desserts. "Get the ice cream out of the freezer, will you," she says composing herself again. "They are all going to wonder where on earth we've gotten to. We'll take these in first, then I can make the coffee, we've been ages, haven't we."

On cue, Adam pops his head around the door.

"Everything all right in here?" he asks, brow furrowing slightly.

"Yeah, all good, mate." Jarvis smiles reassuringly and places his hand on the small of Louise's back gently again as he brushes past her towards Adam. "Is Armageddon happening in the other room or have you managed to smooth things over?

"Him?" Louise says, managing a small smile. "You're joking aren't you?"

"Shut it you." Adam smiles at her. "Need any help?"

"No, we've got it covered," she says, willing him away. He nods, leaving her and Jarvis alone again. Finally, desserts prepared, Louise walks behind Jarvis as they leave the kitchen, each holding two Eton Mess desserts in glass bowls. She can't help glancing down at his pert, beautifully peachy behind, so tightly fitting in his jeans. She can't remember ever feeling so turned on by any man she's ever met. And now she knows he likes her – for a while she'd been secretly worried it was all in her head, but after their conversation in the kitchen she's sure it's mutual. He's fascinated with her, it's like he's trying to see into her. She's never met a man like him, not Tom, not Adam, none of her delivery-man flings or fumblings in the store cupboards or hotel-toilet cubicles. She can't get enough of him, she wants to be with him every living, breathing moment of the day and she's convinced he feels the same. He's slotted into their lives perfectly, like he was always supposed to be there.

As they walk back into the living room, they can hear Imogen holding court again, clearly having moved on from John's earlier insult.

"We have to accept everything nowadays don't we," she's saying, her tone reasonable, "but I'll tell you one thing I'm not, I'm not PC. I hate PC, it's like we're not allowed to say anything about anyone anymore."

"It's not about being PC, it's about being respectful of people," Alice starts.

"Oh, Alice, you're the PC poster girl, you're so..." Imogen starts, but sees John shoot her daggers and stutters to a halt. "... I'm just saying, that's all. I'm allowed to say. We don't all have to accept everything that's all. You already can't make any jokes unless someone thinks you're racist..."

"Oh God, here we go," John says.

"...and now you can't even say anything about the gays," Imogen continues. "And we've got to pretend it's normal and we don't mind them. Why can't they keep it to themselves..."

"Why should they have to," Adam is saying and Louise can hear the strain in his voice; he's struggling not to get angry. She knew this dinner party was a mistake, she should have cancelled it. Adam's too drunk and it's a terrible mix of people. But she wouldn't have had the chat in the kitchen with Jarvis if she hadn't had the dinner party and she wouldn't have seen how much he's growing to care about her.

"I'm just saying, I'm allowed to say. We've all got to be so PC nowadays. Why should I have to accept things?"

"Do you even know anyone gay?" Jarvis says, standing still in the doorway and blocking Louise from getting into the room. She looks in over his shoulder to see Adam standing and downing the remains of his glass of wine and Alice and John still in their seats looking directly at Jarvis. Imogen is sitting with her back to them and cranes around, slightly flushed as Jarvis questions her.

"I don't have anything against them, that's not what I'm saying..." she starts.

"Me. You don't have anything against me," Jarvis says.

"What?" Louise feels likes she's just been punched in the stomach and actually recoils over double, her chin banging against Jarvis's shoulder.

"I'm gay," Jarvis says, glancing back at Louise and continuing to walk in the room, placing an Eton Mess in front of Imogen. "You don't have to accept anything, Imogen. But I would appreciate you saving your comments for dinner parties where I'm not a guest."

Louise stands winded in the doorway, leaning on the frame, feeling slightly dizzy. He's saying it to teach Imogen a lesson. It can't be true. If it's true, why would he have been flirting with her like that in the kitchen? *It's not true*, she thinks, standing upright and walking into the living room, tattooing her best smile on her pale face.

"Come on, everyone." Her voice is strained, like a teenage boy's voice on the cusp of breaking. "It's a dinner party. Let's not keep fighting."

He's her soulmate and he wants her, she's certain he wants her. He's definitely not gay, how can he be? Or if he is, she's his exception, the woman that's blindsided him and made him re-evaluate his life. Oh God, that's it, she's the one. She's his one.

She smiles, a little more genuinely this time, sure she's right. Either he's lying all together, or he's falling for her anyway, despite being gay. God, it's so romantic she could cry. If anything, it makes their love story better. Stronger. More complete.

Filled with a confidence she hasn't felt for ages, Louise braces herself to take control of her dinner party again.

"Imogen, shut up," she says, plonking a dessert down in front of her. "John, no more swearing or insults. Adam, you've drunk enough. And, Alice…" Alice looks at Louise with something like fear in her eyes and Louise flicks Jarvis a look before continuing. "Alice, keep being you," she says, reaching out and stroking her arm lightly. "This is my dinner party and frankly, you're all ruining it. Now have fun, everyone. I demand it." She smiles and gradually, the room begins to smile back at her.

"You don't look gay," Imogen says eventually, as Jarvis takes his seat back at the table. Adam groans, but it's good-natured. They are all feeling a little more relaxed now, Louise can tell. Adam chuckles as he sits back down to eat dessert and Alice is grinning at John with a look that says 'Now what's she saying?'.

"What does gay look like?" Jarvis asks. He's not annoyed, not being argumentative, he's a gentle, wonderful man and Louise loves him. She loves him with all of her heart.

"In all fairness," Louise says, smiling knowingly, "she's right. You don't seem gay at all. Are you sure you're not playing with us?"

"Louise," John interrupts, "I think he probably knows if he likes cock."

"So vulgar, John," Louise says. "I thought he might have been putting Imogen in her place. Is that it, Jarvis? Were you trying to shock Imogen? Because she's right, you don't look gay at all, you're too…manly."

"Louise, you're embarrassing yourself," Adam starts.

"It's all right." Jarvis grins. "I am manly, it's true." He lifts his arms up in a mock showing off of his 'guns'.

Then it's true. She's the one who's making him re-evaluate things. He's falling for her, she's sure of that. Forbidden love. God she's hot. What could be better than forbidden love like this? If anything, his gayness makes it more exciting, more like it's meant to be.

It's more common than people think. Louise remembers reading an article about it in the *Guardian* about a guy who had always been gay but met this woman and now he can't stop thinking about her. Mariella Frostrop advised him to go with it and see where his feelings took him and to stop putting labels on himself. Now Louise wishes she'd paid more attention to the article but she's sure she'll give the same advice to Jarvis when he brings it up. He'll pretend he's talking about a friend who is confused about his sexuality, but Louise will know he's talking about himself and his feelings for her. And as they sit and chat, a little too close to each other on the sofa, he'll lean in and she'll feel his breath on her face and then his soft lips will brush against hers and...

She loves him, she knows that now. How can she continue a lie with Adam when there's a man like Jarvis in her life?

"You only live once," Tom used to say to her. And he's right. If the people she's lost have taught her anything it's that. She's not going to waste another second. She and Jarvis are going to be together, she knows it. And the kids will get over it. Adam will get over it. In the long run, they'll all be happier. It's the best thing for all of them, they just don't know it yet. But she does. She's never been more certain of anything in her life.

Chapter Eighteen

Things have been good since the dinner party. They've had Alice and Imogen over for dinner loads of times before and Adam can't say he's ever enjoyed their company, particularly Imogen's, but with John and Jarvis thrown into the mix it was so…divisive. They lit the touch flame and turned out to be the best evening Adam's had for ages.

They haven't seen Imogen since that night, however. He's pleased with this. Even ignoring the possible pass she'd made in his direction when Louise was away, he's never felt Imogen was a healthy friend for Louise anyway. Adam keeps laughing to himself at how Jarvis casually came in and came out as she merrily gay-bashed. In fact, he keeps having bouts of sponta-neous laughter, picturing the horror on Imogen's face as Jarvis called her out, or remembering the shock in the room as John called her the C word. Eventful nights like that don't happen anymore, everyone is usually so…civilised. It was fantastic.

That was weeks ago and since then he's been going running three or four times a week, and it's amazing how quickly Adam's fitness has improved. And it's had knock-on effects to his mood – he's happier, more content and he thinks that's having a knock-on effect to Louise as well. They're both eating more healthily because he wants to be able to run with Jarvis properly, to do a decent distance without wimping out. He isn't drinking too much and work on his new novel is going well after a long dry spell. When he puts his fingers to the keyboard, he feels alive again, filled with purpose. Like the world is full of possibility.

* * *

"You've only got one life," Tom said to him once.

"All right, Tom Tom. Bit deep for lunchtime."

"I'm serious," Tom said, leaning in and grabbing him by the wrist, staring into his face, a mirror of Adam without the imperfections. "We only get one shot at this, there's no *after*, you can't wait for that. You've got to grab it and live it and stop wasting time stressing about everything."

Adam hadn't realised it at the time, but of course Tom had been dealing with his own mortality first-hand. Until now, Adam hasn't been successful at taking that advice. But Jarvis seems to have exploded into their lives and everything seems to be moving again; the stagnant water that had seemed to threaten their marriage is being flooded by a fresh, clean river, torrential in its power. Adam feels amazing, like he can achieve anything, anything at all.

He's even contemplating signing up for his first half marathon. Even Louise seems to have a spring in her step, like Jarvis is working his magic on her too – and Adam doesn't even have to worry or be jealous because he's gay. It's a perfect situation. His only bugbear is Louise's obsession with Jarvis's sexuality.

"I'm just saying I don't believe it," Louise says to Adam, a little too often, like she's trying to convince herself.

"Don't believe what?" Adam replies.

"That he's gay, he's so…well, he doesn't look gay at all. I think he was saying it to shame Imogen."

"Louise, don't be ridiculous."

"I'm not being ridiculous," she says, a dog with a bone.

"Well, call him out on it if you don't believe him," Adam replies.

"Don't be ridiculous, Adam. You're his running buddy, surely you must talk to each other? Does he mention it?"

"What, that he's gay? It doesn't come up. Besides, we don't talk that much, to be honest, we just run."

And that's true, they don't talk much. They meet up and run, they grab a coffee or a pint, but it's a friendship of few words –

and they both like it that way. They don't explore each other's lives, they don't ask unnecessary questions. They feel comfortable with each other, without any weight of expectation. It's the closest relationship with a man he's had since Tom died and while nothing would ever recreate that relationship, he's also never had a friendship like it, one so comfortable and easy. When Tom was alive, they were such a unit that all friends were secondary. And after Tom, he'd focused on Louise, then the children. Meeting Jarvis was a revelation, filling a hole in his life Adam hadn't admitted was even there. Friendship.

But that's not the whole story, there's more going on than he'll admit to. Part of him knows his friendship with Jarvis is taking him down a dangerous road, one his marriage will never recover from – but he's enjoying the ride so much, he's wilfully ignoring it, enjoying it while it's still good, while it's still positive.

* * *

Take last week, Adam and Jarvis sat in the pub, quietly drinking a pint.

"Ten K today, see," Jarvis said.

"Yeah, can't believe it," Adam said, smiling and leaning back into the swirled red-and-gold fabric of the pub booth.

"Told you your fitness would build up quickly."

"Yeah," Adam said. They lapsed into silence, sitting side by side, watching the people around them, sipping their pints, not talking, not feeling the need to.

"Kids okay?" Jarvis asked eventually.

"Yeah, good," Adam replied. "Maria is reading already, it's mad how quickly time flies."

"And Louise?" Jarvis asked, leaning forward slightly, looking at Adam, his brow furrowed. "How's she?"

Adam couldn't tell where the concern came from – was Jarvis becoming too close to his wife? They were always having little chats. After a run, Jarvis often pops in to say hi to Louise while Adam showers. Adam hears the two of them downstairs, laughing and chatting like the oldest of friends.

Friends. Just friends. Sitting there in the pub, Adam couldn't help feeling a tiny stab of jealousy, a feeling he didn't want to explore or explain. Things were so much better with Jarvis in their lives, he didn't want to ruin it with jealousy or paranoia. He wanted things to carry on like they were, so the best thing was to push the things he was thinking and feeling to the back of his mind so they didn't take hold and spoil everything.

"She's good, I think," Adam said. "Things are good with us." And then, because he couldn't help himself, "I mean you know that, you talk to her a lot, don't you."

Jarvis smiled, a wide grin crossing his face. "Are you jealous, Adam?" he said lightly. Adam squirmed slightly, annoyed at himself for letting his paranoia show.

"No, I didn't mean that."

"Good, you don't need to be."

"Yeah, I know, I didn't mean…"

Jarvis chuckled lightly. "Another pint?"

"No, better get back," Adam said.

"Okay," Jarvis said. Then, "Seriously, you know you don't have to worry about me and Louise, don't you? That's the last thing you have to worry about."

* * *

And Adam did know – it was the alternative he didn't want to admit. When did he realise it was happening? Before the dinner party, maybe? Perhaps the first night he met him, if he's honest. But that's just it, Adam isn't being honest. He isn't acknowledging what's going on at all. At least he wasn't until today. But something happened earlier that means he can't ignore it anymore and now he has no idea what to do. It wasn't a big thing, no lines were crossed, nothing explicit was said or done, yet everything has now changed.

"Looks like it's gonna snow," Jarvis said, glancing at the sky. "Want a drink before you head back home?" They'd finished a run and were getting their breath back by the garage under Jarvis's flat.

"Yeah, why not," Adam replied. Minutes later, snow started falling and the world was blanketed in big fat flakes dropping from the sky.

"Here," Jarvis said, wandering into the living room and handing Adam a steaming mug of coffee.

"Cheers," he replied. They both surveyed the snow-covered scene through frost-rimmed windows.

"I hate training in winter," Jarvis said.

"Yeah," Adam replied.

"I had a friend who got married in the snow."

"Yeah?"

"Yeah." Jarvis paused, cupping his coffee in his palms. "Weird, eh? Most people don't marry outside in winter, do they?" They stood side by side, watching the snow being blown from Jarvis's windowsill into the air, swirling and dropping out of sight.

"Is that it?" Adam asked comfortably, still staring from the window.

"Is that what?"

"The end of your story?"

"Yeah." Jarvis smiled. "Is that all right?" They stared at each other, relaxed smiles on their faces. After a few moments, they turned back to the window and watched the world. Every now and then, they'd sipped their coffee, letting the warmth travel down their bodies. At some point, Adam doesn't know when, he realised they'd leant slightly into one another, as he could feel Jarvis's shoulder pressing ever so lightly against his, making his skin tingle.

"I'd better get back and have a shower," he said quietly, not moving a muscle. "Before I cool down too much."

"Yeah, Louise will wonder where you've got to," Jarvis said, leaning away and breaking contact. He held his hand out for Adam's cup. "Maybe see you later?"

"I don't know," Adam said. "Depends what Louise's got planned for me."

As Adam left Jarvis's flat, he knew their relationship had shifted. Nothing had been said, nothing had been acknowledged. But he knew what was happening. It scared him as much as it excited him. Uncharted territory. That spark of desire, the fluttering heart, the blood flowing through his body... Adam hasn't felt that kind of passion since he coveted his twin brother's girlfriend. The forbidden, there's nothing quite like it, nothing that can preoccupy the body and mind more effectively than that which you must not yield to, must not contemplate. And Adam's always had a self-destructive streak – the drinking, the marrying Tom's girlfriend. He never takes the easy route in life, he takes the path with pitfalls and grief and guilt and hardship. That's what makes him feel alive and that's what's been missing for so long.

It's weird, he hasn't even given much thought to the fact Jarvis is a man. Adam isn't gay, he doesn't think about other guys in that way, but he's never been repulsed by it either. He had a thing with a friend when he was at school, nothing much, nothing he'd have thought twice about if his mum hadn't caught them at it. Tom took the piss out of him for months after that, but only because he could, not because he particularly cared. They'd never had any secrets from each other...well, not until Tom found out he was dying and committed the ultimate betrayal – dying without telling Adam it was going to happen.

And now, Adam can't stop thinking about Jarvis. The first time they went running, Jarvis had bent over to do some stretches and Adam had noticed him. More specifically, he'd noticed his arse. As weird as it sounds, Adam had shaken the feeling off and hadn't given it much mental space. It was just…a thing. Sometimes, everyone thinks weird thoughts, thoughts that are out of character. And Jarvis arriving had already been changing things for Adam and Louise; they were already happier and more positive. So he'd put it down to the excitement of a new friendship, or the fact he was starting to take charge of his life again.

But the thoughts had kept coming, popping in at inopportune moments, as if there were opportune moments. And the wanking…that's when he knew something was going on.

"Oh fuck," he'd whispered to himself, immediately overcome with guilt as he'd wiped himself clean, realising Jarvis had featured a little too heavily in his fantasy. He'd glanced over at Louise asleep next to him in bed and leant over to kiss her cheek, as if this could undo the thoughts he'd been having. It couldn't, of course.

But he'd never act on it. It was a crush, a stupid crush that he'd get over. He'd definitely never act on it. He could never do something like that. Not to himself. Not to his wife. Not to his children.

Interlude

It's a terrible sound, your own scream. At first the howls are loud and anguished, but quickly – more quickly than you'd ever imagine – you can't find the strength and you become silent, voiceless, letting death happen to you.

I'm about to be nothing; a misremembered phantom photographs won't accurately reflect. But the memories I'm experiencing now seem real, like I own them fully, like they're the ones I've never discussed with anyone, the untainted, pure ones. If I could live, I'd take more care of my memories. I'd keep more of them to myself.

"Leave." A voice from another time now. It wears no flesh, it's a disembodied sound, something I can't grasp, can't hear properly. Won't hear properly. "Just leave," it persists. What if I'd done it? What if I'd left?

"I can't," I hear myself reply. But you know what? I could have. It would have been the right choice. I could have avoided all of this.

Choices, life is all about choices in the end. Sometimes we act like we don't have them, that other people rob us of our choices, overwhelming us with their own desires – but you know what, that's a lie. If it's taught me nothing else, my imminent death has taught me that. We always have choices and other people are not in control – we like to live that lie because being in charge of your own destiny is so scary. Just because some choices seem difficult doesn't mean they aren't available to us. Looking back, I always made the wrong choices, allowing bad 'luck' a greasy foothold in my life time and time again. But I'm to blame, nobody else.

I must be feeling, mustn't I?

My head is bleeding.

"Yeah, it's been bleeding since this morning," a voice replies, not my own. Someone I love, someone I haven't seen for so long, too long.

What now?

No breathing.

No sensations.

Am I dead?

"Nearly. You were never the survivor."

No, I don't suppose I was.

"Try and switch off, this next bit is horrible."

But I don't want to miss it.

"Don't say I didn't warn you."

I want my life back, I want another chance.

"No second chances, not this time. Not any time, actually."

But it feels like I can still smile.

"You can't. I'm sorry… Hush now, it's nearly over. And you've got to be ready."

Part Four: Falling

"I don't blame anyone. Not even myself."

Chapter Nineteen

"You may be feeling shocked, sad, distressed, or angry following the crime you have just reported." The policeman stares at Adam, smiling widely and inappropriately. Adam squints in the weird strip lighting of the police station.

"No, I'm okay." His voice sounds dry and slightly warped. The desk sergeant smiles again, too young to be old and too old to be young. His muscles are pushing at the fabric of his white short-sleeve shirt, Adam can't help noticing.

"Just take a seat for a second." He indicates a row of seats opposite the desk. "I'll get you a victim-support leaflet."

Adam still feels lightheaded, but at least he's been looked over by a doctor and knows there's no lasting damage. He and Louise turn and silently move towards the plastic chairs, sitting down next to each other despite the fact that neither wants to.

"Adam, we can't go on like this," Louise says. "I know it hurt you, but it was a year ago. If we can't move on…"

Hurt him? She says it like it was nothing, a minor misdemeanour. She tried to take her own life, to remove herself from the world and leave her family behind. He knows he's supposed to be supportive, that he's supposed to understand that she wasn't in her right mind, that she'd had a terrible shock, but deep down inside, in the place he tries to hide things, where all nice people suppress the truths that would overturn their lives, he hates her for it. Nothing, not even Jarvis, could have been so bad that you could inflict that on your loved ones.

Oh, his rational voice overpowers those thoughts: she was temporarily out of her mind; she didn't know what she was doing; she couldn't process what she'd learned; she couldn't blah blah fucking blah. She was prepared to leave Adam and their children the legacy of a suicide wife and mother. He's already lost his twin and she wanted to leave him a widower and single father as well. He says he doesn't blame her, that he's there for her, that he understands. But he's lying. Emotions aren't as easily persuaded as the mind. His mouth can say things his mind and body don't feel with worrying ease. Given that she's never actually told him why she did it, he can't *feel* the things he knows he should. He can't feel pity or forgiveness or love. Of course, in reality, he knows exactly why she did it. Maybe if they'd talked about it, even once, the past year wouldn't have been so excruciating for them both.

"Adam, are you listening?" Louise says.

"What?" Adam replies, pressing the towel against his head to soak up the blood still seeping out. Lots of veins in the scalp, apparently. Nothing too much to worry about. No concussion, just a lot of blood. A lot. Easy for the doctor to say there is 'nothing to worry about' but what does she know? Adam doesn't feel great at all. In fact, he feels woozy.

"We can't go on like this, what's the point?" Louise is saying, sitting next to him in the police-station hallway, all white walls and yellowing floor and uninviting strobe lighting. She doesn't look her age, Adam thinks, glancing at her and wincing as another bolt of pain spikes his head and eyes. She could still pass for her late twenties still, Adam reckons. But he knows he's looking older now. The odd grey hair already, bags under his eyes. And his hangovers are longer lasting than they used to. When he's sober long enough to have a hangover.

"Well, what do you suggest, Louise? Splitting up?" he says irritably, wanting to shut her down. He's been mugged, he's bleeding from the head, is it really the time for this conversation?

"Yeah, maybe." Her response is quick, like the words have been poised to sprint, straining on the starter blocks at tip of her tongue and his retort was the starting pistol, setting them free to run.

"Okay," he replies simply. He isn't sure he even cares anymore. That's not true, he is sure. He doesn't. He wants her to shut the fuck up and leave him alone. That's all he's wanted for the past year.

The mugging had all been so quick, over in a flash – one minute he'd been getting his wallet out in the street to get a £20 note out and the next he'd been smashed over the head, his wallet was gone and he hadn't even seen a thing.

"We're all done here," the policeman says behind the counter, "unless there's anything else…?"

Adam stands and walks over to the desk sergeant to get the leaflet being proffered to him with twitching fingers, the white-and-green glossy paper glinting in the strobe lights as Adam squints at the front cover. Louise stands up and moves quietly next to Adam, looking down at the counter, not offering any comfort, not seeming like she's mentally there at all. Adam notices her eyes flicker down and hover over the policeman's toned chest for a moment before she looks away again. Nothing has changed, she's still the same old Louise, looking for something – someone – better, shinier, newer and more exciting.

"No, no I'm good," Adam says.

"Good," the desk sergeant replies.

"What?" Adam says, slightly confused.

"You've been mugged," the policeman repeats, as if it's necessary, as if Adam might not have realised. "It's a shock, but you're lucky, it could have been a lot worse. No lasting damage." He nods towards Adam's head. "And you've cancelled all your cards?"

"Yes," Adam says, trying to break eye contact with him. The policeman waves at his leaflet as he begins to speak again.

"Feelings of anger after such incidents are common and…" the policeman pauses, taking the leaflet from Adam and opening it up to scrutinise it, running his finger down the page until he finds what he's looking for, "…victim support are willing to help wherever they can." He looks up at Adam, frowning.

A long pause draws out until Louise eventually says, "I'll look after him, he doesn't need victim support."

* * *

Their walk home is silent, both of them trapped inside their own thoughts and memories, not wishing to open them out to each other – it would be too damaging now anyway, they have too many secrets, too many lies between them. Nice people's lies, aimed at protecting each other but actually driving them slowly but surely apart. Sometimes, Adam thinks it would have been better if they'd never met Jarvis at all, if they'd carried on living in greyscale. Better that than the brief, intense burst of intoxicating light he brought them that turned out to be tumescent. But in the end, Adam can't regret it, no matter how screwed up that seems to him. Jarvis destroyed everything and still Adam can't regret meeting him. What's the point of life if you're treading water and not living, like they were before they met him? If Adam regrets anything it's not acting on his feelings sooner, it's not going for it and committing 100% before it was too late, before everything else unravelled. The kids would have been all right, they'd have got their heads around everything. Because what was the alternative? What did they end up with but one parent going through the motions, a husk, and the other descending into functioning alcoholism and depression?

Functioning. Such a good word. So descriptive of their lives after Jarvis. So descriptive of a lot of people's lives, he imagines. Functioning. All the moving parts doing what they should but nothing going on behind the scenes, no sparks, no real *life*.

He doesn't know if he wants Louise anymore and even if he does, he doesn't know how to make it work. Sometimes, less and less frequently, Adam remembers the people they used to be. He can manage to keep everything in check and he doesn't start drinking until the kids are in bed, he doesn't sit nursing a glass of wine at lunchtime, endlessly thinking and analysing and picking over the details of that night. He can even keep his feelings for Jarvis at bay if he works hard. But he hates that he's so weak, that he's at the mercy of his wife and her... He's blaming her. It's not her fault. He knows it's not. It was such a terrible shock for her, of course it was.

It scarcely seems possible that they've settled back into ordinary life. But they have. Painful, gut-wrenching normal life, killing them bit by bit as the seconds tick by. Hours pass, days pass, months pass. Life disappears behind them in a trail of sameness, the lies and unsaid truths inside them both growing cavernous, echo chambers deep within to get lost in. And like grey steps leading to infinity, the days stack up and up, identical, cold and unremarkable. Sometimes, Adam can even fool himself that he can feel them pass, that he can brush their rough surface and make himself bleed. But he can't. He can't feel anything, not anymore. Not since Jarvis. He gave up feeling that night. He should blame Jarvis, he should hate him the way Louise does. But he doesn't, if anything he feels regret. He should have been braver.

He can't imagine how it felt for his wife that night. The funny thing is – funny horrific, not funny ha ha – she's never told him what she knows. He'd have thought she'd want to talk about it, to thrash it out, to scream and to cry. But maybe her suicide attempt robbed her of the need to talk. Maybe that left her with nothing to say. Maybe it left them both with nothing to say. Empty vessels, bringing up children. Living, after a fashion. Existing. Going through the motions, pre-programmed, pre-ordained.

Except they weren't pre-ordained, were they. She was supposed to live her life with Tom, not him. She'd only married him because Tom had died, pushing them together in the process. But Adam is starting to feel that his life is unravelling for a reason. He doesn't feel right, like he's an imbalance the world needs to correct. How can his identical twin be dead while he still lives? Maybe that's why he's fucking everything up so badly.

Adam doesn't think it ever occurred to Louise that he might have needed to talk as well after her suicide attempt. That he might have needed help moving on after what she did, after what he'd lost? But no, that's not fair. How could he have asked that of her after what he'd done, what he'd wanted to do? He's lucky she's still with him at all. If Adam hadn't lied, she would have left on the spot – or tried harder to die.

We need to talk. Come over. J x

That text was nearly a year ago, but it's still like yesterday for Adam. He remembers the true, giddy, heart-fluttering excitement. He'd felt sick with it, like he couldn't eat, couldn't sit still, couldn't do anything until he saw Jarvis again. Nothing else mattered but being near him. That day, he'd showered after his run and gone downstairs and picked up his phone and there had been a text message from Jarvis.

We need to talk. Come over. J x

Fuck, it still makes him feel sick when he thinks about it. That's what life's about isn't it? Feeling something. Anything.

"I'm going out with Alice later," Louise had said nonchalantly. "You know, for a drink. I haven't seen her for ages, not properly since that bloody dinner party. And I want to see how things are going with John, you know…catch up with her."

"All right, love," Adam had replied, his heart drumming so loudly in his chest he was sure Louise could hear it. "That's sounds nice."

"Okay, well I'm going to have a shower and get ready," she'd said, leaning over to kiss him on the lips.

We need to talk. Come over. J x

That's all the text message had said. All it needed to say.

"I'll probably stay over with her, that way we don't have to worry about how pissed we get," Louise had said. Adam hadn't even looked up.

"Okay, love."

We need to talk. Come over. J x

Christ, what was he supposed to do? He'd known what it meant, of course. But he'd been adamant: he couldn't risk everything for something so… He wasn't gay, he wasn't even bisexual. It was ridiculous to even think about it. And he and Louise had been getting on so well. Adam would not throw it all away. Besides, he'd told himself, he wouldn't have been able to go through with the sexual side of things anyway. Fantasising about something is different to actually doing it or even wanting to do it. Sometimes it's exciting to think about things you'll never do – that's where the interest lies.

We need to talk. Come over. J x

Fuck. What could he have replied to that anyway? If he could step back in time and change things he would. He'd ignore the message and run upstairs after Louise and grab her and kiss her and tell her that she shouldn't go to see Alice, she should come out with him for dinner instead. But of course he can't step back in time. He can't change anything at all because it's all in the past and it has happened already.

We need to talk. Come over. J x

He'd sat on the sofa listening to Louise singing in the shower upstairs, staring at his mobile screen and resolutely deciding that he wouldn't reply and he certainly wouldn't go over there. He couldn't trust himself to do that. Or maybe he should go over there, to put him straight. To tell Jarvis that he wasn't gay and nothing was ever going to happen so he should stop bothering him and hassling him. Yes, that was it. He'd go over and tell him that he didn't appreciate the attention, it was unwanted. Predatory, even.

On my way over now.

There, he'd replied. He'd resolved to tell him in person what was what. He'd written a few responses before actually sending that one.

I can't, sorry x

No, no kiss.

I can't.

Too cold, it wasn't like Jarvis had done anything wrong, he was barking up the wrong tree and needed to be put straight, that was all.

There's nothing to talk about, let's forget about it.

Forget about what though? Nothing had actually happened. All they'd done is leant into each other while drinking a cup of coffee, hardly the crime of the century. So writing that would have been presumptuous.

Okay, but I can't stay long xx

The kisses again, no kisses.

On my way over.

Yes, that's right. Clean, to the point. Not affectionate, not something that could in any way give Jarvis the wrong idea.

I'll open a bottle of wine, Jarvis's response had said.

Fuck. Shoving his phone in his pocket, he'd gone into the hallway and shouted up the stairs at Louise, who'd still been in the shower.

"I'm popping out for a bit, love," he'd shouted. "Shouldn't be too long, but if I'm not back before you go, have a great evening. Say hi to Alice."

"Okay, love," she'd shouted back as he shut the front door behind him. "Remember you need to pick the kids up from your mum in the morning."

This isn't going to happen, he'd told himself. Deep down, he'd known he was lying to himself. Talking, that was all they were going to do. He was going to put Jarvis right, tell him nothing like that could ever happen. He was happily married and Jarvis was Louise's friend as much as he was Adam's, it would be such a betrayal, it couldn't happen.

What was he wearing, did he look okay? He'd glanced down at himself to see jeans, Adidas trainers and a simple grey t-shirt. He wasn't going to win any fashion awards but he looked okay, passable. *It doesn't matter what you look like, that's the point. This isn't going to happen*, he'd told himself again, less convincing with every step he took, walking down the hill towards Jarvis's flat, opposite Louise's café, heart smashing around in his chest, a boxer being pummelled by his opponent.

He supposes looking back the signs had all been there, but they'd both genuinely believed that Jarvis had met them and liked them. That their friendship was real and not based on a lie. Because you don't expect that in real life – in real life people are usually who and what they say they are. They might be an Imogen or a John or a Janet Gaddis, but they're true to themselves, even if you don't like it. Adam's not sure he's ever come across anyone truly duplicitous before.

Duplicitous. That's how he'd describe Jarvis now, for sure. Except, it wouldn't change anything. Even knowing what he knows, Adam can't get him out of his head. He still thinks about him, even now, even a year on. He can admit that now, even if he couldn't back then. Even that night, Adam couldn't admit it, couldn't open up and tell him, 'Yes, I love you, let's do it'.

Instead, he ended up cowering at the back of Jarvis's bedroom, hiding, terrified and appalled, not knowing what on earth to do. Nothing had turned out how it was supposed to – in the end, Adam suspects that might be life's only truth: things don't turn out how you plan.

Chapter Twenty

Louise isn't surprised Adam got mugged. Being pissed off your face on gin at ten-thirty in the morning is likely to lead to such incidents. He's become so needy, not at all like the man she married. If she's honest, she's not sure she can cope with him anymore. In the past year, he's developed this habit of chewing his knuckles when he gets stressed, which is quite often. He gets bleeding valleys on his left hand and sometimes he doesn't even notice it. Louise has to gently move his hand away from his mouth and clean it up, rinsing the cloth under the tap and watching the pink-red water wash down the plughole.

"Sorry," he says quietly, still lost in his own thoughts.

"It's okay," she replies, not meaning it. With everything that's happened in her life, she's found a way to carry on, to get on with it. She is struggling to respect a man who lets everything hold him back like Adam does. He isn't enough. Maybe she hasn't admitted that to herself fully before this moment, but all of a sudden, she knows it in her heart. Something is missing and neither of them will ever find it. Maybe neither of them wants to. That's the elephant in the room playing a saxophone and smoking thin brown cigarettes. That's why this conversation is right, why they have to split up.

And what about the kids, witnessing their dad turning into a train wreck before their eyes? Louise has had enough. Every time she looks at him nowadays, she wants to smash his face in. The way he eats, the ways he scratches his balls while watching the golf, the way he whines and moans about every last thing in the world and can't see the good in anything at all.

If anyone has the right to feel depressed and turn to drink it's her. Hasn't life thrown everything it has at her? But she's still standing. She's still going through the motions, getting through the day. Why shouldn't he? Why should he have the luxury of falling apart while she still keeps it together?

Okay, she had a lapse a year ago, she had a moment when she wanted to end it all. But that's all it was, a moment. And she's grateful to Adam, she's glad he found her, glad he saved her. But he can't hold on to his anger forever. And who could blame her anyway? The thought of Jarvis still makes her skin crawl. Maybe she's projecting. Maybe she's been projecting for months, pushing all the hatred she feels for Jarvis onto Adam, letting it grow and fester until she can barely look at him without wanting to scream in rage and fly at him, nails sharp, teeth bared. Why can't she get over it and move on? How long before the pain dulls, before she can forget?

* * *

For ages after the dinner party where Jarvis revealed he was gay, Louise hadn't believed it. She'd come up with a million different scenarios as to why he might have said it or what he might have meant by it, but in reality, she couldn't get one simple fact out of her mind. He loved her and he wanted her and she knew it for a fact. She knew he had feelings for her, pure and simple. She hadn't invented it, she knew it in her bones, in her tummy and in the way her skin tingled whenever she was near him.

So what did it all mean? She'd never felt confusion and infatuation like it in her entire life. It encompassed every living breathing moment of her existence. Adam, the café, even the kids didn't exist. The only thing that took up any of her mental space was Jarvis, all day, every day. How he looked, how he'd spoken to her, how he'd brushed against her skin, how he'd glanced at her. She knew he was interested in her, so how could he be gay? None of it made sense and the less sense it made the more excited and infatuated she felt. Maybe she was his 'one' – the exception, the woman he'd unwittingly fallen for.

She had constantly encouraged Adam's relationship with

Jarvis. Their running was a wonderful thing – it meant she'd seen Jarvis in running shorts and tight top at least three times a week. And he'd popped in, for a tea or coffee, sometimes for dinner. Not only that, she'd been able to watch him from the store-room window and there was no way he hadn't known what he was doing, walking around drinking beer with his top off. He'd known, she'd been sure. He'd been getting off on her watching as much as she'd been getting herself off while watching him. He'd *known*.

He'd become part of their lives, a close friend. But she'd felt sure he wouldn't be doing that unless he wanted her. She could understand how difficult it would be for him to accept and recognise those feelings. If he'd spent his adult life living as a gay man, admitting he'd fallen for a woman would be life changing, she could see that. But she knew he needed to accept reality and bite the bullet. They could have a life together, they could be truly happy. Maybe they could even have more kids, she wasn't over the hill yet. And didn't she deserve some happiness? She'd had a shitty life. Why shouldn't she grab happiness when it came along?

"You only get one life," Tom used to say. And he'd been right. She didn't – doesn't – believe, not in the half-hearted Church of England God her parents did or any other God. Okay, so she would still spell God with a capital G, as if it was immutable, as if she'd be struck down if she didn't. But otherwise? No, this was it – her one shot. Why shouldn't she be happy? Why couldn't she grab it with both hands and rejoice in it? Adam would get over it, after all. He didn't even love her. She wasn't sure he ever had – he'd only been with her because his twin told him posthumously that he should be.

But how to broach it with Jarvis? A gay man who couldn't admit his feelings for a woman, who couldn't tell her how he felt, once and for all. She'd have to force his hand, confront him with it. Yes, that's what she'd do. She'd go around and tell him how she felt, tell him she knew how he felt but that he shouldn't be afraid. She'd tell him they could face it together, deal with the fallout together. As long as they had each other, they could deal with anything.

So she'd manufactured a lie for Adam.

"I'm going to go out with Alice," she'd said nonchalantly. "You know, for a drink. I haven't seen her for ages, not properly since that bloody dinner party. And I want to see how things are going with John, you know…catch up with her without Imogen there."

"All right, love," Adam had said, more interested in his mobile than her. "That's sounds nice."

"I'll probably stay over with her, that way we don't have to worry about how pissed we get," she'd said. Adam had hardly registered her, he was so engrossed in his mobile.

Louise had felt sick to her stomach. She was going to tell Jarvis how she felt. She was going to tell him that they didn't need to hide it anymore, they needed to go with it and explore their feelings and…fuck. Oh God she wanted to fuck him more than anything she'd ever wanted in her entire life. Her entire body had been hot with the idea of it, too hot. But he'd like that, she'd told herself. He wouldn't be scared, would he? He wanted it…he wouldn't admit it to himself.

She'd changed her outfit no less than six times that day. Luckily, Adam had been out for most of the time, running with Jarvis, and he'd only come back about an hour before she went. As she'd showered to get ready, he'd called up to her again, telling her he was popping out. She was glad of it, one less lie to think up, one less stress to manage. In the end, she chose a Japanese-inspired flower print dress, quite tight fitting around her still-slim frame; high heels – not too high, high enough to be sexy. She'd looked at herself in it in the full-length mirror for about ten minutes, turning and exploring every angle, especially her bum. *He's probably an arse man.*

And then she'd left, shutting the front door behind her and

standing on the doorstep, making a mental note that when she came home, everything would be different. She'd have professed her love to Jarvis, they'd have consummated it and she'd be coming home to leave Adam. And she consoled herself with the fact he wouldn't care. The kids would get used to it, it wouldn't affect them. They liked Jarvis anyway. There were no downsides to this – yes, it would be difficult, but it was the best thing for all of them in the long run, even Adam. He might not have realised it at the time, but he'd have coped and found happiness without her.

They'd all become so close with Jarvis, the whole family. He'd even come on a family picnic with them to Beachy Head and they'd had such a wonderful, carefree day. Jarvis had got on so well with Matthew and Maria, it had made Louise think… It could work, the two of them. Once the kids got over the shock of their parents divorcing, they'd learn to accept him. That day, Jarvis had snapped a picture of the family while they were there. She wished he'd been in the shot instead of Adam, but even though he wasn't, the knowledge that he took the photo made her love it even more and she'd had it blown up on a canvas for the living-room wall. They all looked so happy. Because they were happy, that's the thing. Jarvis was fixing them, making everything okay.

So why had she wanted to break it? She and Adam hadn't been unhappy back then, not like now. Christ, she hadn't even known what an unhappy marriage was back then. It was nothing in comparison to now. So why had she been craving Jarvis the way she was, fantasising and imagining with every breathing moment? It was like he'd become a constant itch she needed to scratch – sometimes, when it got too much, she'd nip to the toilets in the café to get herself off in the middle of the day because she was finding it so hard to concentrate. If she got it out of her system she could focus on something else, even if it was for a short while.

And so it came to that night, the night she decided to move things forward. To tell him how she felt. If only she could go back and stop herself. She hadn't been prepared for it. She could never have guessed the truth, not in a million years. He should have been honest with her from the start, then none of it would have happened. She still hates him so much she can hardly breathe. Sometimes, she catches herself thinking about him and she realises she's holding her breath. Part of her still wants to carry on holding it, never letting it out, waiting for the darkness to overtake her, to make the memories stop.

She hadn't gone straight to his flat, despite her excitement, she hadn't been brave enough. She'd walked into town first, bought a bottle of wine in the Tesco near the Jubilee Library. Eventually, she'd headed back up the hill to her cafe, crossing the road to stand on Jarvis's doorstep. She'd hovered there for what seemed like hours, staring at the scratch marks around his keyhole, lifting her arm up to press the doorbell, then dropping back down to her side again. *How does one broach a love story between a straight woman and a gay man?* It was unchartered territory for both of them, she'd known. There was no rule book…but how would she start the conversation? He might not want to admit his feelings, it was a life-changing realisation for him. She knew it was not going to be easy, but she also knew they were meant for each other. Reaching out and taking a deep, deep breath, she'd pressed the doorbell. No going back.

"Louise," he'd said through the intercom, sounding surprised, shocked even. Her heart had been fluttering in her chest, she was fingering the ring of bone between her neck and breast, rubbing the skin there, making it slightly rashy.

"Hi, Jarvis," she'd said. "I think we need to talk, don't you?"

"What?" he asked, his voice panicky.

"Can I come up?" she'd said, using her best seductress voice.

"Oh fuck," he'd said. "I'm sorry…look, it's not a good time."

Even then, the alarm bells hadn't rung loudly enough. She'd

been slightly confused, he was acting weird, but she still hadn't guessed, how could she?

"Just buzz me in will you, it's freezing out here, it's been snowing."

"Just a second, then," he'd said. He'd sounded flustered and she'd assumed his heart was pounding for the same reason hers was. This was taboo. And somehow, that made it even more exciting, she knew he was feeling it too.

Should she ever tell him she'd watched him from the storeroom window as he got dressed, as he wandered around his flat in his boxer shorts? Probably not, well not unless he brought it up, not unless he told her he knew she'd been watching him all along. God, it was all so *sexy*. It felt like minutes standing on that doorstep, waiting for him to buzz her up. Should she tell him she'd seen him wanking that time? Sitting on his sofa, with his curtains not fully closed, late at night?

What was he doing? Why was he taking so long to buzz her in? Was he making sure he looked presentable for her? Making sure his breath was okay? Maybe that was it? Maybe he was brushing his teeth and smartening himself up for her. And then it buzzed, the front door gave way and she could mount the stairs to her destiny.

Chapter Twenty-One

The past has always influenced their present, Adam realises. First it was Tom, then it was Jarvis. Always something. Someone. Somewhere along the way, they stopped being able to enjoy the moment, to enjoy each other like they used to. And now they're falling apart. Really falling apart, once and for all.

He'd tried to curb his drinking in the past year for Louise. Not for himself, for her, to shut her up, mainly.

"You need to find yourself again," she'd said cryptically, as if this even made sense. It's not like she'd ever been a new-age woman. He'd been the one who'd dabbled with meditation and yoga, not her. She'd never been anything but functional and now here she was telling him to stop drinking and 'find himself'. He could have spat his gin out laughing. But deep down, he knew he was using drink for all the wrong reasons – to de-stress, to forget, to remain unconscious of the hurt. He knew he was on the way to becoming some sort of alcoholic. So he stopped drinking for a while. And he had felt better for it. And Louise had been proud. She'd thought it had taken him a lot of mental courage to stop, apparently. She'd been 'proud' of him. Like a dog owner is proud when their puppy learns to sit for a treat.

How much mental courage would it have taken for her to throw those pills down the sink and not down her throat? When she spoke to him of mental courage, the rage inside of him bubbled up so furiously he could hardly breathe. It was this, if nothing else that made him start drinking again. There he was, sitting, tongue out, begging for her approval. Begging for some feeling or emotion to reignite and then he realised, like a slap in the face, that it wasn't there. He didn't love her anymore. He didn't want her. He didn't care what she thought of him and he certainly didn't care if she felt 'proud'. As she sat sipping her glass of Pinot of an evening and told him of the immense pride she felt that he'd stopped drinking, Adam believed her. She was swollen with it. He felt that if he'd prodded her, her skin would have split and the pus of her pride would have seeped out to congratulate him.

Why do people turn back to whatever their crutch is? Whether it's drink or chocolate or weed or exercise or obsessive cleaning or sex? People always go back to thing that makes them forget themselves, for a moment. Because that's all people want to do, escape their reality. It's all Adam wants to do. But is he an alcoholic? He doesn't think so. *Look at Alice's boyfriend John – he goes to dinner parties and calls complete strangers a cunt. Now there's a man who should stop drinking.*

"I don't like you when you're drunk," Louise said when he'd poured himself a glass of wine, ending his dry spell.

"You don't like me when I'm sober," Adam replied, flopping back into his armchair and losing himself in some meaningless programme on the television.

He wishes he hadn't stayed. Every single day he wishes he'd left with Jarvis and grabbed a chance at happiness. But if he had, she'd have died that night. He'd have had that on his conscience forever and the bizarre thing was, it was nothing to do with him. Nothing was ever anything to do with him, it never had been. He's always been an also-ran in his own life, a sideshow, something on the periphery of reality. He wasn't Tom, he was a cheap facsimile of him. He wasn't anything to do with his wife's suicide attempt – her love for Jarvis was the reason. Nothing was ever anything to do with Adam, he was just there, lurking on the outside of life, hoping someone would notice him. Like Jarvis had, momentarily, at least.

Louise seemed to bounce back from her suicide attempt, silently withdrawing from him and getting on with her life as if nothing had happened, walking and talking, laughing and wearing a mask of normality. Smiling in the right places (most of the time).

He sees her being supportive to other people all the time. Take Bella who works with her at the café, for example. She's been having problems with her husband – "It's like living with a stranger, Louise, I don't feel anything anymore. And now I'm starting to wonder if he's a bit abusive. I don't mean physically, but mentally, you know? He puts me down all the time, makes me feel like I'm nothing…" – and Louise can sit and talk for hours with her about this, clasping her hand across the café table, earnestly nodding her head and offering advice and hugs. Louise seems to have boundless patience and energy to deal with other people's problems. But for Adam? It's like she can't stand the sight of him anymore, let alone talk to him or support him.

It's the little things Adam misses, like when he was waiting to hear from his agent about his second novel, *Yesterday's Croissant*. He'd been so nervous all week that he'd made himself ill, a cold and a sore throat. He hadn't slept well and Maria had snuck into bed with them in the night, kicking and fussing and snuggling up to Adam, then Matthew had followed. Louise had to open the café in the morning, but once upon a time, she'd have cuddled up to them as well, before getting out of bed. She'd have asked how he was feeling and she'd have reassured him things would be okay. She might even have brought him a Lemsip or a hot honey-and-lemon drink before she left or offered to help with the kids. But on this morning, she came in the bedroom and said, "You need to get up, I've taken the kids downstairs, they're watching *Sleeping Beauty*. They've got breakfast. I'll be back about six." No kiss. No 'Good luck today'. No comforting words. As it happened, his agent said the publishers hated his second novel and wanted rewrites that amounted to nearly a new novel entirely. Not that Louise even remembered to ask him about it, even when she got home.

It's unfair to blame Louise for everything, not after what he did. It's not Louise's fault he drinks too much. It's unfair to blame her, but of course, Adam does. Not explicitly, not verbally, he'd never say anything to her face. But he knows their every interaction screams it nonetheless. He's not his own agent anymore, he has no autonomy over his emotions or self-worth. Louise's mood dictates his own, has done ever since she tried to take her own life. As for Louise, nowadays she looks right through him. When she doesn't, every glance, every word, every gesture masks one pervasive thought, corrosive in its power: *You never should have saved me.*

"I need you to talk to me," he blurted out once, months after it happened. "I need you to tell me why you did it."

"Stop it, Adam," Louise replied. "We are both tired, don't put pressure on me. I've got enough on with the café and the kids hanging off me all the time..."

"Hanging off you? You?" Adam said incredulously. "You're never here, I'm surprised they still recognise you."

"Oh, here we go again, poor little Adam. Someone has to earn a wage, Adam. Your novel money didn't last and do you think your little freelance jobs keep us afloat?"

"I'm saying you can't use them as an excuse..."

"*Me* use them as an excuse? You're the one who uses them as an excuse not to have a life. Then you blame me for it."

"You have no idea what being a parent is, Louise. Do you know who taught Matthew to use the toilet? Me. I sat day after day, letting him watch me piss and shit – he even used to try to wipe my arse for me. You think it all happens by magic. They don't teach themselves things, Louise. I teach them things. You should try it, it's called parenthood."

"What the fuck are you talking about, Adam? You chose to stay at home. Man up, will you, and stop whining all the time."

In these moments, feeling more alone than ever before, Adam has allowed himself to think about Tom more that he used to, letting himself descend into melancholy and depression. And as he and Louise drift further and further apart, he often thinks about the letter Tom sent him.

Adam,

Firstly, I'm sorry. But I know you understand. I didn't want to talk about it. But I need to know you'll find a way to carry on after me. I know how hard that's going to be for you but I've got a plan: Louise.

She loves you. I've been watching you both and the more I think about it, the more I think it's the answer. You can help each other through this. You're the two people I love most in the world – and I want you to love each other. Can you do that for me?

Tom x

At the time, Adam had taken Tom's note as a green card and he'd rushed headlong into a relationship with Louise. But without Tom's blessing...without Tom's manipulation, would they ever have got together? Adam doesn't think so, and that knowledge terrifies him. Maybe he and Louise were supposed to have entirely different lives, maybe somewhere in some other time stream, he's married to someone else, she's married to someone else. Maybe they are happier. Maybe two people with Tom's ghost knitted to them should never have coupled up – it made his spectre more powerful, made them make choices they shouldn't have. And so it's come to this.

"You never talked to me about it Louise," Adam says, sitting down at their kitchen table and glancing over at the bottle of wine on the side.

"Adam, you've got to get help," Louise says, noticing his glance. "Your drinking is out of hand, I can't help you anymore."

"Don't change the subject," he continues, determined that if they're going to split up, if they're going to end it after all these years, he's at least going to get the truth out of her, the truth that unbeknown to her, he already knows.

"I'm trying to help, Adam," Louise is saying earnestly. "You've got to find help, you can't carry on like this."

"Like *what*, Louise?" Adam finds himself raising his voice, irritated. "How would you like me to carry on? Like you? Lying and trundling along like everything is fine when you wish you were dead?"

"Adam, that's not fair, it's not like that. I don't wish I was dead."

"But you *did*, Louise." Adam slams his fist down on the table. "But you never once talked to me about it. Months and months, living with you, waiting. Thinking, *one day*. One day she'll feel ready. She'll open up. But that day's never going to come is it? And you wonder why we can't move on? Why we don't love each other anymore?"

There. He'd said the unsaid. The unsayable. The unthinkable. And now it is out in the open he feels…what? Relieved? Something like that, but something else, something approaching loss as well. They've been part of each other's lives for so long, how could he not mourn their passing? But that's no reason to stay with someone.

"Don't you love me anymore?" Louise says quietly, pulling up a chair opposite him at the kitchen table.

"I don't know," Adam sighs. "Do you love me? I mean really, in your heart of hearts."

Louise shakes her head. "I don't know either, I suppose." They sit in silence, a strange calm descending over the room. The kitchen clock keeps time with and eventually, Louise says,

"Maybe we should have split up years ago."

Adam's head is still woozy from the alcohol and the head injury and he's not in the mood for this conversation any more. He wants everything over.

"Maybe," he mutters, his eyes flicking over to the red wine sitting on the kitchen side again. He has to have a glass. *Fuck it, why not? Damage is done now anyway.*

"Poor me a glass then," Louise says as he stands up and walks over to the counter. "Might as well cheers the end of our marriage."

Adam pours them both a glass of wine and hands one to Louise silently.

"You might have a concussion and you're already half-pissed. Do you think wine is a good idea."

"Oh, fuck off," he replies, or doesn't reply. It doesn't matter, not anymore. For a brief moment he thought she was softening, that she was going to actually relax and have a conversation.

"You can't carry on like this," she perseveres, taking a sip of her own wine.

"I can carry on however I like, Louise. Like you."

"Oh here we go again, poor little Adam, isn't life hard," Louise sneers. "Better have another drink to make it all better. Throw a little tantrum, maybe. Give it a rest, you're a grown man, I've heard it all before. Stop needing something you're never going to get."

"And what's that, Louise?"

"Someone to pick up the pieces. You're just you, Adam, not half of something or someone else. You're responsible for you, always have been. You can't rely on other people the way you do."

"Why not, Louise? Isn't that the point of a marriage?"

Louise doesn't answer him, she descends back into silence. He doesn't know if she's thinking about what he's said or not. The atmosphere in the kitchen slowly strangles them, as the anger in both Adam and Louise gives way to another, much deadlier emotion. Resignation. Lines get crossed with them all the time, but today seems different. Today seems like it's the end. For months now, the boundaries of what is acceptable in their marriage have been adjusted and altered, new lines have been crossed and redrawn endlessly. But today the lines they stepped over were glaring, obvious, neon lines with spikes on. They would never be redrawn, crossing them had been too painful.

This has been their reality for months, the life they built

together after Jarvis. Infinitely worse than before. The kids know something is wrong, he supposes, but they are too little to truly understand it. But Adam does and he can't let go of it, can't get over the feeling of betrayal. What does that say about him that he can't feel sympathy or understanding, only bitterness? It doesn't matter, he supposes. He's not sure what does matter anymore. When Jarvis was still in their lives, they'd felt alive with hope and excitement, like anything and everything was possible. And then he'd ripped it away from them again when his lies were exposed, when Louise had fallen to pieces.

And Adam hadn't grieved. Nobody knew what had happened between him and Jarvis, so in the aftermath, he had nobody to talk to, nobody to tell. So he internalised everything, buried it deep within and tried to carry on. Besides, he had to support Louise after her suicide attempt; he had two children to bring up. But something fundamental had changed for them. Every glance, every look, every lie and half-truth they told each other from that moment on, all in the name of protection…stung. It was like each lie was another barb fired in one another's direction, each one more lethal than the last. He pours himself another glass of wine, conscious that Louise has only had two mouthfuls of hers. He stands staring at the tiles on the kitchen wall, trying unsuccessfully to clear his mind.

"Drinking isn't the answer, Adam. It's not going to solve anything. It didn't solve things after Tom died, did it? It prolonged things, stopped you from dealing with it."

"Oh, what the fuck would you know." Adam reels around on Louise, spitting at her, filled with fury. "We spent all our time after Tom dealing with *your* grief, Louise, don't you remember. It was all about you, it's always been all about you."

Louise shrinks back in her chair slightly, her face falling half into shadow under the hanging light.

"It wasn't like that, Adam, and you know it."

"Oh wasn't it. Really?"

"You know it wasn't. It isn't. I've always tried to support you and look after you. Maybe you don't always recognise it, maybe you don't..."

"How did losing Tom make me feel, Louise? Tell me. How have I always felt? I'm not sure you've ever noticed, I'm not sure you've ever cared." Adam is shouting and he doesn't mean to, but he feels like he's drowning, overwhelmed with...something. Self-pity, maybe, he's not sure.

"Alone, Adam. You felt alone," Louise says quietly. Adam puts his wine glass back on the side and runs his hands through his hair, trying to blink back his tears.

"Louise, I..." Adam starts. But he doesn't know what to say.

"Save it, Adam," Louise continues, her voice still quiet, but not gentle, not kind. "Because you know what, your self-pity doesn't interest me. It never has done."

Adam clutches the kitchen sideboard, feeling dizzy, his head still throbbing. It's gone too far, he knows it has. He squeezes his eyes shut, trying to get rid of the floating black squares in his vision. After a few moments, he opens them again and the dizziness has passed. He stands upright and attempts to let go of the side, to see if he can stand okay. He can.

"Don't leave me," he says quietly. The tears building up behind his eyes are actually painful, like little pins, pricking and piercing their way to freedom. He glances over to the table. Louise is no longer there, she's walked away. He doesn't blame her. He wouldn't put up with himself, either. And that's it, no more words, nothing poetic or ornate. Just life. Real life in all its stinking glory. The beginning of the end.

* * *

As he'd walked into Jarvis's driveway that night, leaving Louise in the shower at home, he purposefully hadn't glanced over the road at his wife's café – he didn't want to feel guilty. After all, he wasn't doing anything wrong, he was going to put Jarvis in his place, to tell him what was what.

"Hi," he'd said into the intercom, standing on Jarvis's doorstep nervously as the sun had started to set blood red behind him.

"Hi," Jarvis had replied, buzzing him in. As Adam had mounted the stairs he'd found Jarvis's front door already open. Jarvis had silently and casually stepped back to let him in. And it all been so natural, Adam had quickly been offered a glass of wine, which he'd sat twirling in his fingers, staring at Jarvis, an irrepressible smile on his face.

"Takeaway?" Jarvis had asked, grabbing the phone.

"God yeah," Adam had replied, his jeans itching the skin of his legs, his cock curled sweatily, twitchily, into his black briefs.

Before he knew it, Adam had felt silly for all of his overthinking. Nothing felt awkward or strained, they were chatting and drinking a glass of wine. It was comfortable, not tense at all. He'd started to think the whole thing was probably in his mind, all that 'leaning in to each other' and 'tingling skin'. Because he couldn't remember the last time he had a friend – a real friend, someone that was his, not a 'couple' friend, not someone who saw him as half of 'Louise and Adam' or worse, the surviving twin, the living half of 'Tom and Adam'. Jarvis was his friend. Someone who asked about him, talked *to* him. Hell, someone who cared about him and vice versa. There, he'd thought it. Someone he cared about.

Adam would be lying if he said he hadn't felt slightly unnerved by the afternoon's events, but maybe it had all been in his mind anyway. But if that were true, why was that other feeling lurking around, no matter how hard he'd tried suppress it. He hadn't felt it since those early days with Louise: the excitement of the forbidden. The feelings he shouldn't feel, the ones he shouldn't give in to. Which is why his chest was dancing a butterfly dance, of course. Which is why he'd come over to

Jarvis's house in response to that text message.

As the night progressed, things got more and more relaxed. Adam was happier than he could remember being in such a long time, even when Jarvis produced a spliff for Adam with a devilish grin.

"I haven't had a smoke for years," Adam had said, slightly nervous. He'd spent a long time kicking his weed habit after Tom died, he didn't want to smoke again. And he was surprised at Jarvis, he was so fit and healthy, it seemed so out of character.

"I used to be a bit too into weed, you know?" Adam had said, inhaling deeply. "Like it took over my entire life."

"Yeah," Jarvis had said, flopping back down onto his sofa. "It can get like that sometimes, can't it. I don't smoke much anymore, but sometimes there's nothing like it."

Adam had stared at a burgundy-coloured square of carpet in the middle of Jarvis's otherwise beige floor. One single solitary square of red carpet, what had that been about? He'd handed Jarvis the spliff back, sure he'd had enough already, making eye contact as he did so.

"I don't want it," he'd said.

"Okay," Jarvis had said, stubbing it out. "Listen..."

"Let's not go there, Jarvis," Adam had said, transfixed again on the carpet, not daring to look at him. "Once we talk about it, it's real. We can't undo it."

They'd both remained silent for a moment and then Jarvis had started giggling uncontrollably.

"No, I meant listen – I think the takeaway man's at the door."

Fuck. Adam had blushed, looked away, not knowing what on earth to do or say to cover his tracks, to...

"But we do need to have *that* conversation," Jarvis had said, standing up and putting his hand on Adam's shoulder as he sauntered past him to open the front door to get their takeaway.

They hadn't rushed towards the conversation at all, though. They'd eaten, they'd had more wine. Adam had refused more weed; he didn't like the way it made him feel, slightly nervous, anxious, paranoid like something bad was about to happen. They'd sat quietly, listening to music, chatting intermittently. People's actions say so much more than words, Adam had thought. And he didn't just mean big things, he meant the little things: a nervous scratch or a nibbled nail, a ring flipped around and around and around between his thumb and forefinger, a low chuckle that made Jarvis's shoulders shake, a smile, a half-smile, a blink, a flick of the wrist, a hand covering a unwanted smirk, a soulful glance and an empathetic stroke of the hand.

In the end, they didn't have 'the conversation' at all – like all things in their relationship, words had never been the most important thing, doing something, anything, had.

"So," Jarvis said, leaning over Adam and, when he realised Adam wasn't pushing him away, kissing him on the lips. He had soft lips, softer than Adam had imagined for a guy, he'd kind of thought a man would have rougher lips but…

"I can't, Jarvis," Adam had said weakly, still not pushing Jarvis away. Without speaking, Jarvis had simply carried on where he'd left off, except this time his tongue had penetrated Adam's mouth. And Adam had given in to it, stopped fighting, stopped pretending to fight – he'd decided to go with it and experience it and see where it took him. Of course, if he'd known where it would take him, he'd have shoved Jarvis off, put a stop to it all. But hindsight is a useless bastard – he doesn't exist in the present where you need him the most.

Afterwards, as Adam did his jeans up and knocked back some more wine to remove the taste of guilt from his mouth, Jarvis said the unthinkable.

"Leave," he'd said, and Adam knew it wasn't something he was saying lightly. "Just leave," he'd said again, almost desperate.

"I can't," Adam had replied, "you know I can't."

"But why not? Seriously, you've got choices, we can make it

work."

And then the door buzzer had rung and all hell had broken loose.

"Fuck," Jarvis had mouthed as Louise's voice came through the intercom. He'd waved Adam back towards the bedroom and Adam had taken a moment to make sure he hadn't left anything behind and he'd gone into the bedroom, crouching by the wardrobe at the back, in case Louise for some reason came into the bedroom. His heart was pounding faster than he'd ever known as he squatted in the darkness, listening to Jarvis trying to put Louise off coming up and failing miserably, finally buzzing her in. Destiny calling, in a fuck-me dress and high heels.

Chapter Twenty-Two

His flat was different in real life. She'd seen it from afar, of course, but as she walked in, she realised she'd never actually been in there in person. Jarvis always came to them – he'd come for dinner, or to pick Adam up for a run, or they'd met in the pub, but they'd never actually been to his flat. Or at least Louise hadn't – Adam probably had. It was smaller than she'd expected, with a narrow corridor leading to the back rooms and the front door opening directly into the living room. The carpet was cream and burgundy and slightly worn, clearly the same carpet the previous owners had laid as Jarvis hadn't been there long enough to wear it so thin. The sofas were leather – they looked nice, but in practice Louise always thought leather sofas were quite uncomfortable – they got sticky if it was too hot and in her opinion, nothing beat a cosy, cushioned sofa. She could see why people with young children had leather sofas – they were a godsend as you could clean the marker pens, food, wee and poo stains off them easily and without fuss. But Jarvis didn't have kids, so he must have bought them because he thought they looked trendy.

Jarvis had stood staring at her, not speaking as she'd stepped into the room. He'd seemed nervous, more nervous than she'd ever seen him. *He's feeling the same things I am*, she'd told herself. Pushing thoughts of Adam to the back of her mind, she'd decided to go for it, to tell him how she felt and see how the cards fell.

"I love you," she'd said, lunging straight for him and kissing him on the lips. He'd jolted back so violently, she'd lost her balance and narrowly avoided landing face down on the carpet with a thud.

"Oh shit, shit," Jarvis had said, grabbing her arm to prop her up. "I'm sorry, I didn't mean... I'm sorry." He'd helped her upright and she'd stood awkwardly for a moment, embarrassed and not sure what to do or say. Looking across the room, she'd seen a bottle of wine on the side, two glasses, both filled. He'd prepared for her, that's why he'd taken so long to answer the door. She'd walked over and picked a glass up, taking a large gulp.

"Look," she'd said. "I know this is hard for you. I know you're gay, so falling in love with a woman…it's not easy. I know that, I don't want to rush you, take all the time you need. But we've got to start talking about it, we've got to be open about it." She'd looked away from him then, making a deliberate attempt not to see the expression of horror on his face, not wanting to accept what was becoming so clear to her, so obvious. She'd been wrong. He didn't feel the same way, he didn't love her, not at all, not one little bit.

"Louise," he'd said gently. She'd stared away from him at the painting on his back wall, a woman with a long cigarette in a long black holder, like Bette Lynch used to have in *Coronation Street*. A weird picture for a guy to have on his wall, she'd thought. She didn't like it at all. It didn't seem to fit Jarvis's character at all.

"I *do* love you," he'd said, and her head had snapped away from the picture on the wall to drink in his face, his beautiful green eyes, so like hers, so unusual.

"I knew…" she'd started.

"No, no listen," he'd said, cutting her off and walking towards her, arms outstretched. "Not like that, it can never be like that."

"I don't understand," she'd said, a coldness running through her body, not shivers, a rigid, cement-like cold, solidifying her to the spot.

"I'm so sorry, I should have told you right from the beginning, I should have told you sooner."

"Told me what," she'd asked, white lips whitening, taut skin tautening.

"I meant to, I mean, when I first came here, I'd planned to tell you straight away. But then it got...I don't know, complicated. You opened up to me, started telling me about your life, your childhood."

"What are you talking about?" Louise had to grab the arm of the sofa to steady herself.

"And then there was Adam, I hadn't expected Adam and..."

"What are you talking about, Jarvis?" Louise had asked, a horrible thought entering her mind. Did he fancy Adam? Was that what he was going to tell her?

"I'm your brother," he'd replied, dropping his arms to his sides and holding her gaze. Nothing in the world could have prepared Louise for that, it was almost literally the last thing in the world she could have expected.

The silence that attacked the room was violent and aggressive, choking the air from Louise's lungs and clouding her vision.

"Your mum..." Jarvis continued. "My mum. But I never knew, Louise, I didn't even know Mum had been married before, it was a complete shock when I found out."

Silence.

"Louise, say something." Jarvis leant over to grasp her arm and she flinched away.

"You can't be," Louise had responded instantly, desperately, making eye contact, hoping it was some sick and twisted joke, some horrific...

It wasn't a joke, she could see it, looking at him. She could see herself there, see her mother there. How had she not seen that before, the similarities. The nose, the teeth even.

"Are there any more of you?" Louise had asked quietly. He'd shaken his head.

"Just me, Louise," Jarvis had answered. "Is that okay?"

Okay? Is that okay? What fucking planet is he on?

"Does she want to see me?" Louise said, surprising herself. Of all the retorts, or all the responses, she hadn't expected that. But her mum had run out and left her, cold and alone, shivering in the street with small stones embedded in the soles of her feet. And she'd never come back, not once. Louise remembered the time when she and her dad had visited her mum; she remembered her mum shouting that she could have more children, that she didn't need Louise. And all of a sudden, she needed to know, had she even cared? Had she regretted it? Had she ever thought about her?

"Oh God, I'm sorry," Jarvis had replied slowly. "She's dead, Louise, last year. I didn't know about you until then and I…"

Louise didn't hear anything Jarvis said after that, her head had been filled with a piercing white noise, so loud that it felt like blood would start dripping from her ears. She'd been looking at him, but all of his features had been blurred apart from his eyes. Those eyes, so like hers.

He'd been talking and talking and talking but she can't remember a single word that came out of his mouth from that point on. That had been enough. That had been too much. How could he be her brother, how could he have done this to her, come into her life and make her feel the things she'd felt? He'd made her…a pervert. A monster. Disgusting.

"Louise, please," Jarvis had screamed. Why had he been screaming, what did he have to scream about? She was the one whose life had been ruined and turned upside down, she was the one…

"Tell me you're lying," Louise had said, glancing down to see a broken wine bottle clutched in her hand, waving it at him. Behind Jarvis, she could see a mirror on the wall. Her reflection was large and smudged and puffy. Disgusting, depraved, irredeemable.

"I'm sorry," Jarvis had muttered, his head leaning back, making his neck more, not less, exposed to the bottle in her hand. "I meant to tell you, but then… I don't know…we got on so well. And then Adam and I became friends and it got complicated. But

I swear," he took a step away from her, "I swear I had no idea you had feelings for me."

"What?" Louise had said. "Of course you did, how could you not?" Louise took a step towards him, thrusting the bottle a little closer to his neck.

"Louise, please, I didn't, I swear. Don't you think I'd have said something if I had?"

"Shut up," she'd snapped, not even able to look at him. "What about all those times in your flat, when you were...when I was...you knew. I know you knew I was watching."

"Watching? What are you talking about? Look, Louise, I'm sorry, I really...I wanted to get to know my sister, I didn't plan any of this..."

Louise stared down at her hand, shocked again to see that she was holding a broken bottle. Her fingers had opened, dropping it to the floor.

"Why didn't you tell me straight away?" Louise had said, almost to herself. *I've masturbated over you*, she thought but didn't say. She'd clutched her stomach for a moment, sure she was going to be sick. She was thinking of every romantic fantasy, every finger-flicking filthy thought she'd had over the past months about him – her brother.

"I'm disgusting," she'd said.

"No, you're not. It's my fault, it's completely, utterly, my fault. I should have told you, I didn't know, I swear, I was so happy we were getting on so well and then Adam and I..."

Silence. No movement. Nothing but a broken woman, seemingly outside of her own body, a quivering husk, shoulders sinking forward, breathing laboured, eye makeup smudging. Nothing but a man opposite her, the object of putrid affection, fetid, stinking affection.

"Did she ever ask about me?" she heard as if someone else had said the words – but they hadn't, she had. Then she felt her own limbs around her again, felt her racing heart, her puffed, painful eyes and the agonising pounding in her chest as the horror of who she was – who he was, sank in.

"Mum?" Jarvis said obtusely.

"Yes," Louise said quietly. "Did she ever ask about me?"

More silence.

"She abandoned me, Jarvis. Didn't even look back, even after my dad died she never contacted me. I want to know…did she ever think about me? Talk about me. Did she regret leaving me like she did?"

His silence answered for him. Finally, he shook his head.

"I didn't know about you until after she died. When I was sorting through her stuff I found some photos, some old letters from your dad. That's how I traced you. He'd wanted her to come and see you, said you needed your mother…but I don't think she…I mean, I don't know if she… I'm sorry. I'm so sorry." He'd paused, his skin pasty, making him seem more ugly than she could ever have imagined. "But she'd kept the photos. She must have thought about you, wondered…"

"Fuck her," Louise had said in a whisper, dropping her head and walking past him to his front door. "And fuck you, Jarvis."

* * *

To this day, the feelings that were coursing through her defy description, at once intense and overpowering yet at the same time almost background, like she wasn't feeling anything at all, like she didn't even exist anymore. Before that moment, she'd always felt strong. She'd dealt with so much in her life and she'd always been in control, always dealt with it head on, in her way, on her terms. She'd read about depression, she'd read about people who said if they had a button to press that would wipe out their existence, they'd press it. These people felt that everyone would be better off without them around, felt like a burden because of the way they felt all the time. She'd never understood that, she'd always thought the world was a better place with her in it. She was a wife and mother, after all. But leaving Jarvis's apartment that night, she'd felt empty, like a vacant nothing. If she'd had a button to press right then, she'd have pressed it without a thought. Ceased to exist.

She was damned, she'd realised, like her mother had said she was after Lucy the suicide babysitter. She could never bring anyone happiness, least of all herself. Everyone – her children, her husband, her friends – would be better off without her.

* * *

After leaving Jarvis's she'd walked the streets for a while, not knowing what she was planning or where she was going. The idea of seeing Adam was unconscionable and she didn't want to go to any of her friends, it's not like she could have told any of them what was wrong. Ha, friends, like she had any, like anyone gave a shit. She couldn't burden her friends with this, it was too horrific, too messy. She had nobody to talk to. She was completely alone. Alone and an orphan. Her mother – *his mother*. Dead. Without a second thought about her, without a mention. Had she hated her daughter that much? What had Louise ever done? She'd never know, now.

And Jarvis. She felt disgusting, used, dirty. Like he'd sullied her and she could never get clean again. The worst part is that somewhere deep inside, locked away in place she couldn't acknowledge, wouldn't acknowledge, she still fancied him. You don't switch that off, no matter how repulsive it is. She'd spied on him. Oh God, that's what it was, spying! Leering at him through the cracks in his curtains like some sort of deviant or weirdo. How could she not have seen that, how could she have thought he'd been complicit in it, that he'd wanted it? She was a peeping Tom. Worse than that, an incestuous peeping Tom.

Repeated action, foot after foot after foot, high heels meeting grey paving slabs. High heels. Heels designed to entice and seduce. She hated them, hated their sleek, feminine design, hated everything they stood for. Angrily she grabbed them and pulled them off her feet, flinging them into the street to beeping and moaning from the passing traffic as they drove over them, crushing and destroying them.

Good. They deserved to be destroyed. She turned the corner into her street, passing a woman silently humming to herself, leaning on the street sign, wearing a pair of enormous black sunglasses despite the fact it was night-time. As she arrived back at her house – her family home – she glanced across the road at the fake owl nestling on the roof opposite. It always seems so real from a distance. When the kids were tiny they used to stare from the window, waiting for it to move and fly away, sure that it was alive and breathing. But it wasn't. It was a silent sentinel. Non-intrusive, comforting somehow, like nature watching over the street, keeping everyone safe from harm. Nothing like her own vigils, she can now see. Louise was never Jarvis's sentinel, she was an intruder, a thief, devouring his privacy like a narcotic, taking more and more until she couldn't think of anything else. How could she not have seen what she was doing? What kind of madness could have gripped her to make her so far removed from the reality she now sees so clearly? She bristled in the winter chill that only hours ago she'd enjoyed. On her way to Jarvis's house, she'd savoured the breeze as it had tickled her skin, creating light goose pimples that somehow made every nerve in her body tingle.

Opening her front door, she braced herself against Adam's presence, planning her route upstairs and away from him as soon as possible, she couldn't cope, couldn't manage to have a conversation with him. But the house was silent, he was out. *Thank God.* Without even thinking about where she was going, she found herself in the bathroom, catching a whiff of her *Oil of Olay*, reminding her of her mother. How funny, that smell had never been a trigger but her mother was dead and all of a sudden it had reminded her instantly. Her mum had always used *Oil of Ulay*, as it was called back then. It had been her go-to gift. She would ask Louise's dad to buy it for her on birthdays and Christmas. It was always the same, every year.

"Oh, don't get me anything much, love. Just some *Oil of Ulay*. I like that."

What had she come into the bathroom for? Oh, that was it, the medicine cabinet. She knew better than to wash them down with wine or spirits, that would make her sick and she didn't want to be sick, she didn't want them coming back up again, she wanted them to stay inside her, to do their job properly. She wanted to sleep forever, unaware and unthinking. At peace. She'd never understood that phrase before but now, staring at her blotchy, puffy disgusting brother-fucking face in the mirror, she under- stood. She wanted to be at peace. She wanted everything to stop. This wasn't a cry for help. She was beyond help, beyond redemption. She wanted it all to stop, she wanted peace from the endless struggle of her life.

Louise had never felt like this before, she'd never hit this low. She'd felt depressed and angry but never hopeless, never... disgusting. That was the thing that was killing the last emotion that could have kept her going, she knew. The self-loathing that was filling her stopped her seeing anything else at all and she couldn't imagine any emotion ever overpowering it and making her feel *normal* again. Because she didn't feel normal anymore, not one little bit.

She couldn't muster the will to keep fighting. Because what was the point in fighting when the battle was already lost? It had been lost before she'd started. Maybe if she'd recognised it sooner, understood what was happening before it reached the untouchable land of 'no return', things would have been different. But she'd been blind and ridiculous and...criminal, actually. Some might even have classed her as some kind of sex offender, someone who should be on the register, all that watching…

She'd never believed people reaped what they sowed, she never believed there was a universal moral compass but she knew right from wrong, at least she used to know right from wrong. What had happened to her? How could she have spent all the time *watching* him? Stalking him, because she had to be honest with herself that's exactly what she'd been doing. Stalking, watching and touching herself over her own brother.

She'd known then that it would never leave her, the guilt, the hurt, the pain. The lust, the sexual excitement she had felt when she thought about *her brother*. How could she purge that from her mind? It was now woven into the fabric of her being, an inevitable consequence of the fact she was still breathing. The more she tried to mute the feelings, the more it was like her body was an amplifier for them, vibrating with the strain of her thoughts and feelings. It was part of her. She was disgusting, pure and simple.

She found herself back in her living room, bland and stark like the property programmes on Channel 4 always told her it should be. She was undressed now, out of the tight dress, too young for her anyway. She found her frumpy dressing gown, the type of thing a woman of her age should be in. She should at least be found in something appropriate, not some wannabe younger dress donned for brother-fucking.

She crunched and chewed, making sure the pills entered her system as quickly as possible. She didn't want her stomach acid to have to do all the work, didn't want there to be a window of opportunity for vomiting or rescue. She stared at her mobile on the side across the room as it started to ring. She exhaled. As she fell back into the armchair, her dressing gown dropped open to uncover sagging breasts. As the darkness descended, she licked chalky residue from her lips and closed her eyes. *All better now.*

Chapter Twenty-Three

Adam hadn't moved after he'd heard Louise leave that night. He'd sat on the floor beside the wardrobe in Jarvis's bedroom, reeling. He'd never known people could actually reel before that moment, never known the lightheaded confusion and horror the term 'reeling' truly implied. It was almost like his world was vibrating, so nothing was still, nothing remained in focus.

He'd felt Jarvis's presence in the bedroom doorway before he looked up and saw him there, silhouetted and somehow *other*, no longer connected to Adam, an outsider, a stranger. A liar.

"Adam, I'm so sorry. I wanted to tell you, I..." Jarvis stuttered into silence. What words could he have said? How could he have made things better? Adam continued to sit staring at the carpet, leaning against the dark wooden wardrobe, heart punching, again, again, again.

"I never meant to fall for you," Jarvis continued desperately, a disembodied voice in Adam's ears, merging with the drumming, the incessant beating, beating, beating of his heart, the rush of blood in his head, hissing, bursting its banks; every sense alive in a way he'd never known before, more heightened, more powerful. More painful.

"I should have told Louise right away," Jarvis had carried on, almost whining, "but the longer things went on, the harder it got and..."

"And what?" Adam's voice had been calm as he looked up, calmer than the churning waves buffeting the rocks inside him should have allowed it to be.

"I hadn't expected to meet you, to fall for you," Jarvis said, sounding close to tears, as if somehow he was the one who was aggrieved, as if he was the victim in need of support. *Fuck him.*

Adam pulled himself to his feet, swallowing down every feeling that swirled inside, crushing each one, burying them, hammering them down, down, down.

"I've got to go after Louise," he said simply, pushing past Jarvis and starting to walk down the corridor back to the living room. Jarvis grabbed his arm to stop him walking away, pulled him around and forced Adam to face him.

"Adam, don't," he started, "please don't leave like this."

"Like what?" Adam's voice was angrier now, the rage bubbling out a little.

"Angry. Upset. Talk to me," Jarvis pleaded.

"What's the point, Jarvis? Everything you say is a lie." Adam erupted, yanking his arm away, no longer happy with the physical contact.

"No, not everything. Not how I feel about you," Jarvis whimpered. "I fucked up, I know I fucked up, but please, give me a chance to explain things, you owe me that much."

Adam doesn't know why he didn't go straight after Louise, he's not sure how he let Jarvis talk him into staying but somehow he'd ended up sitting back on the sofa listening to Jarvis talk. It wasn't even a conversation, it was more of a monologue, a man trying to justify the unjustifiable.

"Thing is, my mum was a bitch. I know I shouldn't speak like that about her, especially now she's gone, but it's true. There was something cold about her, something missing, you know." He was nodding, leaning forward in his seat and pouring himself another glass of wine, offering Adam one. Adam had simply shook his head silently, watching the man he had thought he knew explain things he didn't want to know.

"I didn't even know about Louise until I was going through Mum's things after she died." Jarvis leans back, holding his wine glass below his stained red lips. The lips Adam had been kissing less than an hour ago. "How can someone be that good at lying, that duplicitous?"

"You inherited something from her," Adam found himself saying. Not angry, not anything. Monotone.

"Okay, I deserved that," Jarvis continued. "But please, let me explain. She wasn't warm, you see, our mum. She wasn't loving. Louise was better off without her, I swear. When I told her I was gay, do you know what she said to me? She said 'If only I'd known when I was pregnant…'"

Adam was watching Jarvis's face. An hour ago, this story would have elicited an entirely different emotion from him, he'd have wanted to hold Jarvis, to tell him it was okay, that his mother had been wrong, deeply wrong. But Adam remained unmoved, waiting unsuccessfully for an emotion that wasn't anger to surface.

"She didn't finish the sentence," Jarvis continued, "she didn't actually say she'd have aborted me…but we both knew what she meant. It hung in the air between us, an invisible wall we could never break down again. I mean, what kind of mother could say something like that to her child?"

He paused and Adam felt uncomfortable with his gaze, like something was expected of him he couldn't give. Did Jarvis think he was going to crack, to rush over and comfort *him*?

"Seriously, Louise was better off without her, she was like a poison. I knew if I told Louise who I was she'd want to know more about our mother but how could I tell her that? How could I tell her Mum was a bitch? And the more Louise talked about her past, about losing her dad, about losing Tom, I realised I could never tell her. How would she cope knowing her mum hadn't ever looked back, that she hadn't even wanted her – or that she was dead?" Jarvis had sounded more and more desperate as he explained, his words falling from his mouth faster and faster, as if they were on a treadmill, the speed increasing with every word that escaped.

"Am I supposed to feel sorry for you, Jarvis?" Finally Adam found his voice again, but it didn't feel like him speaking, he didn't even feel like any of this was real, it was like a nightmare from someone else's life. "You came into our lives and now it's like a fucking train wreck. You wrapped us both around your little finger and now look at us. It could have been different, we could have been a family, Jarvis. You could have had everything you wanted. But how the fuck am I supposed to feel now? In fact, sod me." Adam stands up, his anger resurfacing, spitting its way out of him. "How is Louise supposed to feel now? She fell for you and you're her brother. How could you not know how she felt?'

"Well, did you know?" Jarvis says, raising his voice in return. "I knew what was happening between us, I could see you were interested too, but Louise? I thought we were friends. I'm gay for God's sake."

"You're gay, you're not blind!" Adam shouts. "Lie to yourself, but don't lie to me – of course you could see. Anyone could."

"Well, why didn't you say something, she's your wife."

"Because I knew it didn't matter!" Adam shouted. "I knew I'd won. You wanted me, not her..." With that realisation, Adam deflated slightly, punctured by his own selfishness.

"We can still make a go of this, it doesn't change anything," Jarvis said, grabbing Adam's arm again. "Leave, just leave."

"Fuck off, Jarvis," Adam said, shaking Jarvis off and bolting out of the flat into the night without looking back. Jarvis wasn't in the least bit important, Adam realised. He needed to find Louise and make sure she was okay. All of a sudden, life was back in perspective and all he wanted to do was look after his wife. Louise had fallen for Jarvis and she'd fallen hard – but so had he, so he couldn't blame her for it or feel angry with her. He couldn't imagine how it felt for her to learn Jarvis had been lying all this time, when she'd been fantasising about him, her brother. It was making Adam feel sick, God knows how it was making her feel.

He'd called her, leaving a voicemail asking how Alice was. Asking her to call him back as he needed to talk. No answer. He'd known she wasn't with Alice of course, but he had to keep up the pretence – they'd both been manufacturing so many lies, it was important to keep hold of them. He needed to find a way of helping her, of making her open up to him without exposing his own lies. But he had to find her first. He didn't have Alice's number, but he figured if he at least called her to 'learn' Louise wasn't there, he'd have a reason for being worried about her, for forcing her to reply to a text message or phone call or voicemail. So he headed home to get her number, burying any guilt or personal betrayals deep down inside his gut. Louise needed him now, perhaps more than ever before. He didn't want to fail her any more than he already had.

As he'd walked back through their front door, he'd known she was there. He could see her dress strewn on the stairs.

"Louise?" he'd called, trying to sound nonchalant, like he didn't know anything was wrong. "What happened with Alice?"

Down the hall he could see the living-room light was on, the door half-closed and foreboding, not in retrospect but in the moment, like he knew what he was going to find before he walked down the corridor. As he'd pushed the door open and looked into the room he hadn't taken it in at first. He hadn't seen his wife's body inside the crumpled dressing gown slumped in the chair, hadn't seen the empty pill packets. Hadn't seen or hadn't wanted to see.

And then everything had sped up, he'd run over to her and grabbed her, tried to pull her to her feet. He thinks he was speaking, shouting, crying, checking she was breathing, saying her name over and over as he held her under the arms, lifting her from the soft chair, her head flopping listlessly around, almost like it wasn't attached. She'd felt heavy, much heavier than she should have, she'd always been so slight, but she'd felt like a bag of cement. He'd wrestled his phone from his jeans pocket while still trying to hold her, not willing to let her go, wanting to squeeze her and kiss her and hug her and tell her it was all going to be all right, that he was there for her and he was so, so sorry.

The ambulance and hospital had all been a blur, the stomach pumping, the questions, the endless questions he couldn't answer, the endless night dragging on alone, not knowing how much had gone into her system, when she'd taken the pills. It was vital to know when she'd taken them, to know what might have been absorbed but he hadn't known, he hadn't been there, he hadn't been there.

"I wasn't there," he'd told the doctors over and over, omitting to tell them where he had been instead, that he'd been with someone else.

Guilt is a terrible thing. Maybe that's what the end of their marriage came down to in the end. Adam has spent all these months blaming Louise for what she did and for the fact she's never told him why, never opened up to him about Jarvis or told him that she'd found out he was her brother. But that was only part of the story, he now realises. His guilt for being with Jarvis, for staying to hear him out while Louise was downing bottles of pills at home – that's what's been eating him from the inside out. It was luck that had led Adam home in time to save Louise with no lasting damage. Just luck, not judgement, not divine inter-vention, chance. How could he ever have lived with himself if he'd been half an hour later? What would he have told the kids?

* * *

Since that night, Adam's life has unravelled completely anyway. He thinks things would have been different if he'd given it a go with Jarvis but it wasn't a choice, was it? Now he's sitting alone in his kitchen, slightly drunk, nursing a head injury and wondering what on earth to do next. He doesn't know where Louise has gone, but with the kids at school the house feels eerily quiet as he sits finishing the bottle of red they both started. Her glass, nearly full, sits opposite him, a physical reminder of her disdain for him. Could he have done things differently? Was there ever any chance of a different outcome for their marriage? What if he'd actually listened to Jarvis that night, what if he'd said yes? What if he'd made more of an effort to understand that everyone has their reasons, even for lies as big as Jarvis's. He wasn't a bad guy, he'd made bad decisions. But aren't they all guilty of that? Wasn't attempting suicide a bad decision on Louise's part? Wasn't falling in love with Jarvis a bad decision for both of them? None of them came out of this cleanly, nobody was blameless. Maybe that's the thing nobody wants to recognise: there's rarely a single person to blame for most things, life doesn't happen in a vacuum, everyone partakes in it, playing their parts. So people find someone, anyone, to blame when things go wrong. Well, Adam's done with the blame game, it's pointless, it never has a winner.

Too late now anyway, things have gone too far. Looking around at the kitchen, their family home, the scene of mundane domestic life for so many years, Adam feels claustrophobic, like he has to escape, to get out in the fresh air. Not after Louise, he doesn't want to see her, doesn't want to continue pulling things apart when she won't open up to him. *What time is it? Are the pubs open yet?* Maybe a pint, a little time out to think, to cool down. Maybe they'll both see things differently with a little space from one another. He stands up, steadying himself against the table as another wave of giddiness overtakes him. Once he feels stable again he heads out, forgetting to grab his coat from the banister at the bottom of the stairs as he slams the front door behind him.

Chapter Twenty-Four

After her suicide attempt – she can call it that now, somehow giving it a label helps her, makes her *own* it more keenly – things were never the same with Adam, Louise now realises. When they got home from the hospital, they'd both been silent. Not quiet, not subdued but absolutely silent. Adam had simply looked after her, not asking anything of her, not asking her reasons, not pushing her for explanations, not pushing her for anything. And she'd loved him for it. All of a sudden, she'd felt an enormous need for him again, like she had when they'd first got together after Tom. He brought her duvet down and she lay on the sofa watching films. He'd bundled the kids off to his parents and he'd brought her water and soup. He'd sat with her head on his lap, stroking her hair. And he hadn't asked, he hadn't pressurised her.

After a few days, watching a black-and-white daytime film and listening to his heartbeat as she lay on his chest, he'd simply said, "You won't try again, will you?" His voice had sounded strange, vibrating slightly, quivering.

"No," she'd replied, snuggling into him more deeply, desperately, pushing any thoughts of Jarvis from her mind. For two weeks after that night, she hadn't left the house. Adam had simply dropped everything to look after her and she'd held him close, day after day, wondering how she could have forgotten the man he was so fundamentally. When she'd felt strong and in control, she'd started seeing his kindness as a weakness. When he'd taken over when the children were born, when she couldn't cope, she'd seen that as weakness, too, she now realises. But kindness and selflessness aren't weaknesses, they're nothing of the sort. They're the strongest things anyone has to offer another person.

"I've told Jarvis I can't go running anymore," Adam said to her after few days. "Thought you'd prefer not to have any visitors for a while." And she'd nodded, gulping back the acid as it crept up her throat at the mention of his name, but glad she wouldn't be required to make up a lie as to why she didn't want to see Jarvis – not yet anyway.

When she was finally ready to venture back into the outside world, she was terrified. As she'd stepped outside, Adam holding her hand, she'd been in a state of panic: would she bump into him? Would he come into the café? Would he try to see her again? Would he call the police, even? She'd held a broken bottle to his neck, for God's sake.

But then, as they walked down the hill, she'd seen the for-sale sign on the garage and his flat. She'd seen the removal vans. As they walked past, Louise had started crying, sobbing and clutching her husband's arm. Adam had asked her what was wrong then, of course. But she couldn't tell him. She couldn't.

And so months passed and Adam never mentioned Jarvis moving away, but she supposes he had other things on his mind, what with his wife attempting suicide. But he'd never pressed her for an explanation and she'd never felt able to offer one. So they carried on as if nothing had happened and while she felt differently about Adam, while she valued him more than she had since the children were born, she noticed a change in him. An emptiness appeared that she hadn't seen before, not even after Tom. Some days she could see it overwhelming him so much that he could barely speak. And she wanted to help him, she did. She wanted to be able to take the pain away for him, to explain what had gone wrong and where their problems stemmed from. But she couldn't. How could she ever tell him that she was planning to leave him, that she'd wanted to run away with his best friend? That she'd felt their lives were so grey and lifeless that when a man – any man – arrived and offered a spark of life, she took it. How could she explain to her husband that when they'd met Jarvis she'd felt more alive than she had in years and he'd offered her a new direction, a new purpose and she hadn't cared about

Adam in the slightest. All Adam had ever done was look after her and take care of her when she needed it, even if she hadn't realised that at the time. And how had she repaid him? By wanting to screw her own brother.

She would never tell Adam, even if she knew that decision was hurting him and destroying their marriage. Some secrets couldn't bear the light of day because they'd burst into flames and engulf everything in their path. They had to remain in the darkness, even if it was suffocating there.

After a while, she noticed Adam had begun drinking a little too much, a little too often – and she did nothing. She watched from the sidelines, going to work, throwing herself in to the café, ignoring Adam's slow descent. *It's his way of coping*, she told herself. And for a while, that was okay. His drinking was moderate to begin with, but time passed and it progressed. They stopped speaking about anything of real value, they were two people sharing the same space, awkward in each other's company at best, tense around each other at worst.

For months, they went through the motions. Then she'd had the phone call from the hospital, when she'd had to go to the police station with him to report a mugging he'd received at 10am, drunk on gin and she'd known their marriage was over. Everything had gone too far and he needed to fix himself. She couldn't do it for him. Wouldn't do it for him. She couldn't give him what he needed, not now, not ever.

* * *

So here she is, walking the streets of Brighton, not sure where she's going or why, wanting to be away from him, to be outside in the fresh air and free. She rounds the corner past Browns bar, heading towards Ship Street, wandering aimlessly, perhaps weaving her way down to the seafront when she hears singing; a woman singing at the top of her lungs.

Louise looks around, expecting to see a busker with a hat and a guitar, common on Brighton's streets. Instead she sees a beautiful woman wearing a long blue mac, like an old 1950s detective might, coupled with massive Jackie Onassis sunglasses. The woman isn't busking, she's standing on the corner, smiling at Louise as if they know each other.

Louise scuttles past, head down, heading towards a café down the street. It is trendier than Louise's, more 'Brighton'. The two guys behind the counter are clearly stoned off their heads and one of them has the patchy red flaked skin on his cheeks of someone who partakes way too much. Nonetheless, it's got a friendly vibe to it, warm, wooden interiors, dim lighting and loads of speciality teas and coffees on the menu, despite the fact most people are genuinely boring and monotone in their tea- and coffee-drinking tastes. She wonders if they sell much of the speciality stuff, or if it's part of their brand, of their 'We're so cool and stoned and relaxed' façade. Louise orders a coffee and takes a seat.

"You okay, love?" a voice asks pleasantly. Louise glances at the empty seat next to her as a woman sits down, a wobbling Earl Grey tea slopping onto the table as she does so. It's the singing lady from the street with the enormous sunglasses.

"I'm fine thanks," Louise replies quietly, angling her away so as not to make eye contact.

"Oh, my mistake, love. You don't look all right, that's all."

"Excuse me?" Louise replies, looking at the woman indignantly, ready for an argument, ready to tell her what's what. But the woman is smiling at her and she looks kind, not mad. She looks like someone who cares and for some reason, Louise doesn't snap at her, she doesn't tell her to mind her own business. Instead, she bursts into tears, something she rarely does, especially not in front of strangers.

"It's okay, love," Jackie O says, reaching out to her and touching her lightly on her shoulder; comforting but not intrusive, the perfect balance. "It's probably not too late to fix things, you know. Not yet."

* * *

"I've made such a mess of things," Louise finishes, sipping her Americano. "When I think about it, I've never given him a chance. First he couldn't live up to Tom, then he couldn't live up to Jarvis and then, when I finally saw what I had in him, I couldn't open up to him the way he needed me to."

"Things are rarely one-sided, Louise." Jackie O smiles, nodding at Louise to continue.

"Well that's it, that's the whole sordid mess. You know, I've never said it out loud to anyone before. Not once. I filed it away like it never happened."

"You could tell Adam," she says. "He might surprise you. What have you got to lose?"

"I don't know if I want anything from Adam anymore, even if I did tell him. Things have gone too far."

"Have they? If that's true, why are we having this conversation?"

"I've no idea, I don't even know you."

"Shall I tell you something? Maybe the most important thing you'll ever hear? It's about time you gave Adam the benefit of the doubt before it's too late. Tom is only interesting because he's dead. Jarvis is only interesting because he's a fantasy, an illusion of a life more exciting. But it sounds like Adam has always been there, he's always been real – and that's why you don't value him."

"I don't think that's fair…"

"What's fair got to do with anything?" Jackie O asks, almost like she's cross. Louise feels like she's completely misjudged the situation. Of course this woman isn't the full ticket, of course she's not. She was standing on a street corner singing at the top of her lungs but not busking. What on earth is Louise doing sitting unloading all of her problems on her for?

"Look, I'm sorry, I'd better go," Louise says, standing up.

"It's not too late," the woman says again, earnestly. "You've got time to change things, Louise."

"You've been kind," Louise says, feeling panicked to be in this woman's presence, wishing she hadn't let her into her life, even for a few fleeting moments. Now, the woman feels dangerous, like she could unbalance things even more than they already are.

"I'd better go," Louise says again, looking at the darkening clouds outside and grabbing her bag and putting it on her shoulder. "Try and beat the rain."

"Don't try to beat the rain." Jackie O stands up, walks past Louise, towards the door of the café, opening it up as the rain starts to pour down outside. "Just accept that sometimes you're going to get wet."

With that, Jackie O strides out into the downpour with her arms outstretched, leaving Louise standing alone by her table and half-filled coffee cup. She sits down again, looking at her mobile phone on the table in front of her. She wants to call him, she realises. She owes him that. All the times he's looked after her when she needed it and he needs her now. If the only way to fix him is to open up then she'll do it. She'll tell him everything. But not yet, she needs more time. She finishes her coffee and orders another. Then she leaves the coffee shop and walks down to the seafront, standing staring for a long time at the burnt-out remains of West Pier, derelict, rusting, but somehow still beautiful, somehow looking like there may be life left in its broken remains yet, that it could magically be reborn from its own devastation, bigger and better than ever. She walks up the hill, weaving her way through different streets and parts of town, reminding herself there's still novelty in everything, there are still surprises. When she finally arrives home it's afternoon, nearly time to pick the kids up. She lets herself in the front door and shouts for Adam.

"Adam, you there?"

No answer.

"I'm sorry about this morning, I am. Let's talk. Let's talk."

No answer. She walks into the living room and stares at the enormous canvas print hanging on their living-room wall. Louise hones in on her own smiling, windswept face. Beside her, Adam isn't looking at the camera, but instead at her, eyes filled with…what? Hope? Sadness? She doesn't even know. How long since he's looked at her like that? Matthew is on Adam's right, his arm around his sister's shoulder, grinning cheesily at Jarvis holding the camera. The green white hills and the sea in the background are shimmering in the sunlight, a twinkling reflection of the mood of the afternoon. This moment, captured, perfect, pointing to a glorious future for the family. A future that no longer exists. Filled with a sickening clarity for the first time in years, she grabs her mobile phone and dials Adam's number. As his voicemail picks up, she can hear her own desperation and hope.

"Adam, I'm sorry," she says, turning back to the print of their day out at Beachy Head and staring at her husband's sunlit face. "I…look, please call me back. Please *come* back. I love you. I want to tell you everything, I want us to open up again, like we used to." She lets the phone drop into her lap as she sits down in her cracked leather armchair, the same one she slumped into that night all those months ago when she tried to take her own life.

"We can get through this together," she says quietly to herself. "I do love you."

Chapter Twenty-Five

Adam's standing at the bar he and Louise first took Jarvis to, the first time they got pissed together. He remembers it like it was yesterday. At first he'd been so annoyed with Louise for inviting Jarvis out with them when they were supposed to be spending time together and fixing their marriage. He's so lost in his memories of that night, the moment their lives changed course, that when he first hears the voice he thinks he's imagining it.

"Hello, Adam," it says. He's missed that voice, despite the heartache it caused them both, despite everything, Adam would do anything for it to be real, for Jarvis to be standing there next to him.

"You're drinking early."

Adam nurses his near empty pint glass, not daring to turn around, not daring to believe it's true. Then an arm touches his shoulder lightly and the voice continues.

"Adam?"

Finally, Adam turns around. Jarvis has the same smile, the exact same smile he's always had. It's all Adam can do not to grab him and kiss him and hold him tight. It's like someone has opened the door and the stuffy pub is full of fresh, spring air and not the stale, overheated winter air it had moments ago. He doesn't care if it's been a year, he doesn't care about anything that happened, the lies, he wants Jarvis to hold him tight and tell him everything will be okay.

"Jarvis," he says uselessly. For a moment, neither of them move, not sure how they are supposed to greet. Are they friends? Ex-lovers? Enemies? Adam isn't sure, he doesn't know what he's supposed to do or say. After all, Louise tried to kill herself because of this man, so he shouldn't be happy to see him. But Adam doesn't think you can spend your whole life blaming other people for things.

"You just left," Adam says eventually. *God, it was a year ago, let it go, Adam.*

"Yes." Jarvis nods. Silence for a moment, then he does something unexpected but welcome. He leans in and grabs Adam for a hug and holds him close. For a second Adam doesn't return the hug, then he gives into it, feeling the warmth and strength of his arms, squeezing him and feeling safe, so safe, safer than he's felt for months. And then Jarvis disconnects, prises his arms away and stands looking at Adam's face, smiling again, seeming genuinely pleased to see him.

"It's good to see you, Adam," he says.

"You too," Adam says, wishing he was a little more sober, a little less wobbly. They stand comfortably for a moment, and then Jarvis indicates to his pint.

"Another?" he asks.

"Yeah, thanks," Adam replies.

"You're worse for wear for this time in the afternoon," Jarvis says, gesturing to the barmaid for another round, pointing to both of their empty glasses. "Mind you, I'm a bit pissed myself. Special occasion."

"Special occasion?" Adam asks, still drinking in his face, his voice, and his presence. It's like the sun has come out again, shining on him, warming him.

"Stag do," Jarvis says, pulling up the bar stool next to Adam. "I'll have to get back to everyone in a bit."

Adam nods, but doesn't speak. It feels slightly surreal, like this can't be happening at all, today of all days. Jarvis is back.

"I'm sorry I left," Jarvis says eventually. "I thought it was the best thing to do."

"I thought you'd fight for us," Adam says, surprising himself. "Or for Louise, at least. She's your sister after all."

"I did come after you that night," Jarvis says, pausing to pay the barmaid for their pints, then holding his glass up for Adam to cheers, which he does. "But when I got to your street, an ambulance was already there, Louise was being carried out, you were in bits."

Adam nods, a piece of the puzzle becoming clearer to him. He'd spent all these months wondering how Jarvis could give up on both of them without another word, without any explanation, just disappearing and selling up. And now it made sense. Guilt.

"I stood there, not knowing what to do. I wanted to come to the hospital, to make sure she was okay, that you were okay. But how could I? It was my fault. I'd fucked everything up so badly. So I went home."

"And then you ran," Adam says simply.

"Yes, I suppose I did," Jarvis replies. "I thought it was the best thing to do. I'd caused enough trouble and heartache."

The afternoon pub clatters on around them. In the next room, there's a screen showing some sporting event or other, nothing big, nothing raucous but it's got a few of the afternoon crowd in. Behind them there's a number of guys drinking, joking and laughing – Adam presumes they are the stag and party that Jarvis is with. But Adam can't see anything except Jarvis. He's back, he can't believe he's back. Adam's heart is beating so fast in his chest he can feel his t-shirt moving in time. He wants to reach over and touch Jarvis again, brush the skin of his hand. Something.

"Kids well?" Jarvis asks eventually.

"Yes, great. Matthew's started school as well now."

"Good, I'm glad. And you and Louise? Still together?"

Adam nods. "Yeah, well sort of. Last legs probably."

"Oh, I'm sorry."

"No, no it's all right. Best thing for both of us," Adam says.

"At least you didn't split up after me, I don't have that on my conscience as well." Jarvis smiles.

Does he think it's all water under the bridge and that he didn't leave a legacy behind?

"I wouldn't go that far," Adam finds himself saying, slightly angry. "You left behind a shit storm, Jarvis."

"Sorry, I didn't mean to sound flippant, I know what I did."

"Do you?" Adam does feel angry, he realises; he does still need Jarvis to know, even after all this time. "Louise tried to kill herself, Jarvis. Because of you. And you left, sold up and fucked off without a word."

"I know and I'm sorry..."

"We *never* recovered from you, never. You know that right?"

"All right, Adam," Jarvis says, moving to get up from his bar stool, "this was a mistake. I saw you and I thought it was fate or something, seeing you on my stag do. I thought enough time had passed to make amends."

"What?" Adam says, sure he couldn't have heard right, he's drunk enough to be mishearing anything and everything.

"I thought we could say our goodbyes without any anger. But I don't want to fight with you, Adam. I am sorry." Jarvis puts his hand on Adam's shoulder, but Adam isn't listening, he's frowning, confused, not able to compute what he's hearing.

"*Your* stag do?" he says eventually. Jarvis drops his hand away and nods. "But..." Adam continues. "I don't understand. You're getting married?"

"Yes," Jarvis says. "Not that hard to believe is it?"

"But you're gay," Adam splutters.

"Yes," Jarvis says, frowning himself, like he doesn't understand why this would confuse Adam, after all that had passed between them.

"I don't understand," Adam says. "How can you be marrying after all that's happened?

"What do you mean?"

"Me, Louise. You're gay, how can you be getting married?"

"To a man, Adam," Jarvis says. "Times change you know. Keep up."

Adam feels another wave of devastation hit him, like a blow to the stomach. At least he's sitting down; at least it didn't knock him from his feet.

"I still love you," he says. *Shit.*

"Adam, don't," Jarvis starts.

"Call it off," Adam says desperately, grabbing Jarvis's arm. "We were good together, you know we were. Louise and I are over now, the kids would cope. We can make a go of it."

"No, Adam." Jarvis pulls free of Adam's grip and Adam wobbles slightly, having to grab the bar to steady himself.

"Tell me how to make things right with you," Adam slurs in desperation.

"We had our chance," Jarvis says. "And you did the right thing, you stayed and looked after your wife and kids. I was the one who fucked everything up, for you and for Louise."

"Please, Jarvis. I was so much better with you around."

Jarvis shrinks back from him, imperceptibly. "You can't rely on me to make you better. Isn't that what went wrong with you and Louise?"

The pub seems colder than it did before. There's a clattering of glasses and the bustle of a young afternoon drinkers, happy and content. Adam feels like the entire place must have stopped breathing and are staring at them both, waiting to find out what happens next.

"But I'm in love with you," Adam says again.

"No, Adam, you're not. You never were."

"I am… I know how I feel, Jarvis."

"You don't even know me, Adam, you never did. I'm sorry for everything, I am. That's what I came over to say. I got caught up in everything, you and Louise, the whole mess. But now I've had time to see it for what it was – a mistake."

"Don't tell me how I feel, Jarvis," Adam snaps before lowering his voice again, worried people will hear them. "You're like Louise, always telling me how I feel."

"And you're still blaming everyone else for everything," Jarvis says, glancing down at the pavement. "Come on, Adam, be honest. You're in love with the idea of me. You and Louise both were. What do you actually know about me? Tell me something, anything about me other than the fact I run the garage and like running."

"Jarvis, you're being…" Adam starts, but he can see that Jarvis is angry, angrier than he's ever seen him.

"Be honest, Adam. Tell me *one* thing, just one. Prove to me you loved me, that you know me and I wasn't some escape for you, some invention or fantasy to take you away from the boredom of your life."

Adam remains silent, horrified that as hard as he's trying he can't think of anything. Jarvis likes pizza and he had a weird beige carpet with squares of burgundy in his flat. He's gay. He's Louise's half-brother. He didn't like his mum much. What else? He stares into Jarvis's green eyes and gets lost in them for a moment, so beautiful, so like Louise's.

"But I lov…"

"What was my favourite food? Film? Book?" Jarvis is angry and this surprises Adam. How can Jarvis be angry? How can he have the right to be angry after what he did? "No? Something easier then: where did I grow up?" He doesn't pause for an answer, not that Adam could give him one anyway. "Okay, let's make it even easier. What's my surname, Adam?"

Adam stares at Jarvis, dumbfounded. He doesn't know. He literally barely knows anything about this man, but how can that be? How can he have known so little? He tries to get off his bar stool and staggers a little, dizzy again, before righting himself by grabbing the bar.

"It's how I feel that matters, Jarvis."

"Enough lying to yourself, Adam," Jarvis says, a little more softly, like the anger has escaped out of him and he's deflating now, feeling some of the softer emotions he used to feel. "We'd never have worked. You see that don't you? It was never real, it was a mistake."

"That's not true," Adam says. He can still feel Jarvis's lips on his, can still feel his tongue in his mouth that night in his flat, before Louise knocked, before the shit hit the fan. "I..."

"I was an idea for you, Adam. A projection. Go back to Louise, Adam. Repair the damage. You two were always meant for each other, you know. You're both too stubborn and too caught up in yourselves to realise it."

"I don't want to," Adam says sadly. "Jesus, I've wasted my life with her, Jarvis. But with you, I could be different. I am different with you."

"What are you talking about? You've got two kids, you're married to a woman you love... You haven't wasted anything."

"I should have run away with you when I had the chance," Adam slurs quietly.

"But you didn't, and that was the right choice, Adam. Tell Louise I'm sorry I didn't tell her sooner. And I am sorry, Adam. I'm so sorry." He leans over and kisses Adam on the cheek, smiling sadly. Then he turns around and addresses all the guys on the other side of the pub, his stag party.

"Right, next pub, guys." He glances back at Adam and gives him one last smile. "Moving on," he says loudly as he ushers his friends and family out of the door. And then he's gone, disappearing, a ghost, almost like he was never there at all.

* * *

Adam stands swaying by the bar, not sure what to do next. Eventually, he pushes himself back out onto the street, shivering. His t-shirt isn't keeping him warm, but why would it? It's November and by the looks of it, it's been raining while he's been inside. At least he missed the rain. He puts his arm in the air to hail a cab. As it pulls over, Adam realises his hand is stinging and he has developed a bleeding valley on his left knuckle where he's been scratching as he spoke to Jarvis. Old habits.

"Beachy Head," he tells the taxi driver, sitting back and closing his eyes, thinking of the canvas print on his living-room wall from that perfect family photo that Jarvis took of them last year. They seem so happy in that picture, like they have everything. Smiling, windswept faces. His children, young and excited to be having a picnic with their parents. Adam knows it wasn't real – both he and Louise had fallen for Jarvis by that point, but he wants the illusion back, he wants to feel like they did back then in those fleeting, happy moments. Right now, he can't think of anywhere better to go.

Thankfully, the taxi ride is silent, like the driver senses Adam isn't in any frame of mind to make or listen to small talk. He probably shouldn't be taking him there at all, not with Adam so obviously drunk. When he arrives, Adam pays the driver with a healthy tip and walks hunched towards the top, filled with a strange kind of relief. He wasn't meant to survive Tom's loss. They were two halves of the same egg, maybe he was never supposed to carry on regardless after. He was like an imbalance of nature, abhorred, a wound in reality that needed stitching. Maybe this was all a punishment for his continued existence.

His head is spinning as he stands at the top of the white cliffs, taking in the view, the waves and majestic skyline, the vastness of it all making his problems seem that much smaller, that much more manageable. The wind is cold against his face and arms, making him feel alive, like he can feel something other than misery. He loves it up here, always has done. It's such a beautiful spot, dramatic and – if it's out of season, quiet. Somewhere to think, to get away from everything and just 'be'.

He takes a step closer to the edge, glancing down at his trainers and the white rubble and grass beneath his feet as he does so. His mobile, in his pocket, starts ringing. He fishes inside it out woozily to see 'Louise' flashing on the screen, her photo beaming at him, asking him to answer, to speak to her. He clutches the phone in his hand and stares out at the horizon from his vantage point high on the cliffs.

"Go back to Louise," Jarvis had said. "Repair the damage." But he's not sure he wants to, he's not sure he can. How can they repair the damage when she won't speak to him? When she won't open up. But who is he to talk? Maybe the only way forward is for him to be honest with her as well, tell her everything. Then they can decide if they want to try again. But only when they both know the score. They've been hiding their faces from each other for so long, they don't know what each other looks like anymore. He'll tell her everything and in doing so, he'll force her hand. He *knows* she wanted to leave with Jarvis. He knows everything. If he's honest with her, they can at least talk honestly and openly about everything. Maybe then they'll be able to move forward. He glances at the ringing, vibrating phone in his hand again, finally deciding to answer it as it rings off. He brushes it against his teeth, thinking for a moment before it beeps, telling him he has a voicemail. Pressing to hear the message, he lifts the phone to his ear.

"Adam, I'm sorry," he hears his wife say. "I...look, please call me back. Please *come* back." She pauses and Adam squeezes his eyes shut, the dizziness coming again. "I love you. I want to tell you everything, I want us to open up again, like we used to."

He reaches out his hand to steady himself against something, anything, as his vision blurs again and he stumbles, losing his footing. But there's nothing to grab, nothing to hold on to. The phone falls from his hand and he staggers forward and topples, his ankle buckling beneath him, his head ploughing straight off the side, his body following after, a helpless hostage to gravity. He's falling, heart thumping, lungs aching, eyes streaming.

Epilogue

Tom and I are listening to our parents singing lullabies over the sea. We're trussed warmly to their chests, watching waves lapping pebbles, lapping pebbles, lapping pebbles. We're comforted by their gentle voices, rocked by their quiet breathing, made drowsy by the sun's fading fingers. Above, we can hear less-fortunate children wailing from deep within graceful, white, feathered bodies. We gurgle. Snuggle into our parents' jackets.

When my body is found, they'll say my death was instantaneous, they'll say my head cracked open on the rocks and there was no water in my lungs, indicating I died instantly and didn't drown.

But an instant is a relative term. A lot can happen in an instant – if you don't believe me, ask your dreaming mind. Entire dreamscapes and adventures and lifetimes can happen in the blink of an eye. An instant could be an eternity in the right circumstances.

I don't blame anyone, not even myself. Sometimes things aren't anybody's fault, they just happen. Events simply cram together, grating against one another like sardines in a can until finally the bloody, fractured reality bursts into the world through the open wounds. It was inevitable. It's almost like my death was the first thing set in stone and everything else sprang from that: effect feeding back into the cause.

Before I go, I've got one more favour to ask. Will you tell them how much I love them? My family, I mean. They shouldn't need to be told, but they'll think I did it on purpose. And in case they never find out, I need them to know I was never going to kill myself. I was always coming back.

– END –

If you enjoyed *Beat the Rain*, please recommend it to a friend
and review it on Amazon.

About the Author

Beat the Rain is Nigel's first novel. He lives in Brighton with his partner, their two children and their greying ginger dog Luka. He's also co-founder and CMO of digital agency, Qube Media. He was previously a writer and editor for Channel 4 Television and a newspaper sub-editor. Find out more about Nigel on his website and social-media pages:

Website
www.nigeljaycooper.com

Facebook
www.facebook.com/nigeljaycooper

Twitter
www.twitter.com/nijay

The Cause
Roderick Vincent
The second American Revolution will be a fire lit from an internal spark.
Paperback: 978-1-78279-763-0 e-book: 978-1-78279-762-3

Don't Drink and Fly
The Story of Bernice O'Hanlon Part One
Cathie Devitt
Bernice is a witch living in Glasgow. She loses her way in her life and wanders off the beaten track looking for the garden of enlightenment.
Paperback: 978-1-78279-016-7 e-book: 978-1-78279-015-0

Gag
Melissa Unger
One rainy afternoon in a Brooklyn diner, Peter Howland punctures an egg with his fork. Repulsed, Peter pushes the plate away and never eats again.
Paperback: 978-1-78279-564-3 e-book: 978-1-78279-563-6

The Master Yeshua
The Undiscovered Gospel of Joseph
Joyce Luck
Jesus is not who you think he is. The year is 75 CE. Joseph ben Jude is frail and ailing, but he has a prophecy to fulfil...
Paperback: 978-1-78279-974-0 e-book: 978-1-78279-975-7

On the Far Side, There's a Boy
Paula Coston
Martine Haslett, a thirty-something 1980s woman, plays hard on the fringes of the London drag club scene until one night which prompts her to sign up to a charity. She writes to a young Sri Lankan boy, with consequences far and long.

Roundfire Books

Paperback: 978-1-78279-574-2 e-book: 978-1-78279-573-5

Tuareg
Alberto Vazquez-Figueroa
With over 5 million copies sold worldwide, Tuareg is a classic
adventure story from best-selling author Alberto Vazquez-
Figueroa, about honour, revenge and a clash of cultures.
Paperback: 978-1-84694-192-4

**Find more titles and sign up to our readers' newsletter at
http://www.johnhuntpublishing.com/fiction**

**Follow us on Facebook at
https://www.facebook.com/JHPfiction
and Twitter at https://twitter.com/JHPFiction**

**Most titles are published in paperback and as an e-book.
Paperbacks are available in physical bookshops. Both
print and e-book: editions are available online. Readers
of e-books can click on the live links in the titles
to order.**